NINETEEN FORTY-FIVE

A SECRET MISSION OUTSIDE THE FRONTLINES

BRIAN STRIEFEL

HILDEBRAND BOOKS
an imprint of W. Brand Publishing

NASHVILLE, TENNESSEE

Hildebrand Books an imprint of W. Brand Publishing

j.brand@wbrandpub.com

www.wbrandpub.com

Printed and bound in the United States of America.

Cover design by designchik.net

Stock images from Shutterstock and AdobeStock

Nineteen Forty-Five / Brian Striefel – first edition

Available in Paperback, Kindle, and eBook formats.

Paperback ISBN 978-1-950385-41-6

eBook ISBN: 978-1-950385-42-3

Library of Congress Control Number: 2020913749

CONTENTS

This story is told from three unique perspectives with the narrator identified at each transition.

January 1945: Alder

April 1945

May 1945

This book is a work of fiction, using research from public domain and free information readily available. All incidents and dialogue, and all characters with the exception of some well-known historical figures, are products of the author's imagination and are not to be construed as real. Where real-life historical figures appear, the situations, incidents, and dialogues concerning those persons are entirely fictional and are not intended to depict actual events or to change the entirely fictional nature of the work, with the exception of factual descriptions of the actions of said historical figures. In all other respects, any resemblance to actual persons, living or dead, events, or locales is entirely coincidental.

This book does not represent personal or political views. It was written to connect the reader to past events and allow them to identify with the characters and the story, regardless of race, religion, or country of origin. The story was written without burdening the reader with too much technical and scientific detail.

When I went to Germany, I never thought about war honors, or the four "coups" which an old-time Crow warrior had to earn in battle. . .But afterward, when I came back and went through this telling of war deeds ceremony. . .lo and behold I [had] completed the four requirements to become a chief.

—Crow World War II Veteran

OCTOBER 1943

ABBY

Wintery weather followed me to the hospital tonight. A surprise blizzard pushed temperatures down thirty degrees, but that's nothing new around Browning, Montana. In 1916, the temperature dropped from 44° above to 56° below in twenty-four hours.

Tonight's not so bad.

I stomp my feet on a wet rug. Snowflakes melt in the pleats of my dress, a minor inconvenience. I always visit John's room before shift-change. I do it out of respect, out of sadness, out of reverence. A fresh dress can wait until break.

My shadow hesitates at the doorway before I push inside. I touch John's cheek. I brush a little snow onto his potted plant, a Christmas cactus that blooms in December because it belongs in Brazil. Sometimes I wonder where I belong.

"Water."

My head turns naturally. For a moment, the radiator tricks me into hearing a voice in a place where there are no voices. Night shifts always challenge my senses.

I stare at his rumpled hospital blanket. Something rattles outside, our ever-present Montana wind making another trip around the world. A cast-iron radiator bumps in response, replacing heat lost to the wind. There's no voice here, always just two sounds, wind and radiators, two opposing forces, my little world at a glance.

The entire world shares my perspective in 1943.

Two opposing forces.

Not that I wouldn't like to hear his voice, to see him stand all tall and handsome. I got over his looks two months ago. Big guys look good standing in your doorway but sponge one off on a hospital bed some time. John won't stand up any time soon, thanks to a sniper's bullet.

Two opposing forces.

John already stood up for us in the war, despite his native heritage and the way treaties became inconvenient at convenient times. That bothers me, especially at night when there's nothing else to occupy my mind.

"Of course he's not moving, c'mon Abby."

I talk to myself all night, just to stay sane.

"Nobody moves on this floor. It's last night all over again."

John started dreaming four days ago, kicking and muttering, maybe the beginning or the end. I think I dread that the most, his final breath, not so much because it connects me to the frightening European War but because I need him alive so I have a reason to drive through blizzards and rush inside and hope that someday he'll say hello.

It's about me. I'm selfish. John's my war hero and he doesn't belong here. I imagine him whole again, what he'd be like—a handsome young man, our special bond, an unexpected recovery rather than a military funeral.

I lean back down to tuck in his covers. Like all Browning hospital rooms, the white walls and antiseptic smells slowly wash away my imagination and hope. The little Christmas cactus and I don't belong here either. I dream of faraway places where a short walk might take you past spacious department stores or fancy restaurants or lively clubs.

"Get outta the church, Abby." He grabs my arm and my daydream explodes. His eyes flutter open then, unseeing to start, pupils narrowing, head turning.

"What did you say, John?"

"I said, I need water."

His words come out a whisper like the first time. His hand slides back down to the bed.

I jump up and down in a complete circle. When I bounce all the way around, he's still looking up at me and he's smiling. *John's smiling.* I dive through the doorway and run headlong to the nurse's desk, where my long red hair catches a stack of paper and spins it onto the floor.

"John Meyer's awake!" My voice sounds like a little girl with her finger slammed in the door.

"Abby, honey, it's just some of his mumbling. You know how long he's been out. John'll never wake up."

"You better come see. He asked me for a drink and looked right at me. He's awake alright, c'mon."

"The bullet fractured his skull. You've seen him walk to the window and stare outside. Then he pees on the floor, and we put him back in bed."

"Yes, yes, I know, but this time it's different. Trust me."

"Alright then, let's go take a look."

Lucy Yellowbird follows me with a sigh. She's really old, perhaps ninety, long-ago retired, then begged back into nursing when all the young nurses left. Lucy always treats me well because I do all the lifting and pushing and anything else that involves hips because hers are shot. She knows I plan to leave town soon, just like her own grandkids. World War II rages in Europe, drawing so many young people away to the munitions factories and to the fighting itself, people like poor John, a casualty in Sicily with the Army's 2nd Armored Division.

Lucy catches her breath when I flip on the light. My comatose patient, John, sits shivering in his white smock. Behind him, our Montana wind pelts the lone window with sleet that courses down the glass in wavy fingers.

"That light pokes right through my head."

Lucy leans in front of him. "John, can you hear me?"

"Of course, I can hear. Who are you anyway?"

"I'm Lucy. A nurse, John, and this is Abby. You've slept for a long time."

"How long?"

"Eleven weeks."

A blank stare.

"It's October, John," I say. "You've laid here in a coma since August, and in an Army hospital before that. My Lord, we never thought you'd wake up."

"My brother's still out there."

I hesitate before answering, "He disappeared about the same time you were injured."

"Disappeared, yes."

"I'm so sorry, John, the Army presumes the worst."

"He didn't die."

"John, I'm sorry too," Lucy says.

"No need to be sorry. You don't know where he is."

"He disappeared in Sicily, almost three months ago. Half the unit didn't make it out alive."

"You aren't listening Lucy, my brother isn't dead. You say he was *presumed* dead in Italy?"

"Yes."

"Did they find his body?"

"No, but you must understand the carnage."

"Where's my unit now?"

"Still in Italy, as far as I know, and that's just the beginning, I hope."

John's awake, although he looks terrible. The scar starts above his right eyebrow and angles back toward his left ear. We kept his head shaved, and it healed in a sense, as much as a body can. The first bullet removed his helmet. The second bullet ricocheted off, shattering an area the size of my hand into a dozen jagged pieces and ripping a hundred tiny tears in the brain below. His skull will never heal completely, according to the doctor. Thin stubble grows across most of his head now, surrounding a scar that only hints of the damage below. His right arm suddenly goes rigid in some unknown spasm.

"Abby, right?" he says. "I have a very big problem."

"Is your brother part of this problem?" I ask.

"My brother, Robert, is part of everything, yet he needs my help very soon."

"We're all so proud of you." My voice trails off as his body twists again.

"Oh, that hurts." He struggles to breathe. "Our father died in World War I, Sergeant Ed Meyer. This is what we do."

"It was in the papers, all about Ed and how you and your brother took Basic together and went away to fight. Robert carried you out in July. Lois visits you every day, exercises your muscles like the doctor showed her."

"I know my aunt comes here. You too, Abby," John says. "I could see you like a dream, yet I couldn't wake up. You thought I would die."

"Yes, John, the Army assumed you would die when they placed you here. A lot of good men already died. How do you feel?"

"Dizzy, a little nauseous. I have to get to Italy."

"John, you can't even walk yet."

"If we lose the war, that really won't matter."

Violent shivering rattles the bedsprings. I wrap a blanket across his shoulders, and he stands, wavering like a drunk.

"Whoa, careful, you're gonna fall, John."

"I'm not gonna fall, Abby, I'm going to walk out that door."

"I can't let you do that quite yet. Besides, it's freezing cold outside. Another day can't make much difference."

"I wish that were true." He takes a deep breath and sits back down. "Can I have a drink now?"

Two headlights pierce the first snowfall of 1943. Snow doesn't fall here, it streaks left to right, or right to left if you face south.

The temperature continues to drop, and all around me, snowy shelves gather on the wall. Builders used local granite on most exterior surfaces, finishing this hospital in 1937. The Helena paper called it "the most beautiful reservation hospital in all of the country."

I walk back inside, my impatience quelled by his arrival.

Doctor Bill Jennings stops his car just opposite the white railing. He steps out, his hair disheveled and coat unbuttoned, his lips curled in a broad grin I seldom witness. I push the door open creating a little snowy cyclone. Dr. Jennings stomps his galoshes on the waiting room rug.

"Lucy got him back in bed, but he won't stay there long Doc. He insists on joining his brother, no matter what we say."

I follow Bill at a brisk pace down the hall. Overhead lights cast his shadow across the freshly waxed tile. His Old Spice cologne always keeps me grounded—a functioning man in a broken world.

"Weather's hell tonight," he says.

"Dad built his snow fence early this year. He says it helps keep the chickens from blowing away."

"So, your folks still live on their ranch, Abby? Your father's getting right up there in age."

"He wouldn't know what to do if he stopped ranching. Dad's that guy that straightens bent nails when it rains."

"I'll be the same way about this hospital, I'm sure. Good work gets in your blood. So John stood up? I guess that's happened before, on and off, right?" Dr. Jennings asks.

"We find him standing every couple days with no sign of any real brain function, just looking out the window. I don't know that we did anything right with him. Tonight it's much different though."

"Musta' done something right," he says, turning into the open room. "Good evening, John."

"You're the Doctor? Hey, I need to go!" John tries to stand again.

Jennings motions him back down and settles into a chair.

"You aren't going anywhere quite yet. They've explained how long you laid here unconscious, right? Your muscles need retraining, your stomach and intestines have to relearn some things, too. Remember, everything slept like your mind."

"Retraining, huh? How long?"

"Weeks, maybe months. John, we still don't understand the extent of your injuries. A bullet fractured your skull."

"I don't have *weeks, maybe months*."

Jennings lowers his voice. "Your skin healed, although we don't know what happened inside. The injury looks bad enough for three dead men, so sit back down."

John never really made it up.

"My brother's one of those dead men if I don't leave now," John says.

"How do you know he's still alive?"

"Identical twins, Doc, and damn annoying at times, let me tell you, but besides my intuition, this all makes sense. You see, he was supposed to disappear."

"Why?"

"That's classified, even from his unit."

Silence.

"They didn't recover my brother's remains."

"Technically, no."

"That means he made it in. So how do I get back to Sicily?"

"In the morning, you start with some broth and some toast or whatever you can chew. You'll move to all solid food and start exercising. Nurses and supplies are short with the war and all, so we'll have to make do."

"This is morning, Doc. I slept for eleven weeks, and I'm pretty rested up, so how's about some food?"

"We don't have anyone downstairs."

"I'll make something," Lucy says. "It takes me a while to waddle down there, and I'm a lousy cook, so don't get your hopes up."

"I hope you didn't hear the broth and toast suggestion," John says.

She smiles and limps from the room.

"Fine nurse."

"She takes good care of you," Bill says. "Abby here does too, so let them help you. Abby can fill you in on what you missed."

"I need the help," John says. "Eleven weeks, that's way too long. Abby, can you please get me back on my feet? I can't explain how important this is."

I almost regret his awakening.

Before, he drowsed peacefully, suspended in time, protected within the privacy of a Montana town where memories of the outside world couldn't hurt him. Now his pleading eyes belong to another man, a lesser man than I imagined before. In times of deep despair, even a man like John reaches the bottom. I watch his eyes and realize that whatever waits in Europe is already consuming him. John's look, that question—this moment will soon change my life.

"I'll help you, John."

John's arms bulged with muscles when he arrived. His chest still holds those ripples, unlike so many old men tottering about. He won't be here long.

"Time to get up, daylight's wasting."

I throw back the curtain with a *whaaack*. John's already awake, or still awake, sitting with his head in his hands.

Sunrise to sunset gives us twelve hours now, and as much as I've outgrown Browning, I love the Rockies. The most beautiful mountains on Earth stretch horizon to horizon, north to south, heavy woods below, and early snowcaps above. All my days off start in the mountains, until today.

"Abby, you just left, at what, four?"

John reclines on a hospital bed surrounded by the aftermath of Lucy's valiant breakfast. She skipped the broth and went with bacon, eggs, toast, and milk: an entire quart of milk. She told him he wouldn't keep it down, but it looks like he did.

"Today's my day off, which usually means a hike up there." I point. "See that opening way up high, right above the hospital van? There's a little lake filled with cutthroat bigger than my arm. Lonely Lake, it's called."

He follows my gaze—mountains, my arm, mountains, my face, mountains. He settles on me.

"I see the mountains, Abby. For some reason, you don't have the mountain look right now."

I laugh, and he watches me laugh like someone watching a sunrise.

"Whatsa matter, you never heard a girl laugh?"

"I'm sorry, Abby. I haven't heard someone laugh for real in years, and you do it better than anyone."

Today I wear my favorite red sweater instead of a flannel shirt and black ACME cowboy boots instead of the Boy Scout hiking boots my cousin outgrew.

"No, these aren't my hiking clothes. I'd rather be outside getting dirty than in here tidying up almost anytime, but today's different. Hey, do you want to catch up on the war or not?"

"Actually, I was catching myself up on the war before you arrived."

"How did you catch yourself up?"

"Over there, we fight and die and sleep, with no time for anything else. Back here, the voices find you, the dead and dying. You remember last wishes mumbled in words you couldn't understand, but you nodded anyway. Your brain can't process the horror then, so your mind saves it for later."

A wind gust rushes across John's window. My excitement at his awakening suddenly collides with John's reality. Our little town already suffers from the loss of two young men, their vigor replaced by telegrams—pastel papers dropped into the Montana wind by distraught mothers.

"When I wake up in a quiet place, I get time to live those war days all over again," John says.

There's no win here. John wakes up from a traumatic brain injury only to plan his return. He'll die in Europe to protect me here in Browning, Montana. All of this flashes through my head quickly and very, very thoroughly. I stutter for a second until my real job still pushes through—it has to.

"Then I guess I'm here to distract your memories. If I get you far enough away from the war, maybe those voices will fade."

I'm operating on momentum now, not the enthusiasm I arrived with. He can't know.

"The voices need their time," he says. "I do have other things to consider right now."

"Here's the deal, I'll work with you and get you back in shape. You have to tell me what happened in Sicily, though. I'm a bit obsessed since my cousin started fighting."

"You know much about WWI?" he asks.

"How much do you want to know?"

"How did Germany lose the first one and come back so fast? The Army never told us."

I grab his shoulder. "Right now, we head to the cafeteria for breakfast. Then I'll explain it, walk around the halls, whatever you want. Ready to eat again?"

John swings his legs over into some waiting slippers.

"Need a hand?"

"Nope." And somehow he stands up, no shaking, no unsteadiness.

"The hand you held out, it looks like you cut it, Abby."

A band-aid wraps around my right pinky.

"Oh, this? Look at the other hand, too. I crawl up some canyons that require both hands and both feet. This broken fingernail and the scratches get me into beautiful places where nobody else goes."

"I'd like to see your secret places, Abby."

"I'll take you there someday, John. You look a lot better in the last few hours."

"Bacon and eggs and milk smooth out the wrinkles, Abby. Bacon is my favorite food, and poker, my favorite hobby."

"Poker, I would never guess poker."

"Nobody really has a poker face. When they turn a card, I know if they want it."

"Ha, well, remind me to never play poker with you, John."

He's watching me again, not weird watching, kinda curious watching. He looks away when I catch him looking.

"Would you like a shower?"

"That would be nice."

"I'm supposed to help you, so you don't fall."

"That seems awkward."

"Well, awkward or not, I bathed you a hundred times already."

"Take me to the shower then, or a bath, that would feel good. You take me there, and I'll be fine."

He walks alongside—his gait surprisingly smooth like a dancer, his smile genuine, a handsome man that would turn heads in any crowd. My brain adds another conflicting emotion. I draw him a bath in the appropriate room. Clad in white underwear, he moves carefully into the tub. The water continues to gush in at his feet. He watches it rise across his stomach, toward his bellybutton, and when it reaches his ribcage, he arches his back and slides his shoulders in.

"I'll give you ten minutes." I plop a bar of soap onto his stomach. "See this cabinet? Robes and underwear are in there. I'll come back to help, and don't get out if you feel dizzy because you'll fall down."

I feel a little jealous of his natural good looks, his dark eyes, high cheekbones, and strong chin. If someone described an outdoorsman, John could fit that description just laying in the bath. John's muscle tone still tells of the shape we first received him in, and the shape to which he will likely return. I look down at my own curvy hips, and I twist my lips in consternation.

He meets me in the hallway ten minutes later. He looks refreshed, rejuvenated.

"I smell bacon frying, Abby. You wouldn't be part of that, now would you?"

"Maybe. You know I like bacon almost as much as you do. Bacon and eggs and hashbrowns soaked in butter."

"I'd never know that by looking at you."

"Yeah, right."

"I am right. Do you weigh a hundred pounds?"

"More than that."

"Not much more than that."

"Well, I know one thing for sure, John. You can use a big pile of buttery hashbrowns way more than I can, so get moving."

Another smile spreads across his cheeks at the lunch-room door.

Every hospital employee and a third of the town stands around the circumference. A spontaneous cheer goes up when John's aunt hugs him. He kisses her head as she sobs into his hospital gown. The crowd moves around him: men in farm coveralls, ladies in pleated dresses, old men in military uniforms—Indian and white—Browning, Montana, here to celebrate.

"Thank you, Lord."

John sits at a table of honor, sipping coffee between handshakes and kisses. I refill his cup, and he blows hard on the steamy black liquid. There isn't a dry eye in the place while Dr. Jennings reads the War Department letter describing intense battles near Sicily. A hero, John is a real hero.

The applause eventually ends. An hour later, the lunchroom clears, and I lead him away.

"Ready for a nap?"

"We're walking now like you promised."

"After all that hoopla, you still have energy to wander the halls?"

"You tell me about World War I, and I'll follow you."

He talks confidently, yet he concentrates on every foot-step like he's not sure the next leg will take its turn. He soon eases back into his natural gait.

"Alright, here we go, your WWI answer. We stayed out of that war for a long time, made a lot of money selling Britain and France supplies. Eventually, these countries borrowed money, giving us an interest in the war's outcome, so to speak. Germany sunk some U.S. ships, yet most people here still didn't want war. Good so far?"

"Fair enough, keep going."

"Then British code-breakers intercepted Germany's Zim-merman Telegram about a Mexican, German, and Japanese alliance against America. The U.S. government finally had enough, along with Australia and Canada—half the world versus Germany."

"And the world destroyed them."

"The world destroyed them, and the Treaty of Versailles required staggering payback from Germany to cover Allied damages and costs. That's after we killed all the able-bodied German men. Alright?"

"Reparations."

"Yes. We turned Germany into a bomb crater and billed the next generation—the widows and children left behind. Those people lived hand to mouth like some primitive cul-ture. All the big magazines did stories. Now the children grow up, and years of unrest open everyone's ears to a man named Hitler."

"German people are very industrious," John says.

"And Hitler is powerful, insane—coming into this war with their complete allegiance."

"We started the war ourselves."

"Well, the U.S. didn't sign the Treaty of Versailles, although we didn't stop it either. Now you understand why the Germans fight so hard too, why the whole country follows Hitler without question. We created this monster."

"And with the monster running Europe, we need our very best men after him. That is why my return is so very important," John says. "One of our best men is in trouble."

We stop near a large window. The mountains capture morning sun in deep greens and sparkling whites framed by an impossibly blue sky.

"Help me understand, John."

"I have to get over there very soon, certainly within a couple weeks." He walks closer to the window, where his breath condenses for an instant.

"I'll do everything I can, but I need to know something. Our country promised your people land, reserved for your future. Our government signed legal treaties, then peeled that land away like an onion. Why do you rescue us now?"

"It's the right thing to do. And why do you care?"

"It bothers me. Breaking the law, breaking treaties, that's not right. This is taking your home."

"I appreciate your sympathy. Life goes on. Everything changes."

And suddenly the mountains disappear. A heavy snow flurry surges across the hospital grounds. Coarse flakes smother anything not already white: a few pine branches here, a shoveled walk there. Several robins flitter into a Russian Olive tree.

"The landscape changes quickly sometimes, the things you took for granted," he says. "You adjust because today doesn't care what happened yesterday. The tribes don't surrender land or send men off to war easily."

"My dad talked about Blackfeet men returning from World War I—officers who led and were respected by white soldiers," I say. "Back here, the same prejudices waited. It must have been heartbreaking."

"Swim or drown," John says. "I remember the emotions when people talk about losing reservation land. I remember men consumed with anger. I choose to live with the memories, but sometimes memories kill a man's will to live."

"I admire your character, John."

"And I'm a better man for carrying these memories. A man with honor cannot be broken by dishonest men. There are men like that on both sides of the reservation boundary."

"Most people only see issues on the opposite side."

"I identify more with my Blackfeet heritage, but I had many advantages because I was raised in both cultures. Our white government treats us poorly while some Blackfeet tribal leaders take almost as much from the tribe as the white man they point to."

"Your memories survived the coma."

"Yes."

"Do you remember what you said to me when you first woke up, John? Something about a church?"

"I don't remember anything until you and the other nurse came in together."

"Do you remember dreaming before you woke up? You started dreaming four days before—let's see, Wednesday, Thursday, yes, four days."

"I don't remember dreaming. You sure about four days?"

"Four days, yes, I'm sure, why?"

"Probably a coincidence. Blackfeet customs and superstitions, that's all, nothing to worry about." He stares at me now. His eyes scrunch, his head tilts. Outside sunlight leaks through puffy gray clouds.

"What is it, John?"

"Have you ever visited our ranch?"

"No, why do you ask?"

He thinks a minute. "Maybe those dreams, I guess. Probably nothing."

"Alright, just wondering," I say. "You've been through a lot, John, an awful lot."

"*Herr bitte helfen Sie mir,*" John whispers quietly.

CHAPTER 3

L *ord help me.*

John grew up in a German-speaking household like half the population up here. His aunt speaks German, English, and Siksika, the native Blackfoot tongue. Her husband taught her German, so they could communicate in the early years, but eventually, they switched to English like everyone else. When visiting the hospital, John's aunt often brought an older friend, a kindred spirit that shared her love for Siksika, their spirited dialogue rambling at John's bedside.

My household also spoke German until I went off to school, and I converted my parents to English. Mother already spoke German from her mother's side and Italian from her father's side. She spoke Italian to the farm animals just to maintain familiarity.

A loss of language is a loss of identity.

John's mother and aunt are Blackfeet Indians, originally a nomadic tribe—skilled huntsman, fierce fighters, intelligent craftsmen—a wealthy, successful society before white laws arrived. White laws clashed with centuries-old native customs. Land ownership didn't exist in the Blackfeet world, an illogical change, but white laws favored those who made the laws and then changed the laws. Without recourse, the Blackfeet acclimated.

They did understand, however, the value of a man's word, at least within their own culture, and that was part of their undoing. They acclimated to treaties and mistakenly assumed the treaties meant what they said. Unfortunately, where white law draws permanent lines in ink, treaty law is written by pencil with an eraser. Still, when everything is said and done, Blackfeet remain the amazing people they were before, and the character that made them great disseminates through generations.

Helping John defend my government seems ironic, but I put all my energy into helping this man because that is what John wants. I'm here for him. His determination and handsome smile help him get what he wants.

I like his smile. I like how he listens to me completely as if there's no one else in the room. I like his brown eyes.

With my help, John develops an aggressive exercise regime. His stamina recovers more slowly than his will, and intense headaches slow his progress. On the fourth day, I find him disoriented in a back hallway.

Short-staffed, I pull long shifts and spend even more time with John. We work out together, chat like old friends. Usually, he exercises all morning and half of the afternoon. His physical condition improves, yet his blood-sugar swings wildly. I sometimes find him standing alone just staring about.

The doctor explains that with some types of brain injury, appetite completely disappears. The staff watches John more closely and finds that he skips meals. We all focus on John's routine and learn that John lost all normal feelings of hunger. His memory serves him well at times, but when he forgets to eat, his sugar runs low, and he loses touch, even exhibits seizures. We discuss this with John, and his eating habits improve.

When he remembers.

Fortunately, his memory improves along with his physical condition. We click. He's kind, funny, intelligent, and interested in everything I have to say. I'm charmed, attentive—smart enough myself to know I have a little crush on John—something I push away because it spells disaster.

We eat lunch or dinner together every day. The dining room revolves around us: the smell of canned corn simmering, spoons clanging in the kitchen, a dish washer splashing away crumbs, busy kitchen staff chattering about the weather.

Every time I talk to John, I take away pieces of this mission in Europe, this urgency to return, and I come to realize that I need to make it happen. I'm not sure if John's perception is accurate, but if it is, I need to set aside my own life. John really believes the entire war could be riding on his shoulders. I know where he came from. Somehow his view seems possible, even from a little hospital in Browning, Montana.

Could John's mission decide the outcome in Europe? Certainly no, yet he believes it might.

October 18, 1943, is a Friday, the last of a ten-day shift, and soon to be the last day of my sheltered Browning existence. I work from three to one, then stop in John's room. John's dressed in a white shirt, baggy pants, loafers, and the faded baseball cap that his aunt dropped off. He stands with his hands in his pockets, the man I pictured outside of a hospital: tall, dark, and handsome, very handsome, curvy dark hair, dimpled smile, and muscular chest. His duffle bag yawns open near the door.

"Can you drive me to Dupuyer?" he asks.

"What? Why?"

"I need to visit my mother's grave."

Lost for words, I turn away. *What is it about the time your fears turn to certainty?*

"Please?"

"You aren't ready to leave, John."

"I know, yet there isn't any choice. And my aunt cannot know about this."

A snow dusting swirls around my '34 Ford coupe when John slams the trunk. He opens my door and takes my hand as I step in. The hospital transport vehicle rolls by. County taxes purchased the twelve-passenger van—enough space to act as ambulance and coroner's wagon, and enough capacity to transport all the local widows to their respective churches on Sunday. We call it the old-lady bus on Sunday. I sometimes drive the old-lady bus, and I love the ladies, especially Elise, the oldest and most thankful one.

John enters the passenger side of my car, and we drive a short distance to Kramer's Wigwam for gasoline. My fingers tingle on the icy steering wheel. The Wigwam perfectly befits tourist expectations of Browning, Montana; a large concrete teepee certainly doesn't belong just anywhere. Outside, snow collects on the glass crowns of each gas pump. A small family exits the restaurant, and their little girl stops midstride to capture a snowflake on her tongue.

"Good morning, Abby," the gas attendant says. "Your parents stopped by last week, and I asked about you. Sounds like nursing suits you fine."

"Everybody finds their place, Lester. How's Anne?"

"Her hip gets a little better every day, and she sure appreciated such good care, Abby. Stop in sometime and say hi."

"I will stop in, Lester. Please greet Anne for me."

I will stop to visit Anne. The Depression transformed her home into a post-Depression temple where organized hoarding fills every available space. Canned food becomes spotless glass jars afterward. The jars jostle for space among Anne's own canning obsession, which will soon manage to refill every glass container completely. Shelves hold used flour bags, worn-out clothing, and off-white blocks of homemade soap—so much soap that Anne could clean every towel in Montana twice. Anne's diligent saving obsession will ensure her family's survival in case another Depression hits. Everyone her age assumes it will.

We pay our gasoline bill, and on a whim, I drag John inside. I ate here almost every Saturday night as a child. I always squeezed up against my father to scan the familiar menu together, and we always started out by picking something different, like fish or chicken salad, yet the smell of french fries prevailed, and eventually, he slammed the menu closed, and we both ordered cheeseburgers. The jukebox always played the same songs, the ones the owner liked because most farmers wouldn't part with a nickel. I hummed "Thanks for the Memories" and "Mexicali Rose" with my mouth full of those crispy fries.

"Here, John, sit on this side with me. Now I hear the fish is good, and the chicken salad, too." The sun bursts through outside.

"They both sound good after hospital food, Abby. What is that delicious smell?"

"I know the answer. It's a dangerous answer."

He laughs at my faux-serious brow. We chat amiably about our favorite foods. We greet people we know, all outgoing and friendly like most rural Montana people. We eat and enjoy the time away from our worries until a young mother comes in with her two children. She wears the

Purple Heart looped through a gold necklace. The crowd hushes at her passage to a corner booth.

John's silence lingers, the remaining food forgotten. He gives the waitress an extra ten for the widow. He tips his hat to that little family before we leave, a touching tribute that hushes the restaurant once again. They all know who he is, who she is, who they were before. This fall, our newspaper printed a front-page article about two heroic returns: one dead and one nearly dead. Most people kept the newspaper.

Our stomachs stuffed with cheeseburgers and fries, I drive ten miles letting the scenery heal us both. Yellow grasses blow like ocean waves. Patchy snow hugs tree trunks and ditches in places the sun can't reach.

"John, did you ever travel outside of Montana, before the war I mean?"

"Never. I couldn't imagine anything better than Montana outside of Montana."

"Same here, I guess, at least in high school. Lately, I think I'm missing something, though. The magazines show all these beautiful people in beautiful cities."

"I bounced through some big cities the last couple years, Abby. I think the magazine photos might be staged. All I see are crowds rushing about and hardly anyone smiling."

"I guess we both come from ranch families that can't leave. They gotta stay home and feed the cattle. So neither one of us had much chance to travel," I say. "Ranch families don't wander very far."

"My family never left the county most years. How about you, Abby? You finished high school then went to nursing school?"

"St. Patrick down in Missoula, then training here. I liked Missoula quite a bit. Everyone smiles in Missoula."

"So you're what, twenty?"

"Yep. And you're twenty-five, John?"

"I feel like an old twenty-five."

"Are you still having seizures?" I ask.

He stares straight ahead. "Well, not really," he hesitates, "not at all lately."

"I watched you have one last week. You talked to a deaf woman in a wheelchair, and the longer you talked, the louder you got. If someone isn't around to keep you eating, it could be bad."

"I don't get hungry."

"And you're so preoccupied that you don't care for yourself. Now you board a train full of strangers and head off to Italy?"

"Don't have much choice."

"I ask you questions when you run low on sugar. You always look confused and go off on a tangent. Last week you told me about a lost General. General Rose, is it?"

"I talked about Rose?"

"Yes."

"I'll get my diet on a timetable."

"You owe me an explanation, classified or not. You know you could trust me with your life, John, and when you lose touch, people across the street see it. With a brain injury, you have to eat."

"Classified is classified."

"If Europe depends on this mission, they're dead. This whole classified thing only works when you eat; otherwise, you talk. You'll tell some housewife about General Rose in Chicago, some GI in London, and if you aren't locked up by then, some Nazi sympathizer, eventually."

He fidgets. We pass ten mule deer, an extended family group foraging in the clearing.

"Is the mission important, or can Europe just hope you eat?"

He inhales. "I talked about General Rose."

"Yes, you did."

"That's not good."

"I'm listening."

"Alright, Abby. The Germans captured General Maurice Rose, the Allies' most powerful commander. He always leads into battle, a fantastic soldier, but this time things went horribly wrong."

"Will they kill him?"

"They'll torture him. He's part of the Allied inner circle, and drugs make people talk. Officers carry the dog tags of a private because Germans don't follow the rules, and a Jewish General could face unlimited hell unless he kills himself. We don't want any of this."

"So, the Army hasn't announced anything."

"Absolutely not. Someone filled in, and everything looks normal. They tasked my brother and me with a rescue or, well, let's just stick with rescue."

"The Army knows you're here. That means everything is off."

"The Army didn't make this assignment; the Office of Strategic Services assigned us. All my sergeant knows is that we will disappear without warning at any time. I doubt anyone in the OSS knows where I am. My brother doesn't either, so everything is far from off."

"Do you know where General Rose is?"

"Stalag VII-A."

"Will the Germans figure out that he's Jewish?"

"If they figure out he's a general, they'll have a dossier on him."

"And how do you rescue an American general from a German prison camp?"

"That, my dear, is way beyond classified, and we are already far beyond the information you should know. Let's just say my brother and I have some unique skills that drew the attention of the armed forces shortly after we entered the Army."

"How does the Army keep this quiet?"

"Right now, the 2nd Armored Division has someone filling in for Rose."

BRIAN STRIEFEL

CHAPTER 4

John's family homesteaded in a Scandinavian postcard. Emerald green meadows wrap around rocky cliffs that rise to dizzying heights above the ranch. Beyond the meadows, pine trees cover any place a seed could possibly take root. A faint trail curves up the mountain—so far it disappears into low hanging clouds. Alongside the trail, snowmelt rushes down a steep ravine.

Color reinvents itself when immersed in mountain dampness: a magical transformation of greens and browns here, grays and pinks there, but all grandeur fades when my eyes reach the center of this natural frame. Nothing on Earth anchors a place so completely.

A little church reaches skyward without waver.

Its flawless lines command a landscape of twisted angles. The whitewashed boards reflect an aura so luminous that the entire valley seems suspended in time, waiting for direction. My breath stops, too, part of the collective reverence, the simple serenity of this place.

My breathing returns, harsh and surprising, as this crude white church, nothing more, holds me completely captive. The world rests while we look at each other for the first time.

I walk away, unnerved from the encounter.

To the south, a log house blends into a handful of deciduous trees still holding the last fall leaves. John and his brother live inside, although neither slept here this year.

My Rocky Mountains rise dramatically behind the house, dwarfing the structure and the lives within.

I peer back at the church. That glow still captivates something subconsciously: the thought of a joyous wedding and a tragic funeral, of white flowers and babies, and God. *Why would God tear them apart?*

I turn away once more and look east. A creek cuts sharply away from the mountains to my left, then quarters southeast and out of sight. Scattered trees grip the shoreline in one place or another, the adjacent water a welcome oasis in a surprisingly dry land.

I finally walk up to the church. Snow or wind dislodged a wooden cross and left it hanging upside-down on the door. The odd angle feels like a distress flag, a symbolic reminder of a family tragedy. Bachelor Buttons push through the adjacent gravel. They seldom blossom in fall, but if cut earlier, a blue explosion erupts again. I suspect deer may have trimmed the summer growth.

White Yarrow and ivy grow here too, against the church itself. Most nearby vegetation withered and died from frost, yet somehow these plants cling to life. John watches me putter about.

"This place amazes me, John."

"When the war ends, Robert and I need to fix just about everything around here."

"Your ranch takes my breath away, John; I didn't expect this view. The church outshines the Sistine Chapel. What is it about this little building?"

"I know. It never fades, never loses that radiance. We don't paint it or clean it ever, yet somehow it stays like that, almost suspended in time, like it's waiting for something."

"Waiting for what?"

"I don't know."

"Is this the church you mentioned when you awoke?" I run my finger down the cross.

"I have no idea what you're talking about."

"The morning you woke up from your coma, you said 'Get outta the church, Abby.' Is this that church?"

"Well, this is the only church I spend time around. If I talked of a church, I don't know what other church that could be. My parents married here, and my mother's casket rested here briefly, too, so it is a special place."

"I feel your mother here."

"See that ridge? I understand my mother walked up there every morning to watch the sunrise. Aunt Lois said that Dad kept her path open all winter. Sometimes I wonder what she thought about."

"A young woman full of hopes and dreams," I say. My eyes follow the ridge down to another cross near the cabin, an ornate pewter cross wrapped with delicate white beads— ten strands, maybe twenty.

"They buried her in her garden. There aren't many places up here where you can dig far without hitting rock. Robert still plants some tomatoes there when he's home."

"She liked tomatoes?"

"Yes, nothing better than fresh tomatoes."

"What else do you know about her?"

"She shot an elk every fall and cured it in the way of her people. Dad didn't hunt all that much because he was so busy at the ranch, yet Mom told Lois that she loved the crisp fall air and the high pines. Dad always helped her pack the meat back out. My aunt repeated these stories so often that I almost feel part of their early lives."

"Did you and Robert ever hunt up there?"

"Yes, we probably followed the same trails our mother did. Robert and I ran cattle up here, even in high school, then spent a few years ranching full-time before the war. I wish I knew her."

He turns toward her grave. He shuffles away, inviting no company. John lost his parents long ago and now his brother. *Does he really believe Robert survived?*

Somehow, after spending this short time with John, I believe.

I step inside the church and close the door.

Very little light trickles in. I'm sure Ed Meyer left the door open for light and for the grand view when he worked here. The construction misled me from outside, not a framed structure but stacked timbers a foot thick. This fortress includes a door that certainly weighs more than I do. Ed reinforced the door with steel mesh and used hinge bolts as thick as my thumb. The door fits perfectly.

I prop the door open.

The ground itself makes up most of the left wall. Outside, rock protrudes from the earth at a crazy angle, and the church was built to enclose this geological outcropping.

Inside and to my left, white quartz surrounds a gaping hole.

A mine shaft starts four feet above the floor like a dark eye peering into a curious room filled with furniture and memories. Floor anchors hold steel cables, each passing through large pulleys, then down into that mine. The structure supported whatever weight Ed pulled from the ground.

Lois said the mine was Ed's intended salvation even before the Lord moved in. Ed's ranch furnished enough grass for fifty cattle, not enough income to expand, but with a gold mine, anything seemed possible. He rented two quarters from a widow. He ranched tirelessly and mined so he could buy those two quarters. He told everyone the mine would get him there long before the cattle.

Tattered cloth partially obscures the mineshaft. Six press-back chairs and a small table crowd the pulley system. On the table, long-dead flowers droop over a few lost petals. I approach the table and the picture above it. Ed and Agnes stare back from a lovely wedding picture, both clearly ecstatic about their bond. He stood almost a head taller than her, and her beauty takes my breath away. A single daisy adorned her hair, matching the plain white gown that hugged her tiny waist. He wore a darker shirt and tie, his grin almost impossibly wide.

I look down at the flowers, carnations—funeral flowers rather than wedding flowers. Profoundly sad, I hurry from the little room and secure the door once again. John kneels in front of his mother's grave, his shoulders slumped, a light breeze pushing his hair back across one temple. I have no idea what I can offer him, but he can't leave U.S. soil alone. There are memory lapses, yes, and something more, something still not completely right in his head. The war in Europe terrifies me. *Can I keep him alive?*

Outside Ed's church, the rock outcropping meets earth six feet from the structure itself. From most angles, you can't see the wall irregularity at all. Looking east, there's very little on the horizon to deny the sun's arrival each morning. Vast grasslands, white and green and yellow by season, stretch all the way to Minnesota.

I close my eyes to think.

I don't know John very well, yet he's the most amazing man.

I don't understand his mission, but I know he won't get there on his own. His brain won't work every time it needs to. If I let him go alone, the mission is effectively over.

I don't know anything about Europe.

I don't have a choice.

He's moving toward the car now. I descend a path strewn with loose gravel that moves down the mountain with each rain. It's predestined—the changing mountain, my changing life.

John stops beside several aspen trees crowded into a rock fissure. He runs a finger across the powdery bark. He stops on a little raised bubble and pushes his fingernail in, taking sap from under the bark and slipping the sap under his tongue. I watch him curiously.

"It's medicine," he says. "My grandfather taught us the healing properties of local plants." He methodically gathers sap from several trees. He puts each little ball in a paper envelope. "When it's hard to keep a wound clean, the aspen will help ward off infection."

"We didn't learn about aspen in nursing school."

"Our tribal school stretches back a thousand years. It's all around you, the plants that serve our people, passed on generation to generation. The mountains are my chapel, much like God's little home on our ranch. See this?" He shows me a pocket full of leaves.

"What is it?"

"Yarrow leaves. They stop most bleeding almost immediately."

"You plan on some more bleeding?"

"I hope not. Somebody's always bleeding in Europe."

He continues when I start the car.

"I remember quiet afternoons here," John says, "when I'd sit near that church with a hundred miles of snow-covered mountains all around. The church made me sad. I thought about everything that had happened, then I realized it was me that changed, my family in this place, not the place it-self. In a thousand years, it will look exactly the same, Abby. Somehow that still comforts me."

"I feel the same about these mountains. They're my best friends."

"Best friends, yes," he says. "What are people to moun-tains? Maybe that's why we adore them. Mountains keep our secrets, and that makes them endearing, grand, almost God-like."

Then we ride with our emotions, and our emotions are enough. The car leaves a dust cloud spreading south across little-used pasture land. Rocks click up against the door panels. The road commands my full attention, straddling the "hump" where deeply worn wheel tracks threaten the car's undercarriage.

Our ride back to Browning further cements my courage until I finally speak up.

"I'm coming with you, John."

"That's not a good idea."

He says it without any conviction.

"So leaving the hospital with seizures is a better idea? You won't get halfway across the country before they slap you in another hospital, John. And you'll forget who you are, and they won't know what's wrong, and that will be the end of your brother."

"I'll watch my diet."

"Maybe you will, maybe you won't, maybe there's more to it. You can't do your brother any good unless you arrive. Do you think that will happen?"

Gravel sprays against the wheel wells again.

"I read you like a book, John. Your sugar drops, and you say whatever comes into your head. You can't sneak into

Germany like that. I don't know your plans, but at some
point, you won't know them either."

"You're right, yet I'm making life and death decisions every day I stay here. I can't afford to wait around, Abby."

"When do we leave?"

"You can't come."

"You are not listening, John. If you leave here alone, the
mission ends because your brain will slip at the worst possible time. If I come with you, maybe I can do whatever it
takes to keep you functioning or cover for you. I'm your
insurance policy, and if whatever you have planned is important, you need me. So when are we leaving?"

"Tonight."

"You're kidding."

"Nine o'clock. The train will deliver me to New York
via Minot, Minneapolis, and Chicago. There's a blizzard in
North Dakota right now and rumored delays in Minot, but it
should blow out before I arrive."

We park my car next to the hospital's blue panel van. I
leave the keys inside, just like always.

"I can get you wherever you need to go. I can do this, John."

"I know you can. I'm still worried about you, Abby."

"You sound resigned to my company."

"I don't mean it like that. I know you're strong, Abby,
stronger than I am."

"You overestimate me. We'll see."

"In the hospital, you took charge. You gave me space, yet
you watched me. You knew exactly what I did and when I
did it. I owe you a lot, Abby."

"We all owe you more, John, so let's get on with it. Remember what the doctor said; if you reinjure your head, it's
over, so we have to be very careful."

"A man can't go through life worrying, Abby."

"I'll worry enough for the both of us then. Whatever happens, we'll make it work."

"Abby, you've done a lot for me, but traveling through a war zone into Nazi Germany, I can't ask that of you. It's a suicide mission, Abby."

"We'll make it work. Trust me."

"I can't say no, because you're right, I need help. I can't say yes, either, because I know how dangerous this is. Getting shot as spies might be a secondary danger with bullets flying everywhere else. It's not fair to you."

"I'm very well-equipped to take care of myself, John. I'm more bulletproof than you realize. Ranch girls grow up like that." My confidence doesn't quite match my words.

"We probably won't survive. I don't expect it."

"Maybe your odds just improved."

I understand John's struggle to refuse my help. I consider the looks we exchange, the guilty pleasure I take in staring when he doesn't think I'm looking, and sometimes catch him looking back. My own conflicting emotions twist up into my throat.

We sit in silence for several long minutes.

"I can't stand the thought of anything happening to you," he says.

MAY 1945

ALDER

BRIAN STRIEFEL

CHAPTER 5

They came from Montana.

Eighteen months ago, Abby traveled this same route in the opposite direction. She traveled with a man so grievously injured that he belonged in the morgue. It is a long way from Montana to Germany, riding trains, ships, buses, and trucks. They came to save a man they never met.

Someone should have caught them, perhaps me.

I spotted them right away in Stalag VII-A, more correctly I spotted Abby right away, but it did not matter because everything happened too fast. Their simple plan put me in a very difficult position and set off a *kettenreaktion*, a chain reaction none of us expected. I could argue that it saved me or destroyed me and be right either way. Sometimes we destroy the best part of our lives.

Abby surprised everyone, including herself. I helped her, unwittingly. She agreed to a debt she didn't understand, but the war is over now, and she will pay me back. She still calls me Colonel Alder, never uses the word Nazi, yet still respects or fears me. Either way, it serves my purpose. Our arrangement has evolved though, now that she's back in her home country.

In Germany, I held every advantage, her life, and the life of her companions. Here in the U.S., she operates purely on hate. In Germany, I very carefully orchestrated this hate, but the leash grew much thinner when we reached her soil. I feel a bit anxious today.

Today the train coasts into Minot, North Dakota, largely the end of the line for this nation until Seattle. The porter just announced a delay, overnight in Minot because of spring flooding further west. Abby traveled through Minot eighteen months ago and experienced similar delays: that time a blizzard. She told me all about it. She told me everything.

Since Abby passed through here last, her life changed dramatically.

I first met her at Stalag VII-A, a large German prisoner camp holding 80,000 soldiers, some of them very important men. The most important prisoner, U.S. General Maurice Rose, carried the papers of a lesser man, but I knew General Rose. I just didn't know what to do with General Rose.

Two days after I found Rose, I met Abby, an Italian nurse that did not speak Italian. Rather than confront her, I hesitated. A charming woman can manipulate any man; they trigger a hidden ego that we thought we had mastered.

Abby's quiet innocence masked a calculating, very intelligent young woman. Her *unerfahrenheit*, her lack of experience, never showed. Two brothers helped her. I discovered Abby just after I discovered General Rose, but I didn't connect them, and she moved quickly—even though their plan now seems reckless.

Maybe that's why I missed it or dismissed it back in Germany. Very soon, we will reach Montana. I wonder how much Abby missed or dismissed since Germany.

She acts very strangely today, yet I cannot confront her without alarming the others. I'm sure her hate will see me through. After all she endured, Abby could break, although she is much too strong to break down. If Abby does break, she will leave a very large crater.

I need to reassure her somehow.

Minot's checkered past and checkered present offer a girl like Abby options without limit. She told me all about Minot before they announced today's delay. She spent twelve hours here on her way east when she scratched Minot's underbelly, in her words.

I can't afford to lose her.

Abby passed through Minot eighteen months ago, in the fall of 1943, on her way to Germany.

She witnessed and agreed to some very bad things in Germany.

OCTOBER 1943

ABBY

CHAPTER 6

"Abby, do you ever sleep?"

"I sleep when you sleep, John."

John and I left Browning, Montana, on an evening train, and I slept all of ten minutes. The magnitude of my commitment hit me again as soon as John fell asleep. We're going to a German POW camp to rescue an American general? I couldn't rescue a cat in the tree behind my house, so what gives me the idea I can take this broken man to Germany and infiltrate some big prison? Infiltrate sounds very secretive, and the only secret I brought would scare even John.

In truth, I've never traveled outside Montana.

In truth, I grew up on a ranch near Cutbank and probably would have spent my whole life in sight of the same mountain, driving the same roads, and dreaming of big cities, yet never leaving my comfort zone. Even at work, John's mission in Germany seemed far away. I spent all my time focused on the man and his overwhelming problems, nurse stuff.

Germany versus John and Abby. That's a lopsided clash.

You may ask why a woman who never ventured outside Montana could leave the country with an injured soldier. There's no single answer, but my life changed dramatically at age eight when my little brother died. People say there was little love in our family that first year without him. But if they view it from my perspective, there was, in fact, a lot of love. The parent-child roles simply changed.

Eddy choked to death on a vitamin pill. That pill wasn't quite down when he turned around with his eyes so big. Mother knew right away what was wrong, yet there was nothing she could do. He collapsed in her arms. By the time she yelled for Dad, Eddy's arms had grown limp. By the time Dad rushed a car through the snow, Eddy had turned blue.

The hospital pronounced him dead on arrival.

So began my life of caring for others.

When there's nobody to blame, you blame yourself, and with overwhelming pain comes dysfunction. My mother didn't talk for almost a year. My father said very little, his own sorrow channeled into the land. Mom cried. Dad farmed. Abby loved. I cooked, cleaned, and did all the talking. We ate normal meals like a family, and I asked Dad questions about his day like mother used to, then I tucked my mother into bed, kissing her on the forehead, and telling her I loved her.

At eight years of age, I became a caregiver.

My father built a new house along the main road. In springtime, with Mother visiting her sister, he moved our belongings and burned the old house to the ground. Life returned to a different normal after that. I became the child again, in a sense, but only after learning how to care.

Many journeys end where they start.

Ten years later, innocent people began dying in Europe.

I need to do my part.

When I told my parents, they looked lost. Was it safe? Why Europe? If I wanted to help the war effort, why not find a nursing job stateside, in a military hospital or veteran's home where all the bullets had already landed. I assured my parents as best I could.

The train finally departs well after midnight, and by dawn, we roll into the first snow squall. Four days on a train sounds straightforward, but North Dakota storms completely erase the landscape, and by Minot, a full-blown blizzard halts our progress. The early blizzard will hold us up twelve hours, according to the engineer. Truthfully, I need those twelve hours to reload. I need some time to get my confidence back. I'm fearless in Browning, why not the world?

The train chugs into town. I stare through the window at snow blowing parallel to the train, lifting up over the top into a swirl on the other side, changing directions like the thoughts inside my head.

I close my eyes. The falling snow disappears, replaced by my own swirling doubts, yet there's nothing out there that I can't face, step-by-step.

I need my feet firmly planted, and my eyes open, all of the time.

The porter's familiar limp moves up our aisle. I've heard about Minot's side streets, places that few outsiders see. Channeling those thoughts, John asks a simple question.

"Hey Charlie, what would you advise for supper here?"

Our amiable black porter thinks a minute. His eyes scrunch at both sides, and his constant smile widens a bit.

"You a little adventurous, John? 'Cause the best places here call for a little adventure. The best places here is on Third Street, 'High Third'. Now, if youz more the Bible type, I can tell you 'bout a couple restaurants right here on Main Street that serves up some pretty good home-cookin'."

"Charlie, I would say a little adventure might be in order tonight, so what can we get on Third Street?"

"Y'all can get anything you want on High Third," Charlie says, "and I mean anything. Saul's is an excellent choice. Try

Saul's Barbeque and tell 'em Charlie sent you, they'll take good care of you for sure. Tell 'em Charlie asked about Luella and her pet mouse, ask 'em about that."

Charlie laughs, maybe remembering some dalliance from the past.

"What do you mean anything?" I ask. "Anything that might get John in trouble?"

"Not that John looks to stay out of trouble," John says.

"Well, you do have a pretty lady on your arm, so you don't need none o' that. So let's say a little liquor even though it's Sunday, and a card game if that catches your fancy."

"Oh, no," I say.

Charlie laughs out loud again. "Men likes poker," he says, "all of 'em, black men, too."

The storm already passed through Minot, and a warm south wind reminds us that it's only October after all. We walk up Main Street as directed, past Saunder's Drug Store, and across Central Avenue.

Peals of laughter halt us at the door, temporarily propped open by a slim brunette waving at some friends inside. She holds the door open for us.

"Are you going in? Good luck with Al, and don't say I didn't warn you about his jokes. Nothing's sacred in this town."

I shrug my shoulders and pull John inside the Terrace. Glass blocks scatter natural light around an elegant circular bar. To our right, a hundred bottles of wine and liquor wait for purchase inside a glass display case.

"You come in for the joke?" a large man asks. "Well, it's no joke. I'm Al, Alfred Emil, and that was my neighbor, Bette. I've been trying to ask her sister Bernice out for some time. Bette always promises to line us up, but she's kinda protective of her big sister."

"Maybe her sister needs protecting?" I ask.

"Oh, Bernice can take care of herself. Anyway, I went to the doctor today, and he wrote me a prescription, are you ready?" Al sits on a leather bar stool near the door. From the looks of his biceps, I guess he owns a farm or works the railroad.

"Sure," John says. "I'm definitely ready for a joke."

"Alright, I go to the doctor about all my aches and pains, and he looks me over a long time, and he writes me a prescription, you know what it says? It says, 'Prescription to cure a bachelor's aches; deliver to the man ten yards of silk—with a woman wrapped in it.' "

The small crowd erupts again, more to Al's delivery than the joke itself. His mischievous smile and his exaggerated gestures endear him to anyone he meets. Al buys us each a beer, a Schlitz, because that is what Al thinks everyone should drink.

I quiz him a bit about this woman he wants to date.

"You got to see Bette on the way out, just change the brunette hair to blonde. One sister is as beautiful as the other. Their mother died young, and those girls kinda raised each other, so they're pretty tight."

"Bette's beautiful, that's for sure," I say. "You live around here?"

"Southwest about thirty miles. You traveling through?"

"Headed east," John says. "All the way to New York."

"Best food around is over that direction a few blocks." He motions west with his thumb. "Any business along Third Street."

"We're heading to Saul's," John says. "How's that?"

"My personal favorite," Al says. "Saul's barbeque could make a grown man cry."

"As long as I can keep us out of trouble," I say.

Al looks around the room. "Keep your nose clean. Saul's is a fun-loving place."

Twenty minutes later, we thank Al for his hospitality. He directs us west on a path already trampled through the snow toward High Third. Brick buildings hold the smell of coal smoke and vehicle exhaust.

John pulls me close, and I feel warm. He walks in deeper snow and guides me down the beaten path. A slushy pool blocks our way, and he carries me in his arms. I wonder how our lives would change if this war ended today.

The Avalon, the Coffee Bar, the Twilight Inn, the Parrot— Third Street bustles with brightly lit signs that overlook a broad river valley north and west. Cars pack every side street despite the storm. We walk into Saul's Barbeque. The floor is worn-clean, the odors smoky-tasty, the atmosphere abuzz with lively chatter. This isn't a church convention crowd for sure, but some of those folks are here, the fun ones that don't talk about High Third when they leave.

Saul's menu sums up his establishment well. John holds it in one hand. The index finger of his other hand taps some interesting offerings: pork hocks and cabbage, pork rinds, sausage and grits, chicken feet. We order the smoked pork hocks. John mentions that Charlie the porter sent us, and a shot of whiskey accompanies John's coffee.

Middle-aged businessmen crowd the tables, along with a few couples, and a handful of military men. Four black waitresses rush about, keeping tables full and customers satisfied—our waitress visits near the end of the meal. John deals an imaginary card deck by his lap where nobody else can see. The young black waitress studies him. One hand drops to her hip, the other rests on our table.

"What'choo trying to show me?"

"Charlie the train porter sent us over. He loves everything about this place."

"Describe Charlie for me," she says.

"Well, he's about your height, twice your weight, with a hearty laugh almost like a crow, and he said to ask about Luella's pet mouse if that's helpful."

"Oh, you know, alright," she says, her voice dropping. "And I'm Luella, by the way. Tell you what, make sure there's an extra dollar in your tip, and you both want to use the washroom down that hall to the right."

"John and Abby here, Luella," John says.

"Nice meeting you, John and Abby." She departs with a practiced sway. Several men follow her gyrating hips across the restaurant.

"C'mon John," I say.

"Oh, just for an hour, Abby. We've got nothing else going on for the next ten hours."

The tip turns into a five. The washroom holds a toilet and sink opposite a broom closet, but one minute after we close the door, the broom closet opens from the other side, and a muscular black man eyes us both. He's stout, athletic, handsome, and well-dressed.

"You friends of Charlie?"

"Yes sir, we are," John says, "John and Abby from Montana. We're acquaintances of Al Emil, too. He bought us a Schlitz down at the Terrace, told us a bad joke."

The man looks us up and down. "Well, come on in, John and Abby, I've got a chair for you, sir. Ladies are not allowed at the tables, but you are welcome at the bar, and we have anything you might like to drink tonight."

He leads us through a false door sealed from the backside with wooden blocks. We walk down a stairway and into a lively poker room filled with cigarette smoke. Two black girls in skimpy outfits hustle drinks out to four crowded gambling tables.

"Right over here, sir. My name is Saul and welcome to my establishment." A familiar laugh roars above the rest. Al Emil slaps his cards down on the nearest table.

"He beat us here," John says.

"He'll beat you in cards, too," Saul says. "Don't tell me I didn't warn you."

"John plays pretty well," I say.

Saul smiles. "Not tonight. I'm gonna start you off at a different table." He motions John toward an open chair.

I sit down next to a pretty blonde at the bar. She looks familiar.

"Oh, another gambling widow for the night. They take us out for supper, and this place just pulls them away. My name's Bernice."

"I'm Abby, nice to meet you, Bernice. You've been down here before?"

"Oh, several times. My husband and Saul were good friends, which isn't really a good thing, but whatcha gonna do? I know my way around, yes."

"You know Al Emil?"

"Everyone knows Al Emil."

"Let me buy you a drink, Bernice."

"Well drinks aren't cheap, dear. It's Sunday, but Saul has no liquor license anyway. You know, this place started during prohibition and didn't bother with a license when the government changed their minds. The gamblers don't care, though. Booze helps empty their wallets; booze and the girls here, luring a few away for a little passion."

"You live in Minot, Bernice?"

"Right on Main Street over a clothing store. My first husband wrapped his drunken carcass and our new car around a tree a few years back, so I'm raising a little girl myself. Her name is Dorothy."

"So, you and Al got a thing going?"

"I work as a railroad ticket agent and help the girls down here on weekends. Al here treats Dorothy and me very well. He's a gentleman, and after the first man, I know what I want."

"I'm glad you found him, Bernice." I look around the room and laugh. "We met him downtown at the Terrace. He's quite a character, a very likable character. He keeps looking over here at you. All the men sneak a peek over here every couple minutes."

"How about you girl, and this handsome serviceman, best-looking guy in the place. He couldn't take his eyes off you when he followed you in, let me tell you that. He keeps glancing over here too, gonna lose his ass at cards."

"His name's John, and we met a few weeks back."

"You really like him."

"Oh, I don't know."

"Well, you make a perfect couple, this big handsome guy and a beautiful redhead, almost like a picturebook. I can tell right away you know your way around men too, around people. You're a little salty. Redheads always come out a little salty."

"I don't know about that either."

"You're sitting in an illegal gambling hall, drinking bootlegged liquor with a stranger, and you could own the place."

"Actually, my confidence needed a boost, and you sure are helping. You see, I've never left Montana until now, never done anything to speak of, and now we're riding a train to New York. John must return to the war, and I'll volunteer as a nurse."

"I've been all over, girl," Bernice says. "My father, Bill, liked to travel, and I can tell you right now, you're spirited, bright-eyed, good looking—you can get anything you want anywhere you want it. Use those eyes, use those curves, a little demure smile. Never, never let them see you sweat."

"Anybody ever see you sweat, Bernice?"

"Not since I grew up enough to know how men work. I married too young, thought that men made all the decisions, but that's what they want you to think. They'll do anything you want IF you let *them* make the decision that *you* lead them to."

I laugh a long time at her words. She's beautiful, that's for sure, not with the haughtiness that usually accompanies beauty. She's lived her share of heartache. She's cleaned manure off her shoes. She's coughed on dust along gravel roads, cried during childbirth, and buried an unwholesome husband. She's a good sister to the brunette named Bette and probably a very good mother, too.

"You're right, Bernice. They'll do anything you want if you let them make the decision that you lead them to. I know you're right, but I never heard it in words. Thank you."

"You are most welcome, my dear. Just remember that the men are in charge, but they're still men. Think about how you look at them, then hang on certain things they say. Derail their agenda, then rebuild it very slowly."

"Have you rebuilt Al's agenda?"

"Al has no idea what his agenda even was six months ago."

"It wasn't all that hard then?"

"No. Listen Abby, men have good traits and bad traits. You don't want any of them at face value, yet with a few adjustments, they will wind up tolerable to wonderful, depending on your needs. You have it in you—your natural beauty, your ease around people, your spark. Men want an equal, although most men like control, too. Give them both."

"Play them."

"In a sense, because they play you, too. We all offer ourselves to others, even you and I. We share what we want, then maybe something comes of it. You control your own destiny."

"Oh Bernice, this advice is all wonderful. Now, where does a girl pee down here?"

"Let me show you because this is a place where a girl should not pee alone."

A roulette wheel spins round and round. "Come on red, gotta be red," a white-haired man chants. His handlebar mustache gives him an air of distinction. "Good evening, Bernice, nice you could join us tonight."

"Thank you, Leonard. Here, let me touch your chips for luck." She leans over a bit further than necessary, pats the chips, kisses his cheek, and then leads me away.

Beyond the bar, Bernice swings another door outward into a lighted tunnel. The wooden floor shows signs of frequent use by a drinking crowd—cigarette butts, bottle tops, and even a broken red shoe. I perceive the direction as north.

"Right down here, Abby. There should be two drinks waiting for us when we return, gin-tonics, my favorite."

Bernice locates a fully functioning bathroom framed in large wooden timbers. There's even spray cologne and a mirror near the door. We take turns using the toilet and Bernice leads on our return.

"Leonard buys you drinks sometimes?"

"Leonard's on the city council, which means Leonard drinks free. He's also the fire chief. Say the cops plan a raid down here. They all get ready at the station, all these extra men and everything. However, the fire station shares the same building, get my drift?"

"I get your drift, Bernice. So how does Saul get rid of liquor bottles and stuff, you know, without alerting the law?"

"Take a lookie here, girl."

She does a one-eighty, back toward the bathroom, and continues down the passage away from the poker room. A single suspended wire connects light bulbs every twenty feet, illuminating damp walls, old pipes, and rusty metal.

"These tunnels started out as service corridors, running steam all over this part of town from the power plant. Once abandoned, the tunnels were condemned and blocked off until all the businesses on Third just cleaned 'em back out."

She stops at a dark passage forking right.

"Can you smell it?" She reaches around the corner and lifts a flashlight, but the beam hardly cuts the darkness.

"It smells awful."

"That's where everyone dumps their trash, the stuff they can't put out, like liquor bottles and Lord knows what. Saul took us on a little tour once. What you have back here is an old underground coal mine, a pit."

"Their own private dump."

"And I'm not sure what all lands down there, maybe a body every now and then, that's what Saul alluded to. He's never done it, although he's heard talk. Man loses at poker, spouts his mouth off about going to the cops, you know, the underworld operates here like any place."

"I'm not surprised."

"You're new, dear, you and your man, and I want to look out for you. This town doesn't follow the rules so keep your fun secret and make sure you both get out safe."

"Thanks, Bernice. I love a little adventure."

"C'mon then. I'll show you some more. I'm good friends with Erma, the lady that does laundry for lots of the girls. I help her out on and off, so I know my way around. Turn back down this tunnel here."

"Not as tall as the last one."

"It's all old heating tunnels. They fixed some of them up to move things business to business." We walk further away from Saul's into a narrow hallway leading to another restaurant, bigger and brighter than Saul's Barbeque.

"This is the Avalon," Bernice says. "They have the second-best chicken in town, and this place is packed at one in the morning. You can get things at one in the morning that you can't get anywhere else." We're staring at a diamond sky from the rear hotel entrance. A row of houses populates the street behind us, and the valley stretches out immediately beyond.

"I heard that," a skinny waitress says. "Who's the meanest man in town, Bernice?"

"Not Al Emil, that's what I think," Bernice peers down the hallway until the black waitress reaches her.

"How's y'all doing this evening, Bernice? And who's got the best chicken?"

"Fine, Etta. Your tag's sticking out. Just a second. There, got it. The Parrot's got the best chicken."

"Heck, Bernice, our chicken's always been better than the Parrot. You stop here next time, and I'll make sure we get it right."

"How's Erma's little boy doing, Etta?" Together they look out the window.

"Still colicky, up half the night. She turns on that porch light," Etta nods, "and one of us goes over and walks with her. I'm thinkin' babies might be a little too much work."

"She's lucky to have you girls."

"We all love Erma. She takes good care of us, too."

There's movement on the porch, the brief flame of a cigarette.

"Her husband, Selmer. He's out there smoking now, but sometimes he's outside with that child half the night."

"I need to stop over and see Erma," Bernice says.

Etta walks back into the kitchen. Bernice shrugs her shoulders.

"Out the front door then, Abby."

Bernice leads us down the hotel corridor. We pass a crowded lunch counter where an elderly man in a black bowtie greets us in passing. Bernice pulls the door shut behind us, and I find my directions accurate; the Parrot Inn sign glows almost two blocks south.

"C'mon, let's get back."

"So this little boy with colic, does she swaddle him tight?" I ask.

"I don't know, Abby, it's the first I heard about the baby's colic."

"Swaddling really helped with babies in the hospital. Anyway, what else happens above-ground on High Third?"

"Alright, across the street and up those three stairs, that's Tuepker's Grocery. All they sell is canned goods and bread; their 'blind' because the grocery business covers for gambling and drinks downstairs. The owner kinda runs things on Third, 'the Mayor' we call him."

"What's a blind?" I stop.

"A blind is what you want people to see rather than the real business that you keep out of sight."

"And what things can you get at one in the morning?"

"Lotsa things. Booze, drugs, and more gambling if that's your thing. People come down late because it's a big damn party when all the legal businesses hafta shut down. Folks that aren't ready to call it a night don't hafta and let me tell you, this place hops on the weekend. Of course, one main attraction is always the girls. Men can get a girl all night."

"Call girls."

"Pretty much all of them, all the waitresses you have seen tonight. Waitressing is a blind, too."

"Got it."

"Back on this side, we got Metro Barbeque, then the Coffee Bar," she points right as we walk. "Just stay out of there."

A passing driver toots his horn, and we wave together.

"Finally, Ma Butler's place. She's got the best barbeque pit, and those are my favorite places besides the Vendome Bar and the Point Hotel way down on the end there. Now back to the bar before they miss us."

"Evening, Bernice."

"Good evening, Dee D. There might be a button down at the Avalon."

"Thanks for sayin' so," the black man continues on his way.

"That's Dee D. Govan," Bernice says. "He's buying in at the Parrot."

"How about the Parrot?"

"I never spent much time across the street. My friend Erma lives behind the Avalon, and she introduced me to the owners on this side. Everyone but the Coffee Bar guy, because he's got a temper."

We zig-zag through a path of shoveled snow, back into Saul's, down the stairs from another false door, and into the gambling area.

"Why didn't we go back downstairs at the Avalon, Bernice?"

"Remember what Etta first said at the Avalon?"

"You mean the beautiful girl talking about the meanest man in town?"

"Yeah. That means there's an undercover cop in the Avalon. Better off using the front door."

"Wow, how'd you get to know all these people, Bernice?"

"Well, like I said, my friend, Erma introduced me because I was pretty broke when my husband died. Ma Butler and her girls found me extra work, and they were so generous when Dorothy got sick, buying food and toys and clothes. They had money when nobody had money, you know, during the Depression. Good friends to have, those girls, intelligent, generous, not what people might expect. I love them all, and we keep each other out of trouble."

"Bernice, do you keep Al Emil out of trouble? Maybe another marriage on the horizon?"

"Oh, everyone knows Al and Al knows how High Third works. He ran booze out of here during Prohibition. Al likes the girls, but not for keeps if you know what I mean."

"Never say never."

"Did Al put you up to this?"

"No, I swear to God, no. We ran into Al at the Terrace, seemed like a good guy."

"Yeah, like I said, everybody knows Al."

Saul's Barbeque seems normal enough upstairs, and although we didn't appreciate the "anything" portion of the railroad porter's advice right away, it doesn't take John long to settle in. He plays for two hours. He wins fifty bucks, tips five to the dealer, five more to Luella, and we both shake Saul's hand on the way out.

"Thanks for coming in folks," he says. "Your handshake is your word, and I appreciate your discretion about the entertainment this evening."

"I really enjoyed the game Saul, and I assure you we will keep our night to ourselves," John says.

"Is a girl welcome for a drink if her man finds himself indisposed, Saul?" I ask.

"Anything for you, my dear. You brighten up the room with that red hair, oh my, you are lovely." He closes his eyes and shakes his head.

Saul's my father's age, mid-40s. I know Bernice steered me right. Offer a man what he wants to see, and he lets his guard down. Once you discover what's back there, the rest shouldn't be all that hard.

"Good night, then." John leads the way up the stairs.

"Flip the wood right to left, and I'll close it behind you. Wait until you hear me knock before you enter the hall, and then walk out the back door."

High Third accelerated into the evening, more boisterous than when we arrived. A fistfight draws a crowd near the Parrot, where Dixieland Jazz floats out from the open doorway. The outside temperature dropped after sunset, so John wraps me in his overcoat and holds me close.

"How was your pork?" I ask. "You seem quiet."

"Hocks, yeah," he says. "That was quite a place. It's the whiskey in their drinks; actually, I haven't tasted whiskey in over a year, and I'm still savoring the flavor. That woman you visited, what was her name?"

"Bernice."

"Did you notice the black girl, the one at the counter when we came in, Luella? She worked the downstairs later."

"Looking for cash and carry romance."

"Yeah, I believe you're right, and I wondered about that. She came and left and came back and she's gone again with another man," John says. "She seemed trustworthy, despite the circumstances."

"You think so."

"Yes. Beautiful, too."

"Why does it matter?"

"It doesn't matter," he says. "Just thinking about how you run a business in the shadows."

"Well, for what it's worth, I trust Bernice, and I suppose Luella, too. What did you think of High Third anyway? Are you glad the porter told us about Saul's?"

"I am glad. Thank you so much for accompanying me to-night, Abby, you were charming and beautiful."

"You looked dashing yourself, John. Bernice even commented."

"Thank you."

Our stroll puts us near the Avalon Hotel when my eyes drift to a lit porch.

"C'mere." I pull John off the sidewalk. "There's a baby over here."

"How could you know that?"

"Bernice showed me around a little when we went to the powder room."

"More than a little, I think."

"Yeah, more than a little." We move through the shadows into a neat back yard.

"Hello, Erma," I say. "Etta told me your baby gets to cry-ing at night. I'm a nurse."

"He can be such a sweet little boy, and then something gets into him." The young mother looks endlessly adoring. A young black girl waves goodbye and heads toward the Avalon.

"My name is Abby, and this is my friend John." I lead up onto the porch. "May I hold your baby?"

"Sure."

"Alright let's wrap him up even tighter." I pull the blanket. "No, let's start all over."

I quickly rewrap her crying infant on the porch floor.

"Almost like a papoose," John says.

"Almost." I pick the baby up and snuggle him to my chest. "Or like a hot tamale. When I wrap them like this, they don't unravel."

"So tight is good. I've heard that," Erma says. "Maybe I didn't go that tight."

"It's calming," I say. "They can't thrash about, can't get excited about anything."

"The Avalon girls make me gripe water out of soda water from their bar."

"That's good, too. Rub his back, keep him warm, I'm sure you've heard endless advice by now. He'll get better before you know it."

We visit about the baby until he falls asleep, and I hand him back to Erma.

"I think your swaddling really helped." She examines my wrap.

"Probably just cried out but bundle him like that. It's always helped me."

We turn to go.

"It was nice meeting you, Abby, John. Stop in again sometime."

"Nice meeting you, too, Erma. Your baby is adorable."

She smiles a sweet smile and holds him close. In a moment, we're back on Third.

"She's a wonderful mother. All in all, a lovely evening, Abby," John says.

"There's something else though, isn't there? You seemed distracted when we left Saul's."

"Coming down from the card excitement, my brain lifted some moments from the past. I'm frustrated with my memory and frustrated with the details I used to gather. Once I could read everyone in the room, but now I can't quite file that information in my head. It's maddening."

"Well, don't worry about something you have no control over."

"I keep getting tiny frames of those coma dreams, too."

"And they might help you."

"Or mean nothing like most dreams. My culture believes in dreams, though."

A truck chugs around the corner, spilling a few coal nuggets on the street—the driver waves.

"I know a little about Blackfeet culture," I say.

"My family raised us with one foot in both cultures and my grandfather took us to a Sun Dance. He educated us about Blackfeet visions."

"And you asked about four days, John, when I said you spent four days dreaming."

"A Blackfeet vision lasts exactly four days. I never pursued this part of the Blackfeet world, growing up with a European family off the reservation. I don't see any connection."

"If the dream feels good. . ."

"Nothing feels good about this dream."

"Can you talk about it?"

"I don't have much, just snapshots, nothing like my perception of a Blackfeet vision. Either way, I cannot discuss it. Visions are private glimpses into another place. They cannot be shared under any circumstance, or their power disappears."

"Give it time then, John. Your fragmented memory is a dream and nothing more."

He seems pacified with my statement, and I dismiss his concerns. We rent a motel room with two beds and fall asleep separately, yet something wakes me after midnight. I snuggle in with John and sleep with his arms around me. He wakes at dawn, and we stare into each other's eyes for a minute. I wonder what he sees.

The train bumps and smokes and screeches back to life—a thin fog makes the city smaller, her buildings fading into a monotone gray. An older couple hurries aboard–him with a small suitcase, her managing a hairnet. Our porter waits for the two of them and then swings himself onboard.

Our passenger car smells of strong coffee and a nice aromatic cigarette. Long ago, my father's friend smoked Winston cigarettes when we fished Harrison Lake. They always left an hour before dawn and I, substituting for a boy neither man had, slept in the back seat, or pretended because I never really slept. They talked about man things like cars and baseball and the curvy bank lady. They navigated those little mountain roads while Dad's friend Wayne smoked his Winstons and bemoaned Herbert Hoover's presidency. I always felt special, part of their secret man's world, even if just for an hour, pretending to sleep on a drive into the mountains.

I feel the same sitting next to John Meyer. He's older, worldly, aware of life beyond my cocoon. His experiences thrill me, terrify me, somehow feeding a hunger to know the world and become part of it. I revel in his presence.

Our travel continues east, uneventful, especially after Minot. We switch trains in Chicago. Our hike temporarily makes us part of that city and, in my case, overwhelmed by sights and sounds. Skyscrapers blot out the sun. Every form of wheeled transportation packs downtown streets. It's bigger than I ever imagined, Chicago—tall and busy and full of intrigue.

The journey continues from Chicago through a landscape neither farm nor forest but a shifting mix of the two. I fabricate a rural tour without a tour guide. I create stories of the people who live here through the eyes of their livestock, all scattered about in neatly fenced meadows. My make-believe adventures replace the nagging uncertainties of a poorly planned trip. My orderly world spinning out of control, I try to anchor the journey in familiar things.

We arrive in New York City, where I join the Red Cross. John converts his cash to the German *Reichsmark* while the banker questions him. In his military uniform, John explains he wants some German currency before the rest of it goes up in smoke. The banker laughs much too long as he counts out the bills. He's nervous, like everyone. Any encouraging words, even the confident attitude of a single soldier, make Hitler's war just a little less ominous.

Skyscrapers and crowds capture my imagination once again. When I see a woman my age dressed in flowing silk under a dazzling mink stole, I wonder what her life feels like. She looks confident but more important to me, she looks determined. We all know it's a man's world in 1943. This girl found a place, a purpose, and in her determination, she inspires me.

I'm still collecting inspiration wherever it appears. I'm still scared to death.

Together, John and I march onto the Queen Mary along with hundreds of Royal Canadian Air Force Troops. The October 24th sun greets this human mass, all headed to Europe and an uncertain future. We depart for Scotland twenty-two days after John awoke from an eleven-week coma.

The port authority planted asters in a long row to cheer people coming and going. I smell the asters in port, and the aroma follows me out a mile or more. My mother grows asters too, their sweet sage smell always strongest behind our house in late September. Today, I feel sad when I lose this connection to land. I stay on the highest deck and watch as the skyline disappears next, three towering buildings are the last to go.

I've never been to sea.

I've never seen a real boat, other than canoes popular with certain sporting people in Browning. Finally, alone with the sea, I grip the railing like a newfound friend. Anxious chatter along the gangplank paints an awe-inspiring picture of this friend. She will deliver us, of that I have no doubt, and today she calms me. She fills my inspiration bucket. There's little time left to gather courage.

My boat experience starts right at the very top.

The Queen Mary, born a luxury liner, was recently converted into a soldier transport. The Queen carries her new burden well—her exterior now navy gray, her fancy furnishings replaced by bunks and most woodwork covered in leather. The ship's workers delight in my questions. They're proud of their ship and love to show it off. The luxury liner includes five dining rooms with lounges, two swimming pools, a huge ballroom, and a squash court. Most special areas currently hold supplies.

I peer through a little gap on the top deck. A crew-member identifies it as an expansion joint. "Engineers designed the Queen Mary to brave extremely rough water in the North Atlantic, so these joints help it flex. Under the trappings of war," he says, "the Queen Mary moves faster than any ship at sea." He promises it will outrun German U-boats, and we feel quite fortunate to catch a ride.

With her identity masked for war use, the luxurious dining room still hints at the opulence all around us. Carved wooden columns, leaded glass windows, art deco lighting, and a large alabaster sconce remain—items not removed and hopefully signs of better days to come.

Somehow the ship calms me. She's not supposed to be here either, yet when war called, the two of us took up service. I roam the halls seeking her hidden personality, and I find it peeking out almost everywhere.

The most intriguing hint of Queen Mary's luxury service stretches over a cocktail bar on the Observation Deck. I sit there alone for hours, daydreaming of the happiness in this beautiful scene. The painting, called *Royal Jubilee Week*, depicts two dozen people dancing in a carefree circle that includes women in fancy dresses, men in tuxedos, but workers, too—a chef and a porter, a dowager and a barmaid—all holding hands and dancing around a statue.

I inquire about the painting several times. A former Queen Mary bartender, now pressed into cleaning service, tells me the painting depicts the anniversary of King George V and Queen Mary's reign. He says the painter even put himself into the picture, the stylish man in the emerald blue trousers on the far right.

So I daydream about this wonderful celebration where rich and common people join hands. *Can a girl from Montana really move about the world among the sophisticates?*

One girl, in particular, draws my attention, a girl painted in a plain green dress, white hat, and gloves. I have a similar green dress. The girl reminds me of myself holding hands with a classy woman in an elegant evening gown and a man simply dressed on the opposite side. The painting gives me hope. This regular girl found her way in the big world.

On the second day out, I find John drinking coffee on the top deck, behind the bridge. His chair faces due east, slightly away from our northeasterly travel. He stares out at a faint glow spreading across the horizon, the first evidence of another day. The ship's bridge blocks ocean winds, and the chilly air feels refreshing, at least for the moment. Little gusts blow hair across his temple much like it did at his mother's grave, and I can't help but think of how much different his life would be if not for the terrible world wars. He's a kind man, quiet and gentle, I watch him until he looks up.

"Morning, John."

"Morning, Abby."

"It seems like I'm on someone's shoulders up here, so far out of the water that I should be able to see Europe if not for the darkness."

"One of the officers said you see the smoke before you see the land. So many places are burning that it smudges the whole horizon at times. All this fighting back and forth for the same land eventually destroys everything in between."

"How far can you see from up here, John?"

"Roughly twelve miles."

"So the sun is shining in Europe. Strange, how I associate that with happiness, yet the opposite exists over there. Sunshine reveals last night's carnage and stirs up tonight's revenge."

"Skilled men with killing machines." John pulls out his little envelope and deposits a tiny piece of aspen sap under his tongue.

"You talked of an OSS assignment and some unique skills you and your brother have. Gonna tell me more?"

John laughs, "Right to the point. You look very nice in your Red Cross dress, Abby."

"Thank you, John, and you look rather handsome yourself this morning. I slept well in the nurses' bunks, and you?"

"I slept right in the dining room, on some tarps actually, no snoring up there. I'm still worried about your safety, Abby."

"As I am of yours, John. We all make our own decisions, and my place is with you right now, so tell me about your world."

"Tell me more about yourself first."

"Not much to tell. We lived outside the newspapers, other than births and deaths. Nobody in my extended family did anything notable unless getting good high school grades or helping neighbors or coordinating the church bazaar get you noticed. My parents came from hard-working families, and a farm leaves little time to see the world."

"Sounds like a wonderful family to me."

"It does to me, too. In your teen years, it doesn't feel like quite enough, though. You see the pretty people, and you want to be like them."

"Even the pretty people feel that way."

"I suppose. Maybe even more so. So how about you? What makes you special?"

"Well, it started in grade school. Twin boys can switch identities and classrooms to meet a pretty girl or exchange tests. Robert likes math, and I'm more of a word guy so neither of us worked really hard in school. We expanded our efforts to cover tests for other boys, for a fee, and found we could both take on almost any personality."

"You wouldn't cover for me very well."

"You'd be surprised how we covered for guys that didn't look much like us, at least in our minds. It's in the mannerisms and dress, a game to us. Hooded sweatshirts helped. You think about a school full of natives, sure, but we took a lot of tests."

"Then you should be twice as smart."

"I am, at least, around English. I took a lot of English and Literature tests. I prided myself in learning new words, in impressing the teachers."

"So how did the Army find out?"

"We arrived for Basic flat broke but in good shape. Some of the draftees came from rich families, so we started covering crap jobs for them, sometimes even long runs for men on different squads."

"And eventually they found out?"

"My sergeant figured it out after we both snuck away for other people's maneuvers the same night. Make a long story short, we told him everything. OSS pushed us through a ton of tests, gave us three months of intense training, and called on us when Rose disappeared."

"So go back further, tell me about your parents."

"It's not a happy story. Even though my aunt tried, she couldn't make it a happy story."

Saltwater roars away from the ship's hull and splashes back into the sea. Flying fish rush away too, their silvery arcs landing well beyond the glistening rainbow of the ship's spray. Nothing else lives above water this far from land, just a determined vessel at maximum speed.

"My father, Ed Meyer, grew up in Stuttgart, Germany. His life unraveled along with the economy of the times, so disillusioned and unemployed, he joined a friend seeking work along the U.S. coast. Homesteaders filled the holds on his voyage and their excitement proved contagious: free land for the taking, instant wealth."

I hang onto the rail for stability because even a ship like the Queen Mary rocks in high seas. John moves closer, and I grip his arm.

"As always, rumors far exceeded reality, but Ed decided to travel west and stake out his own paradise. He reached Ellis Island on June 4, 1907."

"Along with hundreds like him. I can't imagine how they felt."

"Homesteading drew thousands like him, yet arriving behind so many others, he now chose from a few marginal areas. Ed found some partially wooded land near the mountains. He bought supplies in nearby Heart Butte."

"Land taken from the Blackfeet Reservation?" A whale surfaces a quarter mile out.

"Former reservation land, yes. His visits included a grocer who employed a pretty Blackfeet girl named Agnes Two Bear. They married in 1913, just days after her eighteenth birthday. She wanted a church wedding, and he wanted to wed on the ranch, so Ed converted his gold mining shack to a beautiful little church."

I nuzzle even closer to John.

"It stood over a quartz fissure that he followed in his spare time. He always said the gold would find him someday, that's how he said it, and he would buy the rented land with gold. He really believed."

John wraps his arm around me, and I feel safe, if just for the moment.

"Agnes worked alongside her husband, expanding the farm twice in 1914 and 1916 with larger herds and more rented land. War broke out in Europe, but it seemed so far away."

John smells like hair tonic and soap and leather. I close my eyes.

"They both seem far away to me," he says. "Like mother is a word reserved for someone that remembers. I remember Agnes, the name, not the person."

I press my head into his chest.

"And Agnes, the person, wasn't allowed enough time with her husband. Fate creeps up on us in the night."

I think of my own situation and how fate found me in John's hospital room. "Fate pulled me near your bed last month John," I say.

"Fate found Ed and Agnes on a fall day in 1917, in the form of a draft notice."

"I'm sure he embraced his duty."

"Absolutely. Ed reached the front lines in Europe before Agnes shared her news. She kept her pregnancy secret, worried that such a distraction might lead to his death. Her letters talked of other things and promised a wonderful homecoming when he returned. Agnes died one day after childbirth, June 28, 1918, asking her childless sister Lois to care for the boys, and begging a promise that Lois would keep the babies a secret until Ed returned."

"I know your aunt and uncle, John. So they raised you boys like their own. Ed vanished in WWI, one of the thousands that disappeared without a trace."

"Vanished without a trace," he repeats my words. "And a tremendous fall blizzard wiped out most of Ed's cattle after Agnes died. Our uncle planned to round them up a week later and bring them down, but an early October storm swept in. Lotsa death at the ranch that year."

John's story makes us both cry on the Queen Mary, October 25, 1943. I cry for his family, yet I cry for myself, too. I cry because I feel so deeply for this man. These uncontrollable feelings could jeopardize his mission and his very life.

CHAPTER 7

W e reach Scotland on November 2nd and board a transport plane sent to bolster the 5th Army fighting near Naples. John convinces a IV Corps lieutenant that we must rejoin our own unit, the II Corps.

John still falters on occasion, mild and predictable, slurring words, a confused look; the thought of him behind German lines scares me. One slip into the English language, and his ruse will end. Still, he presses on.

Once in Naples, we locate a hospital recently repatriated from the Germans. An errant bomb destroyed half the structure. Dried blood covers several rooms, now open to the mayhem where other rooms disappeared.

I find the nurse's quarters and rummage through personal effects until I find identification papers of one Abbigail Rossi of the *Croce Rossa Italiano* or Italian Red Cross. Many lockers still contain purses and makeup. I wonder if these nurses died in the bombing or hopefully, just evacuated Naples in a flurry. Broken glass crunches underfoot.

Abbigail, the name suits me. I slip her papers and uniform under my American Red Cross trappings. This begins a game of subterfuge for a girl who never even lied to her parents.

We soon reach Mignano, an Italian village tucked in heavy trees. Mignano straddles a canyon between two mountain ranges, beautiful, in a word. According to John, the rugged Mignano valley provides a natural barrier for

American troops, and the Germans fiercely guard against any movement up the Italian peninsula.

November 9th finds us holed up in an old farmhouse cellar. I page through an abandoned photo album, something left behind when the war arrived. Little black corners hold each picture in place. The sticky substance on some corners failed, leaving random photographs sliding about, and silver letters emboss the studio name below several portraits.

I page through two decades of family history, starting with high school graduation and subsequent wedding pictures with the same faces. Add babies, grandparents, dogs, horses, a piano—everything photo-worthy in their lives up to a single photo on the final page. The smiling man in the wedding picture is now a solemn soldier in uniform. The empty pages afterward end this family recording, and I wonder how the story ends for all of them. I entertain my anger for the Nazi party then, something my brain usually suppresses because those dark thoughts can overwhelm me. Seething mad, I allow myself to believe I can make a difference here. I'm in this war like the soldier beside me, trying to destroy the tyranny that destroyed this little house and the family so lovingly arranged here, page after page.

Who gave them the right to destroy this beautiful family?

The album slides back into a protected niche, so winter rains won't further damage these valuable contents. Artillery shelling continues up and down the river to our left. The shells whistle in from somewhere downstream, where a German unit apparently still thinks soldiers prowl this deserted valley. John stares at me, and I stare back.

"Tonight will be cold," he says.

"We shoulda grabbed some blankets at the hospital instead of this musty tarp."

"Yeah."

I shuffle over to join him under the tarp. He wraps his arms around me, and it feels so good I almost cry. He kisses the top of my head.

"Thank you for everything, Abby," he says. "You are my hero."

"We know who the hero is," I whisper. "Why are they still shelling the riverbank, John? There's nobody left to kill."

"Nervous soldiers. They probably spotted some movement at dusk, a deer or a swinging tree branch."

He pulls me in tighter, so tight I can hardly breathe, so tight I can feel his heart racing. I grip him too, longing for the one thing we can't have—the word, us. I tremble in his arms, so close to this man, yet with a river between our souls. We can't share our feelings for each other, but we can hold each other in the name of warmth and share the ache of our reality.

I doze off to the conviction that I'm in John's war for better or worse. Like a marriage without any real happiness, we're committed to each other if only to share the prospect of death. *'Til death do we part.* John and I probably won't survive. Those dark thoughts return, the family in the album, the Nazis destroying their home, my eyelids closing. . .

'Til death do we part.

After dawn, more heavy gunfire wakes me. John sits nearby, cooking a breakfast of sorts, two fish, gutted and propped over a small fire. We ran out of rations yesterday, so he walked to the river and found the dead fish, victims of last night's aerial bombardment. They're some sort of sucker, shrunk to almost nothing in their charred skin, the texture, and flavor of a smoked shoe, yet I eat them both. John ate two more when they were still only partially cooked.

"You alright, John?"

"Nothing for almost a week, Abby, I'm good to go. We're good to go."

"What if we're wrong about everything? You're here now, but if the Germans figure us out, General Rose and your brother might die on their own."

"Time's already short. Robert and I planned this out, and it will work. We were supposed to reach Stalag VII-A together, but since that didn't happen, Robert will study the camp until I arrive."

"Alright, I'm in too."

"Maybe it's best if you stay behind," he says. "It's true; I could be walking into a death trap."

"I'm your nurse. This is what we do."

"Risk your life? Try to blend in?"

"Germans have nurses, right? German nurses, Italian nurses, Polish nurses, they all work for the Germans now. My mother was half Italian, you know. Her maiden name was Giacona, back in New Orleans, actually."

"New Orleans, huh?"

"The place is quite a melting pot. Her grandfather, Jesse Kutcher, drowned in the Snake River, and her mother somehow landed up in New Orleans, married an Italian. I guess this Jesse guy had a beautiful compass that's still floating around the family somewhere."

He stares out a small opening in the handmade foundation. "You don't look Italian."

"Neither do half the Italians. Plenty of Nordic blood traveled down the coast."

"I guess you're right. How do you become Italian then?"

"The prison commander probably knows five words of Italian, so I'm not worried about that. Listen, you grew up out in the country like me. You approached the town crowd as an outsider because you weren't part of them, right?"

"That's about right."

"Same thing with me. In town, I listened and watched a lot. I knew what made everyone tick. I hung out with the jocks, the cowboys, the rich girls, the college-bound kids: anyone I wanted. When you're sixteen, you don't want to sit around the farm alone."

"Which group did you like best?"

"You know, there aren't many mean people. I enjoyed the fun sides of these little social circles, and I usually left their issues alone. Kinda like picking the best strawberries from the dish."

"If you pick around the bad ones all the time, the bowl goes bad."

"Oh, I wasn't afraid of standing up for things, yet I did it quietly. Drop a hint and let it simmer. Most people know right and wrong."

"That's a good approach."

"So, what's your approach now that we reached the front line, John?"

"Take the identity of a dead German soldier. I need his uniform, weapon, and identification papers: a *Wehrpass*, *Soldbuch*, and *Wehrstammbuch*. I make my way to Moosburg, a little town by Stalag VII-A. This nasty head wound helps explain why I'm not fighting. I befriend a prison guard, a man without family, learn his routine, and replace him."

"Just like that."

"My brother's already there so, it should be easy. He's already done the same."

"Easy my butt. Then what?"

"Find a way to get Rose out."

"Good to have a nurse along. With all these injured soldiers, people die every day, an opportunity for another switch or something."

John looks at me patiently.

"Listen, I kept you from seizing five times since we left Montana. I'll risk my life to see this mission through because it's bigger than either of us. I'll keep track of you and see what I can offer from Moosburg."

"I hate to say this because I think the world of you, Abby, but Rose's life is more important than yours and mine, if you do this and something goes wrong, I can't protect you."

"*Danke.*"

"You're *not* welcome, but this all comes down to a single problem. I can't remember the little key details that used to give me the edge. I still notice the suspicion in a man's eyes, the emotion in a voice, the subtle cues people constantly deliver. Once I could shape these unconscious hints into a perfect replication of the man himself, yet now a few minutes pass, and those critical details blur. I'm not the man our government sent to complete this job."

"I'm here to help you, John. Remember our discussion. Stick to the facts from here on out. When you get confused, less is more, no matter what. The Germans will sniff you out as an imposter if you ramble."

"I feel that I'm functioning normally, just not beyond the norm where my talents lie. When my brain heals up a bit more, things will go fine. It's a matter of time."

"I'll let you know because I'll stay with you."

"Let's get on with it then. You hear that shooting to the north?"

"It doesn't sound far."

"I'll head out there when it dissipates a bit. I need a dead German, and those are U.S. shells, so there'll be dead Germans. You ready for dead Germans?"

"I'm ready for dead Germans. You know I'm all in, John."

An hour later, we find dead Germans.

A German counterattack met stiff resistance against battle-hardened U.S. troops. The Allies regained their original positions, leaving German corpses scattered all around. In one foxhole, several men took a direct hit, their bodies completely disintegrated across a hundred-foot circle. Shredded trees bear witness to the power of war.

We help an injured U.S. soldier who tells us his lieutenant, Lieutenant Britt, fended off at least a hundred Germans with two dozen men. He points out their primary battle line nearby.

In the fading light, John searches several corpses, eventually finding a *Wehrpass* photo with facial features similar to his own. Andrew Schmidt took a bullet right through the temple. John strips a uniform from another soldier, and I smear blood across John's skull to make his wound look fresh and violent. A nearby trench holds broken guns in pools of blood.

Here, blood smells bitter, metallic, not like I remember back in Browning, where blood flowed under more controlled circumstances. Maybe the carnage changes it. Maybe the fresh air changes it like the taste of a boiled egg. Maybe nothing changes at all except the sadness here, all the young men now dead to this world, and my stomach tied in knots.

I follow John to lower ground after dusk. We share a loaf of stale bread that tastes like mold. John changes into his German uniform. I dress in my Italian nursing smock and wrap those identification papers in oilcloth, another trench find. Hand in hand, we navigate the riverbank. Even the birds have abandoned these trees or the remains of trees, some still smoldering.

The current rushes north through a shattered forest.

John chooses a manageable log, and together we slip into the freezing stream. Icy water attacks my muscles, forcing precious air from my lungs. The river rushes us along, shadows crossing moonlight until suddenly an intense beam blinds me. Whistles screech, dogs bark, and a man shouts something I don't quite hear.

I do understand our circumstance. Men and dogs rush the shore. A German patrol orders us from the water. We kick and sputter and scramble up the bank where John staggers out to collapse at their feet.

Head down, his hoarse voice explains the horrific American shelling. Two Germans check his identification, examine his injury, and rush him downriver to an infirmary. John says that I helped him escape, but the German soldiers give me little more than an appreciative glance.

An hour later, both of us wear cotton gowns and recall our close brush with death to a German officer. The man speaks of a surgical unit in Merano that specializes in head wounds. I fret about John until another firefight erupts, and the officer takes leave. Our wet clothing propped around a roaring fire, John wraps an itchy wool blanket around his shoulders, wraps his arm around my waist and pulls me close.

I could get used to this if we survive.

We stand quietly until a falling star pulls my gaze skyward. John points out Orion, Pegasus, and Taurus. Completely warm now, my shoulder aches from some trauma in the water, and when I tell him so, he walks back to the stream for a willow branch. He forms a little ball from willow bark and places the ball on my tongue while he prepares a similar ball for himself. I feel the pain fade away minute by minute, chewing willow bark in Europe, my body finally relaxing in John's embrace.

"There's no wind," he says. "Shall we share this deck chair?"

"I love the fire."

"Alright, first the blanket, then my tired carcass, now you?"

I settle into his arms again.

"Perfect," he says.

"I'm surprised it holds us both."

"It's a folding chair, too, a quality piece issued to our Air Force, the *Luftwaffe*."

He's already in perfect form: our Air Force the German *Luftwaffe*.

"Your lap feels much better than a cot."

"Get some sleep, Abby. It's been a long day."

I consider our precipitous arrival: the crazy intrusion on a fresh battlefield to steal away some soldier's identity. We dumped that new identity, now John's injured body, into a freezing river. The risks seem overwhelming, but somehow, we arrived behind German lines. We're part of this side now. Our hearts stay boldly across that battle line even as our wits crossed over to do whatever needs doing. My thoughts swirl until even today's turmoil can't stop me from falling asleep on John's lap.

Fighting continues south to southwest before dawn. John and I wake to an empty camp and a reasonably well-stocked supply tent. Canned food fills our bellies. Fresh undergarments wait there, all dry and pressed. I slip my Italian nursing smock on. Campfire smoke left an aroma behind that reminds me of happy nights in the Rocky Mountains, yet a nearby grave reminds me these trees shelter a World War.

"Here," John says, "put this jacket on." A bullet hole punctured the right sleeve.

"Are you warm enough?" I ask.

"Yeah, plenty of clean clothes here for the wounded."

We walk several hundred yards, occasionally glancing back to an empty camp.

"Does my old uniform work?"

"You look like you slept in it after getting shot in the head."

"Perfect, then I guess we're moving north," John says.

"I'm scared to death, John."

"I'm a bit apprehensive, but we're all in, Abby, like you said. So who are you again?"

"Today, my name is Abbigail Rossi. I went through fifty lockers to find a name I liked."

"I like your name, too, and thanks for escorting a wounded soldier to Merano, Abbigail Rossi."

"My pleasure, Andrew Schmidt, a man with your injuries can't travel alone." His confidence gives me hope, and I shake off some fear.

"Alright, if we follow this road a transport will come along."

John's wrapped head and flawless acting move us steadily up the Italian peninsula. For my part, I always explain our destination, a major surgical group in Merano. We travel with other troops eager to share rations with a wounded man and his young nurse. I hoard rations in my pockets for John.

From Merano, our story changes, John travels to Munich and a difficult recovery. The German countryside reminds me of the eastern U.S. seaboard, all these little towns bustling with concerned mothers and old men, but no young men about.

From Munich, we catch a large delivery truck to Moosburg. No one questions us during the entire journey. The

Allied invasion occupies their minds, and a badly wounded soldier fits the landscape.

At Moosburg, we rent a room along the tree-lined Isar River, eat some rich doughy soup, sleep eighteen hours, and get directions from the Innkeeper.

It's a blur. I arrived so exhausted from constantly watching John that I remember little about our arrival. All my energy went into getting him here. When he wakes me, I stare around the room like it's a strange planet.

A half-hour later, we stand together in the lobby. It smells like fresh pastry, strong coffee. The streets outside remain deserted despite the sun's arrival.

John walks outside. I stifle a sob.

After all this time; traveling, talking, and healing, I know he's not ready. I see glimpses of brilliance of what he once was. Sometimes we'll talk a few minutes, and he knows exactly what I'm thinking in such detail—he has to explain it to me. Like a psychiatrist, he can read beyond my thoughts to the very core of my being. He boggles my mind, and then five minutes later can't remember any of it. His talent for reading people will be of little use on this mission.

The master is merely human right now.

I hesitate in the lobby, unready for whatever comes next.

"He looks tough," the Innkeeper says. "All these soldiers live an entire lifetime in a year if they survive a year."

"He's recovering."

"The bullet almost took his head off."

I nod my head.

"My sons fight the fight, too, somewhere out there. Can't say it's worth it. We had a good life before the war."

"It's hard to know what will happen next."

"What happens to this guy next?" He thumbs out at John.

"His injury will keep him away from the front. Looks like he'll work at Moosburg."

He nods his head. "They will leave him there until he's steady enough to shoot. The camp assignment is not a rest, more like another hell."

"You keep this place going yourself?" I ask.

"My wife died many years ago. The boys planned to take over. . ." He shrugs his shoulders.

"I was sent to escort Andrew here. An Italian nurse without an assignment should probably hurry back to the front, but nobody knows where I am. Maybe I can help out at the camp."

"People say they haul bodies out of the camp every day. You can stay here if you want."

"I'd do my share."

"I know you would. You can cook?"

"Yes."

"You seem attached to this man, Andrew?"

"We've been through a lot together."

He nods. "I'll put you up if you wish. Get your soldier situated at the prison."

"I wish we could sleep more."

"So do I."

"Thank you, sir."

My feet move me through the door—my heart races.

I take John's offered arm and walk him toward a massive prison camp. The noise and smoke and smell of it envelopes us before we leave the tidy neighborhood. German families lived normal lives here before the war. The transition was and is abrupt.

Trimmed shrubs end in nothingness, a half-mile scar upon the land, and in the middle, a fenced compound so large that Browning, Montana, could fit inside of it twice.

CHAPTER 8

W e stand near the front gate for morning and afternoon shift change. Like John's, all uniforms reflect the wear and tear of a long campaign. Most guards carry signs of some war-related disfigurement.

Even with sunlight warming my back, the wind bites any exposed skin. Pine trees surround camp in scattered patches, a nice diversion from barren ground, yet not enough to break the chilly breeze. From one perspective, the buildings might house an industrial site, but inside the fence, long barracks line up to house prisoners. The largest tent on Earth covers several acres. Men stand everywhere, 1,000 men, 10,000 men, all suspended in time—suspended and waiting.

Most guards already passed by that afternoon when a lone man turns our way. He peels away from a knot of shuffling old men, disfigured men—soldiers now unable to soldier on the front lines. His own limp twists at a crazy angle as if his hip joint somehow turned inside out.

"'Bout time, hey," he says.

I feel lightheaded. John grips me for balance.

"Sorry, I'm late."

We find John's twin brother posing as a German guard, thousands of miles from Montana. It's just as he told me. Robert could pass for John although he wears his hair longer and somehow carries even less weight—his cheeks gaunt, his skin, tight—yet his lively eyes offer the strength I need to continue.

Robert displays his uncanny ability in this dangerous place. His walk, his look, his odd speech pattern tell of another man now dead to this world. He examines John's bandages.

"Looks like you healed alright. Who are you then?"

"Andrew Schmidt," John responds. "And you?"

"Dietrich Hoffmann."

"This is my nurse, Abbigail Rossi."

"Nice meeting you, Abbigail."

"Nice meeting you, Robert. Call me, Abby."

My response tells him everything he needs to know. He smiles again, a warm smile, and nods toward the guard barracks.

"Come, Andrew, I have someone for you to meet."

That's the extent of their reunion—a quiet exchange of words, an amiable smile, and an immediate switch back to the German language. I know that I won't speak English again for several weeks.

"How was your journey, Andrew?"

"I woke up from a coma last month."

"So, you took your time."

"Most rest I've had in two years. A coma relaxes you."

"Abby helps you, I see."

"Long story."

"I'll say." Robert gives me a look, and I know he's already sensing John's limitations. He pushes open a barracks door and yells in. "Anton, my turn to buy." He lets the door slam back shut. "Study him, John, he's a bad one and he looks a lot like you."

The door swings open, and a young man limps out, his height and face a reasonable match to John.

"Anton, this is my good friend, Andrew. Mother Germany gave him a few days for this," he points to John's scalp wound, "before he heads back to Italy and another bullet. Come downtown with us."

Anton shakes John's hand, "Hello, Andrew. I'll give someone an extra pounding tomorrow for you, an Englishman, perhaps. An Englishman shot off my kneecap and half my ass."

We enter a nearby tavern already crowded with off duty guards. Both waitresses avoid eye contact with Anton. He looks them up and down before shouldering another burly guard. That afternoon and evening, we study Anton's voice, his mannerisms, and the pride he takes in recalling camp cruelties. Robert and John nurse their own beer but buy Anton beer after beer until the man can no longer stand. Robert almost carries him out after dark.

"You ready?" Robert asks.

"Yep," John says.

"Ready for what?" Anton slurs, "One more at the Lavenhouse?"

"Yes," Robert says, "one more beer, Anton."

We head further from the barracks through a residential area and into a factory yard. Tangled weeds cast moonlight shadows on abandoned buildings.

"Gotta pee," Robert says, and the trio slips behind a squat building. Two loud thumps draw me off the road where Anton lies against a broken crate, his skull crushed from chin line to forehead.

"Strip him before the blood pools," Robert whispers, "then help me drag him over to that conveyer."

The men anchor Anton's corpse with two bricks and drop it into a dark tank. The splash ends one version of Anton and introduces another. John changes into Anton's clothes.

"Had this spot picked out for a month, the man, too. He's single with no friends because he's an ignorant ass. You notice the limp? Shelling in France blew his kneecap off, and he thought the English were to blame. You ready for the tough part, though?"

John turns to his brother.

"We have to stage a helluva argument tonight, outside the barracks in the dark. That will explain your change of heart around the prisoners. Everyone knows I don't like his cruelty. A fistfight will help cover any personality changes and the wounds on your head."

"It will take quite a fight to explain that wound," I say.

"Anton wears the hat constantly," Robert says. "John's ugly head will never see the light of day. So back to the barracks, then?"

"After we drop Abby off," John says. He pulls out his little medicine packet, the aspen sap, as I've seen him do quite regularly. "We stayed at the little Inn last night, the red one with the big deck out front."

"Don't hit John's head," Abby says. "His skull will bust apart again. Is there a medical staff inside the camp?"

"Actually, the prisoners include some very good medics," Robert said. "They work in three locations depending on the malady. If you volunteer, I would guess Commander Burger might put you to work. They treat prisoners and guards alike. Unfortunately, there's no place for you to stay."

"And we can't spend time together," John says. "If one of us gets found out, all three of us go down."

"You're right," Robert says. "Tell you what; any communication starts with a note drop. I drink coffee at that Inn every week. There's a worn-out Harley motorcycle out back with flat tires, a souvenir from the last war, and a little document pouch under the gas tank. If you have a note for us, Abby, draw a little bird on the chalkboard menu."

"And if one of you has a note for me?"

"I'll do the same. It's right there in the entryway. A little bird means another fond look at the Harley."

It's all happening way too fast. Together for the last time, I struggle with composure. My voice crackles a bit.

"I talked to the Innkeeper," I say. "Their food business looked pretty steady. It sounded like I could help out in exchange for a room."

"You're an Italian nurse that fled north when the Allies attacked," Robert says. "You can't get back to Naples and need a place to stay until the area stabilizes. If you're a German nurse, you should be working near the front."

"I already told a similar lie."

Robert nods. "You're smart. I can tell that already." He turns back toward the barracks.

"Walk with me, John. I'm scared."

"Alright," John says. "An Italian nurse that speaks reasonable German seems normal."

He holds my hand. We talk of home, of my friend Bernice back in Minot, anything at all to forget where we are for the moment. A billion stars crowd the sky.

We hold each other behind the Inn.

"I struggle to push you away, Abby. I need one hundred percent for Rose, and I fiercely guard ninety-nine, but you sneak in a lot. Please be very careful. I would die if something happened to you."

"We'll have time together someday, John. Right now, you have a job, and I have a job. I will be very careful, and please, please come back to me."

"We'll have little contact these next few months. I'm worried."

"Thank you, John." I kiss him full on the lips. "Thank you for your concern, but until this whole thing ends, I don't know you. It has to be that way. I'll be fine."

He nods his head, and I turn so he doesn't see me cry.

The Innkeeper takes me on for room and board. His two young sons fight for Hitler, at least today, maybe forever, and the business itself feels tired with worry. Each threadbare room carries a sadness, a neglected sorrow that I plan to attack with a vengeance—a thorough cleaning first, a fern sprig on each table, fresh cookies when ingredients permit. Hopefully, it will keep me grounded.

Robert drinks coffee the next afternoon. We have the dining room to ourselves.

"John's sleeping off Anton's hangover, just like Anton always does. You'll find Otto Burger's office inside the gate to the right. He's a nondescript guy, nothing to worry about."

"So he's, what, a bad guy, good guy, smart guy, suspicious guy?"

"Banker or something, kinda boring. From what little I see, he's harmless. He runs a good camp, treats the prisoners and guards well; Burger's heart's in the right place."

"Good."

"So, what do I need to know about John's head?"

Robert's nonchalant attitude irritates me.

"John's head belongs in a hospital, Robert. The bullet damaged something inside there, and if he doesn't eat, his blood sugar runs low, and he forgets who he is. John's pretty beat up."

"I see that. So a twelve-hour shift, I eat breakfast with him, eat lunch with him, eat supper with him, is that enough?" Robert asks.

"That should work. Three normal meals even six hours apart, but stay in touch, especially late in the day. Low sugar makes him slow like he's drunk, watch for that."

"What else should I know about you?"

"John explained the rescue. I'm in."

"Your nursing position intrigues me. Maybe Rose acts sickly, then John or I swap places with him. If the Germans bust you, we lose that opportunity, correct?"

"Correct. I can sell it, don't worry. The only thing I ask is your help with John. I'm afraid he might fall apart or regress, so I want you to consider John the wild card here, not me."

"I'll check on John every hour, literally, if that eases your mind. We always work the same shifts, we cross paths. I can talk to him every time, share snacks, whatever it takes. Satisfied?"

"Thank you, Robert. Now let me ask you something else. This is it? This is the United States government trying to rescue a captured General?"

"It's not ideal, Abby. He could be dead before we even start."

"Rose or John?"

"Either."

"It seems they should send in a crack team of spies or something. It seems like they're giving up on Rose."

"First of all, it's gotta be an inside job, below the radar. You can't go big here because you would never find a single man among 50,000 escaping prisoners. The Germans would kill them all within the week."

"50,000?"

"It seems to you they gave up on Rose, yet nothing is as it seems in this war. The Allies are stretched much thinner than you think. What if Germany conquers Russia?"

"I don't know."

"Germany wins the war. They get all the oil and steel and troops. They become unstoppable in their conquest to rule the world. What happens if the opposite happens, if Russia roars?"

"Then Russia controls Europe."

"Probably not much different from having Germany in control. Europe loses, and so do we."

"It sounds precarious," I say.

"There are three obvious ends to this war, and two are devastating. We're a tiny piece on the chessboard. It might seem the U.S. should come after Rose harder, but they're moving a million pieces at once."

"Every play is important."

"A single pawn moving at the wrong time can lose a chess game. Every move, no matter how small, could change the momentum of this war. Things are not as they seem, Abby. Our mission is critical despite the appearance otherwise. And one more thing."

"Yes?"

"You see John as he is now, yet they called him a master spy in training, the best they had ever seen. The U.S. government sent their best after General Rose. You and I must make up the difference."

I nod.

"I have a role to play. He has a role to play. He still has a lot to offer. "

I cry into my hands.

"This is your last opportunity to cry, so get it all out."

"I know it. I'm worried about John, not me."

"Your role could decide our success or failure." He wipes my eyes.

"Alright," I say. "The last couple of weeks overwhelmed me."

"Understandable."

I straighten up. "Thanks for putting this mission in perspective. I thought we were hung out to dry."

"Far from it. We're good at this, and I've already seen what you're capable of."

I squeeze his hand. "Focus on John. Leave the rest to me."

"That's what I need to hear." He doesn't look surprised.

"The three of us against Moosburg, it doesn't seem fair. You two could have pulled it off."

"Very true. Watch for opportunity Abby, study how the camp works."

That afternoon I volunteer as a displaced Italian nurse at the largest POW camp in Germany. I tell Commander Otto Burger about my job at a local inn, explaining how I still want to help these men any way I can. He's got a baby-face with a strong chin, mid-fifties, a rather handsome man.

"There are good medics in camp yet not enough. Someone dies almost every day. What was your name then?"

"Abby, Abby Rossi."

"Nursing papers?"

"Right here, sir, and your staff will find my skills very current."

He huffs an impatient sigh. "I will put you to work because we need help, and I will keep you secret, so they don't push you up to the battle lines. You must understand one thing. An inspector comes through on occasion, Colonel Alder. We won't acknowledge your nurse training, you are a helper. Do as he tells you."

"What will he ask of me, this Colonel Alder?"

"Probably nothing."

"What does he inspect, sir?"

"No idea, and I never ask. Alder is my superior, and I have no desire for transfer, especially up to the front. If he asks for anything you can't provide, bring him to me."

Behind Burger's desk stretched a spectacular North American map, eight feet across and dotted with tacks, especially on the populated east coast. He follows my gaze.

"That's a hobby of mine, something to pass the time. Every single European has relatives in the United States, you know. I had tickets to visit my sister in Boston before the war broke out. Do you have relatives over there?"

"Yes, sir, I do."

"Here," he hands me a tack. "Put a tack where your relatives are. Sometimes it feels good to forget the war."

I dutifully step up and push a tack near Browning, Montana.

"Oh, Montana, yes? One of my favorite pictures shows swans standing along Yellowstone Lake, you know?"

I nod. Apparently, that postcard travels well.

"So, describe this place, how do your relatives describe it?"

"They talk of a mountain stream shimmering with bright stones and colorful fish moving among the stones. They talk of high pine trees and lonesome meadows and places nobody knows."

"My sister in Boston loves the ocean, just like my wife. I remember fond descriptions of America like your own. Maybe someday we can see this grand place."

Burger's initial impatience dissolves, and we spend an hour talking of family. His brother lives in Detroit. I discuss cousins in North Dakota and Montana. He seems fascinated with his two nephews and their clock business in Green Bay, Wisconsin. The concept of enemy feels foreign.

Our conversation seems to calm him, a diversion from who he is and what he does in his war-time world. He's an electrical engineer outside of the war, a very successful man. His wife teaches at a local school.

Burger turns to the United States map. "Tell me again the name of this place on the map, this place nobody knows."

"Browning, Montana, sir. I have relatives in Browning, Montana."

"Write your name by the place, Abby. It must be very small."

My neat handwriting borders the words "Glacier Park." Both words take up an empty space in the center of our country, a broad space stretching from Idaho to the Red River Valley, from Billings to the Canadian border. Other than a previous tack near Billings, Montana, it sits empty like the broad vistas themselves.

BRIAN STRIEFEL

MAY 1945

ALDER

A bby's demure appearance fits my expectations of a young woman from almost anywhere, a woman raised to comply with the men around her.

By fabricating my expectations, she took the upper hand.

Abby arrived as an Italian nurse with perfect manners. Even though I suspected her Italian heritage, I never expected an American. I never expected the *real* Abby.

Even among American women, Abby defies convention. She grew up outside of convention, in a rural area, where the ways of a young lady did not focus on serving a man. An outsider who learned social expectations from a distance and learned that the roles many women accepted, even strived for, didn't fit her.

I questioned her many times over the last year, and I learned all these things about her.

Abby is a *liebhaber*, an *aficionado*, of the human state. Once she reads you, she can present herself exactly the way you want her, a made-to-order person planned just for you.

Abby creates the perfect Abby to meet Abby's needs.

We instruct military agents to do this in Germany. Abby comes by it naturally, and since she wrote her own instruction book, Abby never hesitates or makes a mistake.

Right now, standing near the train in Minot, I just watched Abby walk by as another man's Abby. I know what she's up to in a general sense, but she flashed me a look that did not fit the general sense.

I have no idea what she planned for today.

This whole thing could blow up in my face, right here in Minot. Abby hates me. Abby hates Josef even more. I depend on that difference to keep this charade alive.

Minot's Main Street runs south from my vantage point, up and out of the river valley.

Even in the late afternoon, cars line both sides of the street and in front of me, a band plays, welcoming soldiers home from World War II. Slide trombones and a cheering crowd inspire all the soldiers that just stepped off the train, yet Abby walked right around them all.

Josef walks down Main Street with the Abby created especifically for Josef.

I can't warn him. I can't control her.

Abby took Josef's arm and walked south. I watched them go. She had that look when they walked by me, the look she first gave me over a year ago, the day I first met her, a few days after I first spotted General Rose.

Eighteen months ago, I spotted Rose my first day back at Stalag VII-A.

NOVEMBER 1943

I visit camp every two weeks. My purpose, interrogation. I'm not a cruel man by reputation, more a quiet, stern man. Some say I report directly to Hitler, and Otto always greets me warmly. I like my persona, it gets the job done. I usually remain in Moosburg for several days.

A good interrogator memorizes the dossiers of top Allied officers. If you know the man, you know something about his soldiers and how they think. If you know something about the soldiers, a subtle question might yield monumental results.

Every dossier includes a photo.

I spotted the man in Rose's photo yesterday. According to our records, he carries the paperwork of a Sergeant, yet he is too old to be a Sergeant. I sniffed around, not enough to spook him, and I know exactly who he is, but I am not sure what to do with him. An officer carries cyanide. I need time to think.

Today, I walk into Commander Burger's office and discover another anomaly.

Otto Burger's imagination takes him all over the world. A man with a serious face and ambitions to leave Europe runs a POW camp while he dreams. He keeps a large North American map right over his desk. He collects information from everyone who passes through—a new guard whose brother lives in Texas, a fresh prisoner from New York. All who pass are begged for information about their homeland or relatives there, information captured with a pin on Otto's map, another escape for his collective imagination.

Somebody named Abby signed Burger's map since my last visit, and the location catches my eye. Montana? Nobody lives in Montana. Almost the entire north-central United States remains empty on Burger's map, other than two red tacks. She claims relatives in Montana.

Burger says this nurse works hard, treating old wounds, frostbite, and trench foot. We keep these men underfed and poorly dressed for a German winter. Nobody finds enough energy to escape.

I spend a short afternoon with an injured U.S. Navy pilot. The conversation goes nowhere, not really an interrogation, more a discussion of United States geography and actresses, especially Katharine Hepburn and Bette Davis. I'm thinking about Rose the entire time.

I walk to Otto Burger's office that rainy afternoon and I ask to see this Italian nurse, just a name on a map, "Abby."

Burger sends for her, and moments later, she knocks on the door.

"Come in. Come in, Abby," Burger says.

"Commander Burger," she says, "I want to thank you for the blankets. Oh, I'm sorry, I didn't know you had company."

She stops partway in the office. Her red hair flows around her shoulders. Her smile reveals flawless white teeth and her green eyes capture my attention. Abby disarms men by being Abby, but I don't know that yet.

"Come in, Abby, this is Colonel Alder of the SS. Colonel Alder, this is the young nurse with relatives in Montana, whom you asked about this morning."

I give her a quiet stare, and she looks back, respectfully demure.

Actually, she's studying me as well.

She looks more Swedish than Italian. There are not a lot of red-haired Italians.

"You speak German well." I contemplate some tough questions for this red-haired Italian.

"Some German, yes," she says.

"And you have relatives in America, in Montana?" I ask.

"An aunt and her children. I miss them terribly."

I hesitate. Abby's eyes look profoundly sad. "This war separates many good families," I say. "Here and abroad, but someday it will all be over."

"She wrote me letters describing the mountains and trees and the winter snow in America. Hardly anyone lives there, you know." A tear trickles down her cheek.

"What is your Aunt's name?" I ask. "And how long has she lived in, what is it called, Browning?"

"Adona Kritzberger," she says. "She was a Rossi until she met a nice German man and moved halfway across the world to Montana. She took care of me when my mother was very sick the entire year before Aunt Adona left for Montana. Now she's bedridden from a horse-riding accident. I saved my money to go care for her, but the war changed everything."

Burger nods. "Yes, many Germans left to escape the first war, and now they live all across the U.S. and Russia."

"And what do they say about Browning?" I ask.

"My aunt talks of a beautiful stream filled with colorful little fish, right in Browning," she says.

"*Pesciolino*?" I ask.

"What?" Abby asks.

"Oh, in Browning, *pesciolino*? Any of those?"

"Nope. That doesn't sound familiar."

"Anywhere around there?"

"High pines and lonely meadows," she says. "My aunt says she can ride a horse all day and never see another person in the most beautiful place on earth." Her dimples slip through a shy smile.

"Maybe it is," I say.

"And maybe a place to visit someday," Burger says.

"Commander Burger, I must get to work," I say.

"Yes, I'm sorry, Abby. Please close the door on your way out."

"Nice meeting you, Colonel Alder," Abby says.

Burger motions her away from his desk, and she scurries out the door.

Abby knew about *pesciolino* swimming in Browning, yet she didn't know what *pesciolino* is. Her German flowed perfectly, yet I knew more Italian than this Italian nurse. How peculiar, a redhead posing as an Italian, and to what end?

Our encounter left me curious about her intentions, but I was focused on Rose.

I granted Burger a week's leave and settled into his office.

It was time to make some decisions about the most crucial prisoner in Germany, General Rose. It was time to push the redhead out of my thoughts.

That was a bad idea.

NOVEMBER 1943

CHAPTER 10

ABBY

I'm the only female nurse at Stalag VII-A. I'm the only female anything at Stalag VII-A.

Burger gives me my own small ward, primarily treating frostbite and trench foot when prisoners first arrive. Burger calls it Abby's *Krankenwagen*, a reference to an ambulance.

Abby's Ambulance.

Soon I get more complicated illnesses that fit my training, like pneumonia. *Abby's Ambulance* becomes the first stop for arriving prisoners, sometimes twenty a day with maladies ranging from gangrene to blindness. I perform triage, stabilize their conditions with makeshift supplies, and send them out into the prison yards until better care can occur.

Time passes much the same as it did in the Browning nursing home. There are two kinds of people in a nursing home: those who lost their minds and those who lost their mobility. It happens to everyone if they live long enough to survive everyday perils like pneumonia, heart attacks, or car wrecks. So a nursing home nurse does what she can to comfort people nearing death. A Nazi prison camp nurse does the same. There are two kinds of people in a prison camp and a nursing home—those ready to die and those fighting it. The people ready to die are always happier.

A tall, German officer named Alder visits camp regularly. His polished black boots arrive in striking contrast to a camp blanketed in dust or mud, depending on the week. His crisp uniform and erect posture communicate power, confidence, ownership.

He interrogates prisoners, and Burger says he might report to Hitler. I asked a young Army private about him. Alder's the most notable visitor, and the private says he treats the men well; his purpose generally unclear. Men fear him because of his presence, yet he remains a mystery to most.

Burger calls me to his office one snowy afternoon. I walk in without knocking.

"Commander Burger," I say, "I want to thank you for the blankets, oh, I'm sorry, I didn't know you had company."

"Come in, Abby, this is Colonel Alder of the SS. Colonel Alder, this is the young nurse with relatives in Montana."

It's about the tack I put on Burger's map.

The room closes in around me—their solemn stares, Luger pistols, the bright Nazi flag above an inspirational photograph of Adolf Hitler. The room whispers organization, purpose, war, and danger. The men represent Hitler himself, a man reportedly prone to a devilish temper.

"You speak German well, my dear," Alder says.

"Some German, yes," I say. Time to wear a different mask.

"And you have relatives in Montana?"

"An aunt and her children."

I smile. I give into their stares. I hold Alder's eyes with my own and make a careful connection, a submissive stroke, a gentle touch.

"I miss them all terribly."

His focus stumbles. He looks away briefly, looks back, and I'm waiting. A single tear slips down my cheek.

"This war separates many good families," he says. "Here and abroad, but someday it will all be over."

Whatever purpose he brought to this conversation falters. His discerning glances turn warm, concerned. He's suddenly more interested in Abby, the girl, than Abby, the Italian nurse with relatives in Montana. Thank God neither man speaks Italian, or this whole sham would unravel before it starts.

"She wrote me letters describing the mountains and trees and the winter snow in America. Hardly anyone lives there, you know."

"What is your Aunt's name?" he asks. "And how long has she lived in, what is it called, Browning?" He's still a little curious.

"Adona Kritzberger," I say. "She was a Rossi until she met a nice German man and moved all the way to Montana. She took care of me when my mother was very sick the entire year before Aunt Adona left for Montana. Now, she's bedridden from a horse-riding accident. I saved my money to go care for her, but the war changed everything."

I call on the tears, just a couple more. Their faces look a little troubled, Alder and Burger, like fathers watching their own daughter cry.

This Alder guy continues his questions from another perspective, distracted, going through the motions. He finally dismisses me. I leave slowly, not escape speed, but sorrow speed. I turn back at the door to leave them with a final impression.

"One more thing, sir," I address Alder.

"Yes, Nurse Abby?"

My lip quivers. "Promise me Germany will win this war and make all the suffering worthwhile. Tell me you have my future in mind."

"The future in a German-controlled world will open many opportunities to people like you, Abby. The party faithful will especially benefit, and I will remember you."

"Thank you, sir. I must get back to my patients."

Alder seems harmless enough. Our conversation wandered, not everything he wanted, yet I put his curiosity to rest for now. I could read it in his eyes, not complete satisfaction because he's still curious, but enough.

My time feels short, and this can wait.

It's time to make some decisions about the most important prisoner in Germany. It's time to push Colonel Alder out of my thoughts.

I need to focus on General Rose.

That very afternoon, John slips me a note at the Inn. After dark, he meets me and outlines a timetable, stretching from Rose's first illness to John escorting Rose, disguised as Robert, out of Stalag VII-A.

"What do you think, Abby?" He paces about a little courtyard near the Inn's back border. "Sometimes Burger oversees shift change. Sometimes he shakes hands with the departing guards."

"I can distract him, John. The question is, how does Robert return to duty?"

"Maybe he doesn't. Maybe he deserts."

"If Rose's departure translates to Robert deserting, then Robert is a camp prisoner with no way out. Robert becomes Rose until the end of the war."

"Nobody said it would be easy. We are tasked with a mission despite the danger, Abby."

"Let me think about it, John. I might have an idea." My breath hangs between us in a tiny cloud.

"Tell me about it."

"Not yet," I look down. "Just in case."

"You're talking around something, Abby. Something makes you uncomfortable."

"It's probably nothing. I visited Burger's office today, and he asked me a few questions."

"Maybe you need to disappear."

"No, I handled him. There's a lot at stake here, and I'm ready."

"You sure? I don't want you in any more danger."

"How will you achieve the switch without using my infirmary?"

"Right out in the yard. Behind a building."

"There are guards and prisoners everywhere, night and day. You can't change clothes someplace random, and besides, you leave no possible out for Robert after Rose's rescue."

He shrugs his shoulders. "War is hell."

"If things fall apart, I'll let you know, but we're on for the infirmary for now." A large cat prowls the courtyard perimeter. "The owner here talks about that cat. It's always killing mice, yet a greenfinch nests in this courtyard every year, and the mother bird leads that cat around almost like it's on a leash. The cat's predictable."

"So, you say Burger is predictable."

"Yes. He's an honest man, and that makes him predictable."

"I'll leave the plan in place, for now, then," John says, "with Robert's fate in your hands."

"You concentrate on your part, and I'll concentrate on mine."

"Tell me you're not hiding anything, Abby. I worry about you."

"I have nothing to hide." It's partially true because I don't know enough about Alder to hide it. I don't think Alder will play into this.

"I'll be on my way then." He looks uncertain.

"What's the matter, this German winter too much for you?" I hug him. "You have plenty on your plate, just leave mine alone. Any misstep on your part or Robert's can bring this whole thing crashing down. We have to trust each other."

"Alright, alright," he sighs. "I trust you'll contact me if anything changes. Let's move our drop back here someplace. The owner saw me milling around his motorcycle last week."

"Right here," I point to a wooden bench. "The center-board is cracked on the bottom. I come back here every day, so any tracks in the snow will seem normal."

He nods his head. His shoulders sag.

"And John?"

"Yes?"

"You owe me a big fat cheeseburger when we get home. Add fries and a malt. Lotsa ketchup and a whole dollar in the jukebox so I can play whatever I want. Deal?"

My enthusiasm brings him back.

"Deal." He smiles. "Anything you want, Abby."

"I want to hike up above your ranch. I bet there's some nice trout in that stream. Trout that never see a fishing line."

"We never get time to fish, Abby."

"You'll take time then. You will take me fishing."

"Thank you, Abby. Thanks for everything."

"Now get back to the barracks before we both freeze our ears off."

I push him, and he shuffles away as light snow falls. This is the only contact we will have the entire time leading up to Rose's escape.

They all look the same, these drab prisoners, these thin men shuffling along with no destination. The smell reaches you some distance from camp. Nobody talks, nobody risks the wrath of certain brutal guards who resent their assignments and welcome a chance to exercise their control. Another thin shape in oversized clothes, Rose avoids contact with guards and prisoners as well.

Robert passed Rose a message several weeks ago.

Their brief interaction lit a fuse that will slip past the camp borders and detonate far-away lives, but for now, it starts as a simple plan, a simple escape plan. Each month the guards receive a three-day leave, with a two-day leave scheduled in between. Robert replaces Rose as a prisoner, and Rose walks out the gate with John. Robert already matched hairstyles and spends time near Rose to learn the other's mannerisms and speech patterns.

This explains Robert's long hair, his gaunt appearance.

The plan might get Rose across the border, yet it leaves behind a new prisoner. The risk transfers to Robert, a new prisoner of war.

Intent on Rose's escape and with no consideration of his own safety, Robert leaves that task to me. Robert must step back into his guard duties somehow. The guards don't sign in each day, so his appearance on duty is simple enough, but Rose's empty bunk will turn the whole place upside down. I have a plan.

And no time to think about Alder.

So it's two days after my encounter with Alder. Those days passed in a blur of sick men, black limbs, and infected wounds. John and Robert's weekend leave coincides with yet another snowfall. Few people move about that morning. Prisoners and guards alike huddle around any heat the camp offers.

Rose coughs uncontrollably near the end of Robert's watch. They enter the infirmary together, change clothes, and John arrives to walk Rose out of Stalag VII-A.

. . .*with my help.*

By design, I visit Otto Burger every week with some minor requests or a word of thanks. A young woman's attention is always welcome in this land of soldiers.

Sometimes Burger controls the gate at shift change and greets his men. He does it two or three times each week, and for this shift change, we think it best that he's otherwise occupied. I wear a uniform with one button missing when I enter his office. The clinic needs more supplies, although our makeshift facility actually stays quite well-equipped.

One of the biggest surprises of my life waits in Burger's office.

Colonel Alder.

"Otto Burger took several days off, my dear, what can I do for you?"

The Colonel invites me to sit. His eyes wander momentarily.

"Colonel, I hate to bother you, sir, but the food in my infirmary, it arrives cold. Sick men can't eat cold food, especially with the threadbare blankets we offer them."

His right hand reaches for a rather large coffee mug.

"Yes, my dear, the winter winds whistle through all these buildings, and a thousand more blankets could not keep everyone warm on the worst nights." His response pulls my eyes down to the mug.

"Is it the mug that interests you?" he asks. "My son made the mug in a potter's class, long ago in Munich. We haven't spoken since the war began, and it reminds me of him as I travel from camp to camp."

"How many children do you have, sir?"

"Two boys, both teenagers, all full of energy like teenage boys." He talks about their escapades with a hidden tree fort, a raft made of fence posts, a blonde girl that torments them both.

"And with luck, they won't grow up in time to fight."

"How long do you think this war will last, Colonel?"

He shakes his head. "Who knows? Our Russia invasion slowed down the Western Front."

He talks about the Russian offensive, a conversation that takes us through shift change and far beyond. I worry about the men but realize that Alder would be the first person notified if Rose stumbles. The longer Alder and I talk, the more relieved I feel. The longer Alder talks, the more upset he gets about invading Russia.

"With Germany winning, an officer like yourself can expect any number of rewards when they divide the new territories. Possibly a mountain retreat in Austria?"

"Germany bit off more than it should."

"Germany can't lose. Your Army fights better than any other."

Alder looks me over again.

"That is what I believe, too. When Germany divides their territories, I would like my own private wilderness. The Nazi party will reward us for our work."

He doesn't believe his own words. He repeats party lines with little zest. I've seen defeated men before, men without futures and Alder already expects defeat.

"You will return to Italy, then?" he asks.

"My hospital in Naples burned completely, Colonel, the entire west side collapsed so the future may have to wait. What kind of coffee are you drinking? It smells wonderful."

"I was about to make another pot. Most coffee comes from the African continent, yet this particular bean grows in Brazil. I purchased it in Berlin at a little shop run by a retired Monk."

We talk about coffee for another hour. He seems relieved to escape the wartime drudgery, and I find his company pleasant though somewhat depressing. He mentions a wife, their own weekends drinking coffee in the Black Forest. He describes their little farm, their own crops, her passion for flowers.

Afternoon shadows cover the snowy camp when I depart. I start the walk praying for John and Rose and all the other brave men in this terrible war. Everything feels normal in a bone-chilling wind. It seems normal walking past a camp full of dejected prisoners without enough food. This is my new normal.

I dance my way down the city streets. General Rose made it out.

I wake to the gentle sound of sleet on my window. My eyes open in full daylight, something that never happens because I never sleep more than an hour at a time. My tiny room looks even smaller in daylight. It holds a bed, a little closet, a window, and a door. The bathroom down the hall serves ten rooms. In turn, the shower is busy at dawn but usually quiet otherwise because most rooms stand empty. The few guests include visiting Nazi officers, an occasional spouse of the prison staff, and displaced families on the move.

Three days ago, we rescued General Maurice Rose.

My warm bed feels good, so I allow myself a brief moment of repose.

The whirlwind leading up to Rose's rescue left little room for any rational thought. Yet, rational thought reminds me that we actually face greater danger now. Somehow Robert's version of Rose has to die so Robert can stand up and return from leave.

This fix belongs to me.

John and Robert officially return tonight.

I usually help serve breakfast at the Inn, but it's already too late for that. The bathroom door stands open when I peek down the hall, so dressed in a thick cotton robe, I rush down the cold passage to my only indulgence each day. The warm shower ignites my imagination. Today I will put everything back in its proper order.

The owner serves a few guests this morning, and he waves off my apology with a smile. The pastries I cooked last night share a platter with thinly sliced cold cuts, usually liver sausage or some other frugal offering. I pour coffee in a mug, cool it with tepid water, and down it with a long gulp.

"They're lucky to have you," the owner says. He tells me that every morning.

The skies part on my way to Stalag VII-A. Shafts of sunlight rush across the houses where families without men prepare breakfasts without meat. Most food goes to those absent men fighting somewhere beyond the horizon. I enter Stalag VII-A with a wave. The single guard waves back from a high-backed chair. His right leg ends above the knee.

A British soldier greets me from his usual morning perch along the fence. He watches the sunrise every morning because it reminds him of that same sun rising at home. It reminds him that the toes he lost to trench foot pay part of the cost to keep that same sun rising over a free London. His wife promised she would watch the sunrise with him every day until he returns.

There's only one soldier in my ward at this hour. We don't expect him to live.

Robert looks anxious on my arrival. He's done his part feigning illness, yet today our performance will ultimately decide our fate.

Today the man in my care must die.

"Good morning, Abby."

"Good morning, Robert."

"You slept well?"

"Unusually well. Normally I would lay awake all night, but after several days of that, I crashed. I actually timed the crash quite well. I wanted to be fresh."

"You always look fresh in the morning."

"That's the benefit of youth, I guess. You ready for the blankets."

"Yes, I am. Let's get the fever going."

"The doctor will arrive in an hour, so we gotta start now." I pull a stack of blankets.

"You ready for this, Abby?" he asks.

"Absolutely." I cover him head to toe. "You need to eat, though. I'll get you some bread and honey. A guard gave me some honey he found in an abandoned garage this fall. I had to treat the bee stings he endured when he raided the hive."

"So tell me again how you were able to keep me in your ward."

"Oh, that wasn't hard. Nobody wants to treat the real killers, the viruses that kill as many people as the shooting itself. Even the doctors don't understand viruses."

"And a guard gave you honey."

"He's a very old man, pressed into service. He stops here to warm up on occasion. We talk about springtime, and sometimes he cries."

"I can't wait for springtime, Abby. What do you like most about spring?"

I laugh at his eagerness. "Just getting outside is enough after our Montana winters. I can stand in a raincoat and still feel wonderful. What do you like about spring?"

"The birds more than anything. When the migrating birds return, the land feels normal again." We talk through our homesickness, each thought making us anxious for springtime and the end of this terrible war. We talk of trout fishing. We talk about horses we knew, and canyons we explored and winters we endured.

So Robert, still impersonating Rose, spends his day coughing and sweating in the infirmary. A doctor checks Robert twice. Each time the doctor leaves, I lay six blankets over Robert's chest. With plenty of water and salt pills, he will survive, but Robert looks deathly ill.

The doctor agrees with my pneumonia prognosis. I volunteer to stay with the sick soldier into the evening. Robert resumes his memories, this time focusing on John.

Like Robert, John never had a girlfriend or *any* friend really, outside of school. Their remote ranch kept them far from town on weekends. Even in summer, the sheer distance made travel unattractive. John developed a soft heart for family pets. He was every dog's favorite: right down to the little house dog that Lois called her own. Robert guessed that John would have been popular in town—his classmates universally liked him—but close proximity develops lasting friendships. John and Robert served as each other's best friends.

John loves chocolate and hates cabbage. He catches fish anywhere he tries. He once rescued a fawn when a car killed its mother, but the fawn eventually died, and John was heartbroken. Robert's stories leave me longing to join him in the mountains for a month or a year or a lifetime.

I put those thoughts out of my mind.

John arrives early and strolls to the infirmary as planned. Robert changes in the dark, and I hug my favorite German prison guards. They visit a few minutes, and after shift change, they leave the infirmary with a dead Russian prisoner in a body bag.

My plan.

The Russian died of sepsis two days earlier, and I wheeled the corpse behind a curtain. When the guard came back for that Russian, I told him the man died, yet showed tuberculosis symptoms, a "lunger" so a doctor must inspect the body. Russians rank below dirt in Stalag VII-A, they were animals from a German perspective. Many Russian deaths go unrecorded. Tuberculosis frightens everyone, so the guard gladly abandoned his responsibility.

After midnight, Robert and John transport a bodybag to the graves. They log this death at the gate using Rose's camp name. When the doctor arrives the next day, I explain how our patient died, the bloody cough, all the classic symptoms. I explain that I had the guards bury him directly, my instinct suspecting pneumonia but fearing some far more infectious disease.

That's it.

John and Robert schedule our own escape in fourteen days—during their next two-day furlough.

General Maurice Rose's alias officially dies in the Stalag VII-A logbook.

Our mission ends, and we remain, just three Americans working in a Nazi prison camp.

Commander Burger and Colonel Alder have no idea who was in their camp.

BRIAN STRIEFEL

CHAPTER 11

ALDER

Y ou can imagine my astonishment.

Abby sat here and we talked about my children while her accomplice walked General Maurice Rose out the gate! She came here specifically to distract Burger. She found me in Burger's office instead, so she made sure I didn't attend Stalag VII-A's weekly shift change.

She didn't want me to interfere with their rescue. She even had a Russian body hidden in her infirmary!

Rose had feigned sickness, so a guard would put him under Abby's care, a guard working with Abby. Two Americans posing as a Stalag VII-A prison guards then made the switch. Both were scheduled for leave, so one changed place with Rose in the infirmary, and the other simply walked Rose out the gate.

Abby paraded that American guard, acting in Rose's place, as a sick man dying of pneumonia.

She created this illusion with our medical staff. When the other American returned from leave, she substituted the Russian corpse for the "dying patient," sent it to the morgue, and her "sick" American prison guard stepped right back into his duties.

Brilliant.

A nurse that never lived outside Montana came halfway around the world, infiltrated a German POW camp, and rescued the most important prisoner ever captured, maybe in the history of warfare, and all of it right under my nose.

I am the intelligence man.

The Nazis commissioned me because my English matched their best, and my knowledge of the U.S. and Europe exceeded their best. I spend my time interrogating prisoners all over Germany. The work suits me, although my allegiance comes and goes. I have no issue with any country—the U.S., the Brits, Germany, or France—only a job to do.

The knowledge I extract goes in many directions, so I know important men in every camp. Most high-ranking officials in Berlin call me by name. I pick and choose what I share at times. A man with knowledge is a man with friends, and in the Nazi party, a man with friends might survive the war.

Otto Burger never noticed any important Allied prisoners in his camp. There are so many prisoners that I doubt he would notice Winston Churchill himself. Still, I found men of interest, three men that held distinct value at Stalag VII-A, all three with important classifications, and I interrogated two of them. The third intrigued me, confused me, kept me awake at night.

I discovered him eight days ago.

Eight days ago, Stalag VII-A held the most important Nazi prisoner in Germany, General Maurice Rose. How we captured a General, I will never know, but I recognized his face because we know the enemy, *I* know the enemy. The SS keeps us well-informed. *I* know the highest levels on both sides.

Nobody else knew about Rose, and I had not shared anything: a man with knowledge. High-ranking officers carry cyanide pills. Rather than giving up information, they often choose to die at their own hand.

So Rose presented a challenge. He did not commit suicide on capture. He carried the secondary ID like most officers, and he seemed relatively comfortable at Stalag VII-A. I watched him for hours at a time. I watched to see if other prisoners recognized him.

One time he talked to a guard named Hoffman.

I missed a big opportunity with Hoffman. I missed with Abby, too.

Opportunity does strike twice.

So. . .how did I finally catch them?

My first clue involved a simple map.

A boring man named Burger runs this prisoner camp and obsesses about the world, especially the United States. Before the war broke out, he planned to visit a sister there. Now a map behind his desk helps him obsess, a huge map covered with tacks. Each tack represents a city where any passerby has family or personal knowledge, any passerby that Burger could chide into a story.

I never paid much attention to Burger's map, but the day after I spotted Rose, I noticed a new tack at the very center, in a place with no other tacks.

Montana.

Nobody lives out there. All the other tacks are on the coasts or along the rivers. The tack struck me as odd.

And I met the girl who placed that tack, an Italian nurse named Abby with a rather inconsistent accent. She did not have that sauciness the Italian girls always have, and she claimed relatives in Browning, Montana. I cannot imagine Italians crossing the Mississippi, let alone wandering out in the wilderness. I asked a few questions and found she didn't even know Italian.

So, I knew Abby wasn't Italian right off, yet Rose kept my head occupied long enough to miss everything. I missed an opportunity to pull her back into a room and find out who she really was, an opportunity to interrogate Hoffman, an opportunity to grab Rose, but I hesitated.

Perfectionists do great work if they ever start.

I spent a week holed up in Burger's office, studying everything on Rose, and ignoring everything outside the room, except for the short time when Abby visited. Even then, she fooled me.

Rose was my catch, and nobody else knew. I considered a hundred ways to approach him. This interrogation would define me, so it must flow perfectly. If I said this, he would say that, yet what if he said something else? How could I plan for every possible direction our discussion might go? How would I execute the perfect interview?

What exactly will I do with General Rose? How will I approach him?

When I shut out the world this week, the world stepped right over top of me.

I finally assemble a plan. I will approach Rose as a fellow prisoner, carefully gain his trust, then settle in for a long visit. When I walk out into the camp, I cannot find Rose in his barracks, near the eastern fence where he usually stands, or around the latrine. I spend three hours dressed like a filthy U.S. prisoner. My search eventually reveals the complete absence of one General Maurice Rose. That leaves one last place to look.

His fake identity, last name Scott, appears on the list of recently departed souls with Hoffman and Rossi's names on the signature lines.

My heart stops completely.

With those names, every clue I ignored snaps right into place.

And I know with the same clarity that Abby played a big part in this ruse. Her demure posture, her captivating eyes, she drew me in. My instincts confronted her, and she distracted me, pacified me, and dismissed me. I suddenly see it all through different eyes.

Before I can draw another breath, their plan becomes clear.

The map, the confrontation, her look, her words, Abby beat me at my own game.

A simple tack on a simple map. An Italian nurse that isn't Italian.

It's my turn now.

I watch the infirmary. Two guards come and go, Hoffman and another, twice each. Her accomplices look alike, maybe brothers. They're both tall men with dark complexions, pronounced limps, nondescript American men playing prison guard in Nazi Germany.

And through my astonishment, an idea forms, a way to salvage this crisis, to make things right.

My emotions run high. Can Abby be recruited, unwittingly, of course? How much is she attached to these American men?

How good am I?

She sweeps when I step into the infirmary. The mud and sand tracked into her little haven dries each night on the wooden floor, so at dawn, she dutifully scrapes and sweeps it into powdery piles in every corner.

I arrive with a trimmed mustache, my best uniform, and a prominent Luger sidearm. Polished officers rattle guilty people, and this girl reacts accordingly. Her hands stop, her breathing slows, her eyes follow my progress toward the center of the room.

"Tell me what you did with General Rose, my dear." I use English today.

The color leaves her face. She wavers and grabs the table for support.

"I can tell by your reaction that this question surprises you, or maybe it doesn't."

Her cheeks turn red. I pace around the room.

"It shouldn't surprise you. Let me help you grasp the question, and I do expect you to answer me, understand?"

She nods.

"I have a rather interesting position with the Nazi party. I monitor each offensive and spend time with captured prisoners, trying to predict the Allied force's next moves. This puts me in touch with many high-ranking officers. Do you follow me?"

"Yes, I do, sir." Her English comes out perfectly.

"Now, most prisoners have nothing of value, but the information in some prisoners' heads could change the war. Certainly, you know this."

"Yes," she whispers.

"General Rose is a very powerful and talented man. The Nazi party faced a much brighter future with Rose here at camp rather than shooting up Panzers, correct?"

She nods.

"General Rose knew the Allied war machine better than almost anyone."

"I can't imagine the General told you anything," she says.

"He was never interrogated."

"Why not?"

"*Today's* interrogation is *yours*, not mine. Rose is back with the Allies, not dead on a battlefield in Italy, as the U.S. claims, or here in a German mass grave, as you say. I know a lot more than you realize, so don't lie to me."

She looks confused now. "If the Stalag knew about Rose, how come he stayed here? And how could *anyone* sneak out someone that important?"

I smile at her tenacity, and then she comes at me again.

"How could a General wander around Stalag VII-A without every eye on him, all the time?"

"Only I knew about General Rose."

"Just you?"

"Nobody else knew a thing."

Her eyes drop. I grab her shoulders and share my fury.

"Your actions put my family in grave danger. My teenage sons will die in battle because you put Rose back on the front lines. You might as well walk into our home and shoot them yourself."

"I had no intention of harming your family, sir."

"I do not share that feeling right now. What is your real name, young lady, and where did you come from? Not Italy, not Germany, you are American." I lean even closer.

"Why did you let me stay if you thought I was American?"

"I underestimated you and your friends."

She stifles a sob.

"How long has Mussolini been in charge of Italy, my dear, and tell me the name of one of his wives, just one."

She shakes her head. "What do you want from me?"

"Where are you from, my dear?"

"Montana, near Browning, Montana."

"And your two American friends?"

"What American friends?"

"The two tall men with dark skin."

She hesitates.

"You know exactly who I am talking about, and they might live if you do not try my patience. So far, I believe you because your name is on Burger's map alongside the town of Browning, Montana."

"The men come from the same area, the Browning area, south of Browning, near Dupuyer."

I smell fear on her breath.

"Your name?"

"My real name is Abby."

"Two men from Browning, Montana, guard U.S. soldiers in my camp today. That is so outrageous that I cannot comprehend it. Who are they?"

"John and Robert Meyer, twin brothers."

"Twin brothers from Dupuyer, Montana."

"Yes."

"How did John and Robert Meyer breach my camp?" My voice trails off to a whisper.

A long hesitation.

"All they needed was a guard to replace." Her answer makes her uncomfortable.

"I'm not convinced I need to kill you and the Meyers quite yet, but one more hesitation on your part. . ."

"I understand." She wavers on her feet.

"Sit down over here before you faint." I guide her into a nearby chair. "Better?"

"Yes."

"So, the Meyer brothers find guards who want to go home or whatever, the details matter not. Then the Meyer brothers waltz the most important prisoner right out of the gate."

"Yes, and I'll tell you everything if you let us live."

"I do not expect you will find more generals to rescue, so I am not in a hurry. That could change in the next moment, though."

She looks me square in the eyes. Her face transforms back to the Abby I know, and I secretly admire her for it.

"What do you want from me, Colonel?" Her voice still carries nervous tension.

"Losing an American general would not go over well with the *Gestapo*," I say. "Unfortunately, Rose already escaped. I can keep this to myself, if I choose, or kill you as a spy with no explanation."

"I'll do anything you ask."

"Tell me about how you got Rose out."

"How much time do you have?"

"If I enjoy the story, you might live. Take your time either way."

"What do you know about the other men?"

"I do not know much. The men are American like your-self. Somehow they managed to become prison guards at one of the biggest camps in Germany, and you some-times move about with them, not enough to trigger any scrutiny."

"Well, I first met John in nurse's training. Browning sits a long way from anything, so we take care of people for miles around. John grew up near Dupuyer, west of that small town, and the Army returned him to Browning after a German sniper hit him."

She explains their connection and their journey. She recalls their plotting, their close calls, and her own satisfaction in helping our sick prisoners.

"And you knew we were here, but allowed us to remain," she concludes.

"I had no idea why you came, and I never expected this. I still do not know what to do with you."

"There might be something you need down the road," she says.

"Like?

"Even something for your own family, Colonel. Anything. Think about it. Think about our connections on the outside."

"My resources are significant," I say. "What could you possibly offer?"

"Take your time and think it over, sir; you have us now, either way. Depending on how the war ends, somebody with connections might make a difference for you or your family."

"I could take some time and think."

"Yes?"

"Any further problems and I will know immediately. Do you understand?"

"Yes."

"If I take time to consider this situation, the only way to keep track of you three, is to separate you, understand?"

"There are things I don't understand."

"You do understand that your actions will decide their fate, those men that helped you. Otherwise, I have no idea what else might happen here, despite your assurance."

"Yes, I understand."

"Say nothing of this to anyone, and have your bags packed in one hour. You can leave those men a note. Tell them you transferred and will return when the war ends. Beg them to wait because if anyone escapes, you all hang."

I leave feeling satisfied, more than satisfied.

Abby is mine.

CHAPTER 12

ABBY

"Yes, Abby, The Auschwitz Family Camp."

"Family camp?"

"Families much like your own. Many Gypsies."

I didn't know anything about Auschwitz. If I *had* known about Auschwitz, I would have killed Alder on the spot with my bare hands. Still, I only knew of our precarious situation, and his threat to kill us all if I didn't cooperate. If the world had understood Auschwitz, the war would have ended much sooner because even Swiss monks would have taken up arms.

Auschwitz means nothing to the world in 1943.

Alder informs me that I will care for families at the Auschwitz Family Camp. With no realistic alternatives, I nod, accepting his assignment. My desk clock ticks quietly. A young medic stands at attention, his hasty tour cut short by Alder's arrival. This British medic will take over my ward.

"Alright then."

Alder opens the door, a gentleman despite the circumstance. Icy snow pellets pound down, stinging any exposed skin, and multiplying my misery. Wind delivers the filthy stench these men must endure. The idling car seems too elegant for its task, a beautiful sedan with a long sweeping hood and gentle sloping curves to the rear. It carried an Austrian banker or a Jewish business owner or a French dignitary in a previous life.

Alder ushers me in. A few turns, and the road opens to a rural wooded drive, not unlike the foothills at home.

"Abby, there is no point in ignoring me. I'm doing what I need to do."

"That doesn't mean I have to like it."

"True, but you will survive. Tell me more about yourself and these men you worked with, the tall prison guards from Montana. You left them a message about your transfer?"

"I left a message that you transferred me to a prison camp for families."

"Good, good, and the men, the guards, who are they?"

"They ranch like everyone in northern Montana—normal people in their normal lives, soldiers in their soldier life."

"So, they raise cattle, outside Browning. Dupuyer, you said?"

"Yes, I visited their ranch with John after an early snow. There's a beautiful little church and mountains all around."

"And you came from a ranch, too?"

"My parents ranch, yes. I planned something else, a future without ranching."

"I, too, come from an agricultural life," Alder says. "Many Germans live on small farms near larger towns. Their city jobs keep the farms profitable."

"Your life sounds pleasant. Your future sounds promising. Maybe Hitler will make you Mayor." My indifference strikes a chord.

"You owe me your life, the men from Montana too. I want to make it clear that your future belongs to me until this war ends, understand? You do exactly as you are told, and for that obedience, the three of you will live, understand?"

"Yes."

"How was John injured?"

"A sniper they say, near Canicatti. When John arrived in Montana, we didn't think he'd ever wake up from his coma. These men fight bravely, like Germany's finest."

"Good men, you say, good soldiers and good men."

"Yes, people from my area think highly of them, honest and hardworking, always ready to help out a neighbor. Like your soldiers, these men didn't choose war but they accept their call of duty."

"I don't see any reason to kill good men from either side, yet circumstances dictate our actions in war. Don't make circumstance a reason for action in this situation, Abby."

"You have my full cooperation, Alder." I turn in the seat. "My nerves got the better of me, and I spoke out of turn. I apologize."

"Tell me more about yourself."

"I'm a nurse, nothing more. I grew up on a little ranch away from town."

"So, you aren't part of the military."

"No, sir."

"The Meyer brothers are part of the military. Obviously, some special part of the military."

"Yes, sir. They had some specialized training that qualified them for this mission. I helped John recover and helped him get over here."

"Thank you, Abby. Now I need silence, time to think."

Four quiet hours transport us deeper into Germany, and further from the Allies. Snow turns to sleet. Ditches shine in bright fall colors, yellow and orange and red, a windblown blanket of leaves soaked by overnight rain. I watch some leaves disturbed by our passage, tumbling off the roadway, and I relax for a moment, almost enjoying the beautiful forests of southern Germany. Occasional rain pushes little streaks of water across my window. I contemplate Alder's plans, what I can possibly do to keep us safe.

We reach a rural inn surrounded by military vehicles displaying small Nazi flags on each front fender. Six officers visit under a trellis wrapped in ivy. The smell of fresh apple pie greets us outside the door along with a man sporting jowls like a bulldog. I spot him first, through the car's windshield, the other men cluster around his lecturing hands. He turns one of those pudgy hands our way and appraises me like a piece of meat. My heart sinks further.

"Good morning, Richard. Nurse Abby, meet Richard Glücks, my superior and friend. Starting tomorrow, you will assist a man named Josef Mengele at the Auschwitz camp. Richard will escort you."

"Thank you, Colonel Alder, this is the one?" Glücks asks. "I watched you pull up."

"Are you sure I deserve this honor?" I ask.

"Yes, your faithful service earned you this reward, young lady. You will be assisting one of the most prominent physicians in Germany for one year. Hush now, and no thanks required. Commander Glücks, as I said on the phone, we waste her talents on Russian prisoners, Josef Mengele's research is much more important for the future of the motherland."

"First let me buy you both lunch, then," Glücks says. "Colonel Alder, have you found any noteworthy information from the latest wave of prisoners at Stalag VII-A? The fighting in Italy moved Hitler to rage last week. He demanded that the peninsula be cleared of those allied invaders by midsummer."

"Our latest prisoners could still be in school without this war. Their young recruits seem hardly worthy to meet the German war machine."

"Then our enemies seem short on seasoned fighters too, good news indeed."

Their conversation turns to more comfortable topics like the bratwurst simmering nearby. When our meeting ends, Alder takes me aside and reminds me of our arrangement. His manner is neither gentle nor brutish. My life now takes a cruel turn as I serve at the Romani Family camp—part of the Auschwitz facility, and indeed the most horrific place on earth.

Richard Glücks fills every passing second with Nazi propaganda. He's a driven man, preparing me for my duty even as the miles slip by.

"Auschwitz may be the perfect internment camp," he says. "I started my career as a trader in Argentina, then returned to Germany as an artillery commander in World War I: ascending to the rank of Concentration Camp Inspector. For this facility, I chose the location and designed the layout myself. Auschwitz gives me great pride."

"A long and impressive career," I say.

"And your assignment will continue the glory of Hitler's vision. We run a very special research program at Auschwitz. The things we learn will extend Aryan lives as we eliminate undesirables from the continent and repopulate with men of proper breeding."

"Alder spoke highly of your abilities, Commander."

"My previous superior, Oswald Pohl, expanded my duties almost weekly. As such, this assignment of yours plays a critical role as chief nurse for our most talented doctor.

Skilled nurses are in such shortage that I wanted to meet you personally. Alder filled me in on your uncanny abilities."

"Stalag VII-A receives a hundred prisoners daily, and half of them suffer some disfigurement. I perform every imaginable procedure with very limited supplies."

"According to Alder, your unconventional decisions save countless lives," Glücks says. "At Auschwitz, a dead patient yields little information but a living patient, no matter how grievously injured—a living patient prolongs the experiment. A living patient explores new limits. How much can a human body endure? Sometimes the results startle me."

"There are moral limits to consider when people suffer."

"Precisely, my dear, yet, what are those moral limits? When does the human body move beyond repair? Josef Mengele solves these questions by exceeding moral limits on people of no consequence—Jews and Russians and Gypsies—inferior in many ways, although physically similar to us."

"Us?"

"The Aryan race. Our utopia awaits this cleansing war. Your children's glorious future will be established on the battle lines, and in the research wards themselves, learning the extent of human frailty."

"I'll do my best to save the afflicted," I say. "If saving lives in dire circumstances can help expand the world's medical knowledge, then I'm your most ardent supporter."

"Not everyone survives the rigors of war," he says. "We built two crematoriums rather than infringe on the local graveyards."

He leads our conversation into aesthetics. He feels the crematoriums are unsightly for arriving dignitaries and discusses a tree row between units one and two. I don't yet appreciate Auschwitz's full magnitude, but Glücks' words fill me with dread.

If my Auschwitz introduction isn't frightening enough, the reality proves even worse.

They assign me to a German doctor, Josef Mengele, a sadistic man who performs medical experiments on otherwise healthy men, women, and children—especially twins and people with abnormalities.

Josef greets me on the very first day. He wears a gray fedora cocked at a jaunty angle when he arrives at the clinic. He spins it onto his desk with the enthusiasm of a confident leader. A tailored suit matches his dark hair and trimmed eyebrows, a handsome man with an infectious smile.

"Welcome, welcome, Nurse Abby! News of your skills reached Auschwitz yesterday, and I can't wait to show you our facility."

"Richard Glücks told me a little about your family camp, Dr. Mengele. I'm here to serve in any way I can."

"I must warn you, Abby, we experiment with all the worst maladies that humans suffer. These prisoners give their lives to science—a noble sacrifice that helps further humanity. The things you will see might seem cruel at first, but if you think of mankind's suffering, and all the suffering of future generations, these lives are a mere pittance."

"So, you perform drug testing, Josef?"

"Oh yes, drug testing, and so much more. As a student of the medical sciences like yourself, you will find our research fascinating, Abby, uplifting."

"And my part?"

"You will care for our subjects, observe their bodies attempt at healing, and record that information for the future of the Aryan race. You will prolong their lives with any

measures necessary, so the physical manifestations continue. Entire generations now put their future in your hands."

He holds out his arm like a kindly gentleman and leads
me into a long hall. With cautious curiosity, I fall into step
alongside a man clearly admired by Richard Glücks. I arrive with no reason for dread, but Josef's words put me ill
at ease. I will prolong lives with any measures necessary, so
the physical manifestations can continue?

With a dramatic flourish, he introduces a long row of
windows.

"Some wards are empty today, but our ongoing experiments progress with one experiment's results soon
leading to more tests. This first ward holds patients in
our high altitude experiments. We put them in a low-pres-
sure chamber for extended periods of time and observe
their tolerance."

"What have you learned here, Josef?"

"The human body can't endure very low pressure. Most
die within a few days, yet some survive, usually partially
brain-damaged. We study them to find what characteristics
keep them alive, lung capacity, and the like."

I swallow and nod. Two young women lay asleep or unconscious on hospital gurneys. He moves away from me to
stare inside.

"The one on the left is a young mother. Her will to live
amazes me." He gestures for me to proceed.

"The next ward houses a phosphorus team, simulating the
effects of incendiary bombs. We expose patients to phosphorus and try to save them. The pain kills many from the
start, but we found medicines that seem to calm the pain, at
least temporarily. Fair skin seems the least tolerant of pain.
That was my big finding. Turn the corner here to your right."

He beams with pride recalling his wards. A total of four patients stare from gurneys in the phosphorus room. Appalling burns cover arms or legs, with a harried nurse tending them in turn. The shivering and moaning tell me little comfort accompanies her efforts.

"In here, we house two men and two women today. Each spent time in ice water yesterday until rigor mortis set in. We then tried different warming rates and various broths, vitamins, and the like. We won't enter the ward because you can hear the woman still screaming, but despite the pain, she survived, her hands and legs were amputated after breakfast. The other three won't make it, I'm afraid. Slow warming seems best, and a concoction of salted vinegar shows promise, too."

"She sounds dreadful, Josef, why not give her morphine?"

"Morphine masks the real nature of healing, Abby, and most experiments don't accommodate pain relief."

I'm too shocked to pursue this question further.

"In this ward, patients are only allowed seawater to drink at different strengths. What levels can they survive? The next door down houses our malaria ward, come in here, and meet a fellow nurse. Here, we inject malaria into patients, and work toward a cure."

Ten children lie on neatly spaced beds. Sweat covers their red faces. Josef greets the three conscious children cheerfully as if they were his own grandchildren recovering from head colds. He pulls small lollipops from his vest pocket, and one little girl looks at him adoringly.

"Survivors always retain some permanent disabilities, yet some get by lightly, like little Ann here. We test various medications hoping to curb suffering, and even cure malaria for future races."

I turn away and slip back out the door.

"It will get easier," he says, "when you understand. Always remember these experiments expand the future, a world when our superior race occupies every territory, and their resistance to disease will be so important."

"Little children?"

"Children have the best immune systems, the strongest bodies, Abby. They give us direction for older patients—the next room tests mustard gas. Be very careful there; we don't want any on your skin, even from the patient's skin because, it's very painful. Then, onto my favorite ward for human experiments, surgery. We swap extremities from one patient to another, researching transplants that can repair damaged soldiers."

My work, as his direct charge, involves caring for these patients, who usually die.

If I do save anyone, they return to camp in whatever condition that remains. I never see them again, but I know they return with nothing left. We don't send anyone back with enough life for another experiment. Their bodies are spent. I'm part of a massive prison system. It's not until years later that I will understand the additional atrocities committed: the gas chambers, and the annihilation of an entire population. Yet even without this knowledge, I loath Josef and the suffering he creates.

In the beginning, these people feel fortunate. Mengele's victims are better fed and housed than other prisoners and safe from the gas chambers for a time. He even builds a playground for children that are the subjects of experiments. He introduces himself as "Uncle Mengele." He distributes candy, but one building away, he watches them through his window, concocts deadly experiments—random experimental surgery, intentional infections, beatings, and exposures—all with sadistic enthusiasm.

He ends each day with scotch and Beethoven, right in his office, with the gray fedora confidently placed on his head. He glances into every ward on his way out, a serial killer with free reign over a subjugated population.

He starts the next day like the last, walking each ward with the air of a general going into battle. Josef reviews the charts of his favorite experiments. They are not referred to as patients because this facility is not about patients. He talks candidly about the future of the Aryan Race when a concerned nurse breaks down. He inspects everything from the cleanliness of the beds to the pleats of the nursing uniforms to the punctuation on the charts. He believes these experiments, this "research," will eliminate future suffering for people that actually matter—the superior race that will soon rule a planet now controlled by an undeserving population.

And his lurid fascination with twins communicates everything Alder wanted me to know. Josef believes twins are the closest thing to identical human specimens. He delights in the arrival of any twins. He transplants eyes, ears, arms, legs, or fingers: twin to twin. In time, he believes the blood vessel alignment, the muscle attachment, the suture patterns used in successful transplants will help enable other transplants. Unfortunately, the transplants never work. Infection sets in almost immediately, gangrene follows extreme pain and death. Smaller transplants, like ears, sometimes look promising, but the body can't sustain this misaligned tissue long, and eventually, the ear dries up like shoe leather and falls away.

If Alder turns John and Robert over to Josef Mengele, their lives will end slowly, brutally. Alder imprisoned me here with psychological brilliance.

My mornings start much differently than Josef's. The previous day's horrors churn through my head until well after midnight when exhaustion reaches up and smothers me. Morning arrives three hours after yesterday's anguish and an hour before another horrific day. I open my bloodshot eyes to escape the nightmares, but my real life waits with more of the same. I pull the covers over my face, knowing what remains in the light.

I won't follow my Hippocratic Oath to uphold ethical standards. I will uphold the Nazi oath to rule the world. I won't heal my patients, or comfort them, or fulfill the hope and trust they place in me.

I'll follow orders and systematically kill each and every one of them.

Alder hands me sixteen months of pure hell and those same sixteen months turn nightmarish for Germany. My strange incarceration keeps John and Robert in place as prison conditions deteriorate. My only joy in life occurs early each morning when I lie in bed, focusing all my anger on revenge.

JANUARY 1945

ALDER

"If you win, you need not have to explain. If you lose, you should not be there to explain."

Now that Hitler's ambitions have fully outpaced his fighting force, his words feel especially cruel. Hitler understood the consequences of failure. Hitler accepted those consequences for 70,000,000 Germans. Seven million died. Sixty-three million must explain.

My own day of reckoning approaches.

I monitor Abby through Josef Mengele. Josef worships her because she does her job; more accurately, Abby delivers the nurse Josef needs because Abby understands the consequences of failure on her part.

Hitler's war machine fares much worse than the concentration camps.

His Russian invasion proves disastrous, depleting men and fuel without any strategic gain—but infuriating a powerful neighbor with unlimited men and fuel. Germany evolves from the aggressor to the defender. Hitler now has too many borders to defend.

Time passes, and I finally revisit our arrangement, January 10, 1945.

My war will soon end.

Abby stares out the window at the cremation stacks. Heavy smoke hurls into the heavens night and day now, a determined effort to eliminate the entire human inventory by springtime. She sits alone at a wooden desk in an empty ward. Two patient charts lie beside her right hand, certainly complete, detailed flawlessly per Josef's instructions. She looks away from the window: her face thin, her eyes tired, her hair subdued under a sagging net. The camp began closing a month ago under advancing Allied movement.

"Hello, Abby."

Goosebumps rise across her arms. I'm sure she likely hoped I would die in a bombing attack or just have a heart attack or really any attack at all would do. I pull up a chair to face her without an answer.

"I need to visit with you. Can you arrange it?"

"There aren't even birds here, you know that? Even the birds stay away from a place this horrible. How do they know?"

"I can't answer your question."

"Are you going to kill me?" Her eyes inventory me during the question. My frayed collar. More lines under both eyes. Thinner gray hair. Scuffed shoes and missing buttons. This isn't the Alder she knows.

"No, I'm not."

"Is someone else going to kill us?"

"You aren't in a position to ask questions, but no, there will not be any killing or torture or even yelling. You owe me your life, your friends' lives, and today I collect on that debt."

"Sounds ominous."

"The Nazi party unravels more every day."

"I hear rumors."

"Your General Rose destroyed us in Normandy."

"I shouldn't comment, but that's the best news I've heard in a year."

"He led the first division into Germany. Right now Germany is losing their final battle of any significance—the

Battle of the Bulge. Rose leads to the south, and he's already insured an Allied victory. Do you want to know more?"

"Why are you telling me this, Alder?"

"Maybe it's best this way. A warrior like Rose can save a lot of lives on both sides, just by finishing the war. I told you he's that good. You know about the Normandy landings that started Allied movement across France and Belgium?"

"I'm exhausted and bitter, Alder, so I won't play any games."

"Your friend, General Rose, pushed the U.S. First Army through Normandy. They welded I-beams to the front of their tanks to smash through hedgerows, the very I-beams that Germany buried along the shore to keep Allied transports from landing. Rose's division advanced a hundred miles a day."

"Maybe he was lucky."

"No, he was good. They fought all the way across France and reached Belgium in September. In Mons, they cut off 40,000 *Wehrmacht* troops and captured 10,000 German prisoners. Then Rose's division invaded Germany for the first time since Napoleon. They crossed Germany's final defensive line, the Siegfried line, before any other division."

"So our rescue did help end the war. The good guys win."

"There are good guys on both sides. Hitler forced every single man into service throughout Germany and all the occupied countries."

"Describe the good people."

"People forced into service with their family's safety in question. People concerned about the future."

"Are you good or bad?"

"It depends on your perspective."

"I can't comprehend any part of the whole Nazi vision, so I can't allow myself to think I understand your perspective."

"Germany still controls most of this continent, but that will soon change."

"So, I meet with whom today?" Abby asks.

"Just me. Line up a quiet place."

"Here and now is fine. We've killed almost every prisoner worth killing, and the rest are going fast." She points out the window.

I wear civilian clothes today. Abby turns her tired-looking wooden chair.

"They burn everyone, you know. Not just the corpses. They burn entire families."

"It's time to abandon Germany," I say.

"I guess I knew it all along even though I didn't talk about it, as if not saying it might make me wrong." She looks back out the dirty window.

"You and your friends need to leave before the Allied forces arrive, otherwise you might get shot by your own troops."

"That wouldn't happen."

"The Russians kill everyone."

"You treated them the worst."

"Agreed, but that doesn't change your situation."

"And you will help us escape? Why?"

"I'm coming with you, along with two other young men—men of less importance."

"Men of less importance," Abby repeats.

"Exactly."

"You're a Nazi, sworn to follow orders," she says.

"I'm German and will always be German, but I'm not part of this lost cause. Many Nazis aren't."

"So, you want me to help you sneak German soldiers out of Germany."

"And I will accompany them."

"Why would I sneak you out?"

"I get you three safely out of Germany, and you help the three of us, simple trade."

"And your plan for this escape?" Abby asks.

"To cross the border, we carry Allied dog tags of a private, much like your little Stalag VII-A ruse. When the Nazi party finds anyone missing, they spare no effort in finding them, so we will move quickly. I can reach the border, but I cannot cross Belgium without your help."

"So, we are met on the other side?" Abby asks. "We can't walk to the ocean."

"I will have a transport waiting at the border, an American truck we captured. I relieve you from duty, and we reach the Belgium border with American papers."

"John and Robert?"

"They escape with us."

"Three Germans, three Americans."

"Yes."

Abby leans forward. "I've got a problem."

"What is your problem?"

"Mengele."

"And the problem?"

Her eyelid quivers. Her jaw clenches, and she turns away. Auschwitz damaged her.

"Tell me about him." I expected this.

Her shoulders sag, closing the distance between us.

"Tell me about, Mengele."

Her eyes don't betray her next move. Her hand comes across my face with such force that my chair tips. I catch myself with one arm and push back up, the metallic taste of blood flooding my mouth.

"How could you," she hisses, "put me with that monster? I endured over a year with an insane murderer, watching mothers and children die—all for his curiosity. With John and Robert in Moosburg, I had no recourse. All I could do is watch."

"I had no control, no influence over Mengele."

"Even if I believe you, nothing explains what you put me through, nothing. They killed everyone in your "family camp" on August 2nd—2,900 people. Since then, they've slaughtered most everyone else, barrack to barrack."

"Maybe I can help you make it right."

"Not in a million years." She looks back outside, thinking of something else, her eyes moving building to building across the Auschwitz camp. German shepherds bay in the distance.

"There wasn't a thing I could do to change what happened. He had the support of high command. This whole camp follows orders right from the top, and Josef would have carried out his work whether you helped him or not."

"He plans an escape of his own. I can't allow him loose on the world."

"Mengele has friends in high places," I say, "so he's untouchable here. He reports in every single day, yet you gained his confidence. Maybe you escape with him, deal with him on your terms."

"Deal with him on my terms."

Her cheeks glow bright pink like I slapped her myself. Her bloodshot eyes, her tangled hair, the lines on her forehead all speak of her year here at Auschwitz. No revenge on her part could ever equal the world she witnessed. I needed her exactly like this.

"He trusts you, Abby. As horrible as your experience was, you gained his trust, you did your job. We spoke about the end of your service, and he talked graciously, so appreciative of your help."

"He's trusted me with his research all condensed to a single satchel, in his own handwriting."

"Excellent."

"I helped kill hundreds of people. They looked at me with hope, and I did nothing."

"They were dead already. You were a witness. Do *you* really want him?"

"I want to kill him."

"The world still frowns on that, and he'll escape or die of old age before the courts deal with all the Nazis."

"I want to kill him myself."

"Every high ranking officer has an escape plan. Josef's plans are real, yet he would follow you anywhere. You have an attraction, a gift. He would trust you to smuggle him to the U.S."

"And kill him there—Josef and that damn gray fedora."

"You said nobody lives in Montana. He would follow you there."

"Why are you entertaining me, Alder?"

"The Nazi party will fall soon, and the world does not need Mengele."

"The world doesn't need any Nazi."

"Some will escape. If this all hinges on Mengele, I will help you."

"He kept their teeth," she says, as though the news is fresh. She shakes off a chill that just climbed her spine. Her lips curl in a look of pure revulsion.

"Whose teeth?"

"Prisoner's teeth with gold fillings, he kept them in his desk. He cracked them open each night like so many mixed nuts and stashed the gold in a box. Sometimes he did it while he reviewed my charts. When Josef escapes, he will escape with his pockets full of gold."

"A man selling gold will be a man under scrutiny when this war ends. German troops confiscated a lot of gold."

"Confiscated seems almost legal, so let's stick with murdered and stole."

"As you wish."

"Semantics aside, Mengele can sell that gold in Montana without raising suspicion."

"You have an idea?"

"Prospectors still comb the mountains. Every fall, they arrive in town with a little jar of nuggets and flakes," she says. "They come in old rusty pickups, sometimes even on horseback."

"Delivering their annual take."

"Gold still entertains a romantic notion out west," she says. "I can't say I haven't panned a few streams myself. Some of these men live hand to mouth, living off the land, but others do pretty well."

"So, you have something that might interest, Josef."

"Yes, I do. It seems I've come into an inheritance, a little Montana ranch with some gold."

"You've already thought about this."

"I've already considered a hundred ways to kill Josef. I've also considered a hundred ways to kill you."

"Which one shall we do first?"

"Fortunately for you, Josef must die first."

"And you need my help."

"Yes, Alder, I need your help."

"I deliver us all at once then, four Germans and three Americans. I deliver us to the Belgian border, and you deliver us to New York. I'll help you with Mengele if you wish, and the others are free to do as they please."

"John and Robert can help me."

"That's up to you, pretty risky, though. If you spook Mengele, he disappears, and he's good at disappearing. He's comfortable with us."

"You really think he could get away?"

"He's as charming as he is brutal, Abby, with perfect English. Yes, he could blend in anywhere."

"Then I need to do this without alarming John and Robert. I'll need to travel with everyone on the way back to New York. You need to find a way that will work with Josef."

"You could be helping fellow Nazis, John, and Robert all the way to New York because their English will not stand up to scrutiny. Josef prides himself in his mastery of English, so this would be something that would feed into his ego."

"If you can sell that, I can sell that. I can get them to speak German with a little broken English when Josef's around. You can keep Josef company until New York."

"That won't work. You must accompany Josef until we reach New York," Alder says. "He's fixated on you."

"So I need to pacify John and Robert instead. That's what you're saying? "

"Mengele must be your primary companion. He'll only follow you."

"John and Robert must accept this," I say.

"Yes. You're rescuing a prominent researcher from the Germans or Russians or whomever. Can you convince your friends that this innocent German doctor needs your full attention?"

"I can do that, yet how do I trust you?"

"I know about Mengele's research, Abby." Just the word starts her seething all over again.

"RESEARCH?!"

She regains her composure.

"He's gone for the night, so I could scream at you for hours, but I don't have the energy. I can't keep food down, and I can't sleep, yet I clean up nice every morning, and I smile so you don't deliver my friends here to Auschwitz. I do all of this to meet your demands, but never use the word research because this hellish place only researches new ways to commit murder."

"You want him dead, and I can't disagree. He played God at Auschwitz while actually doing the devil's work. I will help you end his life."

She slides in close like I did to her earlier. She brings her nose six inches from mine and grasps my shirt with one hand, twisting until a button pops off and skitters away.

"I smell a sincere man now, yet our history reeks. Can I trust your words? All I need is backup, in case I fail. Will you do that for me, Alder?"

I tell her some version of the truth.

"Yes, I will."

"Shake my hand then, because as much as I don't know about you, I do believe you are a man of your word."

"Yes, yes, alright, Abby, I will shake your hand. It will take until April for me to line up everything. The people, the identities, transport itself lay scattered about."

She holds my hand with both of hers, and she stares me down again.

"Then, for now, I must stay with Mengele, on to Gross-Rosen, wherever he goes," she says. "You want us in

Moosburg by early April, Josef and me. I will make sure we arrive at your chosen time."

"Make it April 15th."

"Alder?"

"Yes."

"I hate you. That will never change."

I nod my head.

"Mengele dies. If I get even the slightest notion that you aren't on board with that, any time of the day or night, I'll kill you. You get between us, and I'll kill you. If you aren't sincere about killing Mengele, don't start this ball rolling."

"Mengele dies. I promise."

BRIAN STRIEFEL

APRIL 1945

BRIAN STRIEFEL

CHAPTER 14

ALDER

Stalag VII-A looks the same from afar but Germany finally runs out of everything, and prisoners of war find little consideration in *Gestapo* headquarters. Commander Otto Burger moves heaven and earth to keep his prisoners alive.

Burger's *Gauleiter*, his current overbearing commander, rules with an iron fist. Any sign of insubordination invites immediate execution. Within these dangerous confines, Burger fiercely protects his charges. *Gestapo* leaders and other fanatical groups call for retaliation against prisoners, yet Burger works to ease tension, and secretly establishes contact with approaching U.S. troops—to avoid local bombardment. He then convinces prisoners they are safer in camp than on the outside and within this atmosphere of mutual respect, the prison awaits its fate.

Abby and Josef arrive April 15, 1945.

Abby greets me like a colleague, courteously and respectfully, but as my grandfather always said, a cornered dog is the most dangerous dog. I entertain Josef that day, while Abby visits her old infirmary, now staffed by two captured U.S. medics.

Josef can't praise Abby enough. He's excited about the escape and all the future possibilities it offers. He talks of

New York City and Chicago and the Montana mountains.
He's equally fascinated with Argentina: a beautiful place
with an undereducated population ripe for exploitation—his
words. Each topic returns to Abby's steadfast dedication for
Josef's work. I sense a little infatuation, and I can't blame him.

That night, the three of us dine at a little Inn where Abby
helps the owner cook a delicious meal. Bratwurst served
with sauerkraut complements her buttery mashed potatoes.
Yes, Abby's mashed potatoes steal the show, heavy on the
cream, just enough salt. The owner furnishes his own hidden food stash. We chat like the closest of friends. She grips
Josef's hand when he brags. She adds enthusiastic details to
his chilling accounts. She hushes everyone each time the
owner brings coffee. If I had any lingering worry about her
commitment, her warm admiring smile brushes it aside.

The next morning she rises early and delivers coffee to
my office. She's smartly dressed in a white blouse and gray
skirt. Her hair is gathered under a stylish hat that matches
her skirt in color and texture.

"You look very nice this morning, Abby."

"Nice is not my intention. Try determined."

"Determined then. You look determined."

"Josef bought me this outfit last week. He said, 'Josef
Mengele's head nurse deserves an air of distinction.' I cried,
and he perceived tears of joy."

She seats herself across from me.

"I would kill me, if I was someone else," she says. "Just
knowing what I did at Auschwitz, almost any good citizen
of the world would kill me."

"You aren't his nurse by choice."

"I don't know if it matters. Many Nazis do what they do
without a choice."

"The end justifies the means."

"I don't know if any end will justify what I've done. I'm not like you, Alder."

"You might be wrong about that, too."

"I lost a sense of right and wrong in Auschwitz. I should have killed Josef there."

"You acted on behalf of others. You protected the Meyer boys."

"I would kill me, if I was someone else," she repeats. "I should have killed myself."

"In killing Josef, you will settle that score in your own mind."

She stares at me, unmoved.

"So, what arrangements have you made since returning to Stalag VII-A?"

"I've explained our arrangement to John and Robert," she says, "and they have agreed. I told them that Josef is an important research scientist that we are smuggling into the U.S. I told them they need to speak German around him to calm his nerves. I told them that Josef trusts me, and I need to spend a lot of time with him."

"How did your reunion go yesterday?"

"You want me to tell you about how dreadful they looked? Is that what you want? Because they did look very bad. Does that make you feel good, Alder?" Her monotone words arrive without emotion.

"No. "

"You leave them out of it and let me tell you one thing. I didn't cry yesterday because I no longer have a capacity to cry—you won't get any satisfaction from me. John and Robert know nothing about Auschwitz, only that I spent the year treating prisoners at another camp."

"How about Josef, then? He's with you on this escape?"

"He's already planning how to start up his research again. He gave me his journal, all of his notes for safekeeping, in case he's caught. He wants them available in the future, to the right people, the people he trusts me to find."

"You play this very well, Abby."

"He believes that I inherited a Montana ranch from my aunt. He believes there's a small gold mine on the ranch and that I've seen the gold myself."

"Josef believes in you. His death will go unnoticed."

She gives me a fake smile. "I'm killing you next."

"Anything else I should know?"

"I lectured Josef on his new identity. To Robert and John he's a medical researcher defecting to the United States. He tested war victims that were exposed to phosphorus, high altitudes, freezing temperatures, and the like. He can't mention that he actually exposed people to these horrors himself because Americans are incapable of understanding."

"Robert and John are incapable of understanding Josef," I say.

"Americans can't comprehend how important this research is for the superior race that will someday rule this world," she says. "Small sacrifices for the greater good."

"You're coaching him well, Abby. If you want to deal with Josef yourself, he can't start talking about his real work, no matter how delusional he might be."

"He's the devil incarnate."

"Not in his mind."

"In some ways that makes it even worse." She stands up and walks to the door. "We couldn't administer morphine at Auschwitz. Without pain a human body acts much more predictably. Pain keeps everything real."

She walks to the door with disturbing poise.

"I will be transporting his medical research notes, too. He feels I'm less likely to get searched. Just a leather satchel." She looks back over her shoulder at the Nazi flag.

"May God go with you," I say.

"Maybe God put Hitler here for a reason," she says. "If the world doesn't lose its taste for war after this atrocity, all is lost."

She returns to help out in the clinic that afternoon. I watch her those next few days. The life of her friends seems a sufficient deterrent, a reason she must trust my plan, but trust is relative.

And truth is also relative. Fortunately, she doesn't know that.

We gather four nights later to make our escape. Dazzling stars surround an Earth embroiled in conflict since early men argued over a piece of meat. No lights shine back toward the heavens from Germany. Wartime blackouts cloak the whole country. Darkness cloaks our faces too, a darkness created by Adolf Hitler's vision, an all-encompassing darkness that devours a man's soul when he enters the Nazi Party because there's no escape except death, and more darkness.

Abby joined the darkness in Auschwitz.

Tonight, Abby clings to Josef with both hands as if he alone will protect her from the dangers waiting ahead. She whispers in his ear. His murmured response seems comforting. She straightens his fedora, then tilts it back to where it was. He surveys the area, evaluates the other men, approves their presence with a confident nod.

The rendezvous point served as Moosburg's largest employer, a former toy factory. Toys served no purpose in Hitler's war, and the materials found more appropriate service in a bomb or tank, so the SS shuttered each building, and conscripted the workers into wartime service. That was early in the war. Their names initially listed on a memorial near the gate until each man died, few names remained and everyone presumed the lot of them dead. The town carved "missing in action" over those remaining names and sadly waved as their sons now marched off to war.

Robert and John reminisce about a night of drinking with a fellow prison guard. Apparently, they passed through this abandoned yard long past midnight, and stopped to urinate nearby. Abby admonishes their idle chatter.

I urge everyone into a large armored car.

"Keep quiet and if we run into anyone, let me do all the talking," I say.

Wrecked vehicles litter the empty road. Allied planes took their toll on Germany's war machine here, like so many other places. Allied planes could find us too, driving without headlights down a moonlit road. Abby sleeps.

Exhaustion catches everyone, eventually.

The miles stretch between close calls with road debris. Each time I speed up, another bomb crater or wrinkled fender straddles my lane. Once I see a civilian body crushed under the remnants of an old farm tractor. A dog scurries into the darkness, and I see where it's been eating on the corpse.

An hour later, the trip ends in an old barn that smells of used oil and old hay. I don't know how this particular structure survived, just that it did. We hide the German vehicle inside. Shadows hide another vehicle in a side room used to store grain.

I came here alone, several days ago. With all the fighting elsewhere, this building and the ruined land around it lay empty. A brick chimney marked an absent farm home, and another lone dog searched for scraps in the yard. I fed the dog what little I had, a liverwurst sandwich, yet later wondered if I just postponed the inevitable. The dog reminded me of a German survivor, not responsible for war, yet responsible to deal with the aftermath. I feel regret today leaving so many people in the same circumstance as that dog, picking through the aftermath.

We dress as Stalag VII-A prisoners, complete with camp identification and original U.S. military dog tags. We're an escaped work crew now. Other men whisper in the shadows, but no introductions occur. Abby sprawls across Josef's lap with John and Robert both awake and watching nearby. This sleeping girl with the red hair endured a lot for the Meyer boys.

I visit with our two new companions in the dark.

Three hours before dawn, I uncover the American transport truck.

"Wake up Abby, it's time to go."

She opens her eyes. She takes inventory, one man at a time, ending with Josef.

"It is time to go," Josef says.

She looks at me again and nothing about the look suggests friendship.

"Stand up," I say, "take it easy, keep it quiet, let's drive."

With our headlights covered midway and above, I steer around the remnants of whatever battle occurred here. More than once I stop to inspect divots and rusting machinery. Robert helps me navigate a clear path.

All six men wear Stalag VII-A prison uniforms, but Abby remains an Italian nurse. Some distance beyond the border, Abby engages me. She's back.

"Are you ready for the United States, Alder?" she asks. "Are you ready to travel west?"

"West," I say. "Yes, on to New York City, then west to a better life without Hitler."

Fortunately, she can't see my eyes.

"Your family, what about your family?"

"My family is safe for now, Abby. They can follow when things settle down. I moved them away from our home to a good place."

"I'm glad your family remains important, Alder. Indeed their safety must be in the back of your mind at all times." She squeezes my shoulder. "With the right encouragement, the occupying forces could believe almost anything about anyone."

Abby reassures me that she won't be reassuring me.

"That is why I am glad to have the present company," I say, "of six good citizens whom I trust. I know our secrets are safe."

"Secrets," she says, "bring together the most unlikely of allies."

We cross the German border south of Aachen. Thirty minutes later, a damaged road leads west toward Antwerp and the ocean beyond. I chose an odd route to avoid both Allied confrontation and the renewed German aerial attacks I argued against.

Why bombard our neighbors when the war is already lost?

Smoke hides the city of Liege until we reach the outskirts. I curse the German cruise missiles that continue this needless destruction—V-1 buzz bombs, the V announcing vengeance—one thing a losing army should never consider.

From Liege, I steer northwest toward Hasselt, a town with little strategic or industrial importance. The war largely spared Hasselt. A porch light shines in front of every little home squatting along the roadway. Inside, the family waits for a door to slap hard against the woodwork, waking them from hopeful dreams about the survival of their soldier.

We carry on.

Further west, the winding road reveals progressively more devastation, more shelled towns and dead livestock. Belgium appears a broken country like Germany, but the smell of saltwater revives us near dawn. We stop above Antwerp in a small roadside park. Revealed in predawn light, frothy whitecaps march up the river like so many obedient sheep. Large pine trees flank our vantage point, and together we watch the sun explode across the damaged city.

"A celebration," I say, "to the end of this war."

I hand everyone a candy bar.

"You need energy, each one of you."

They take my offering with unbridled enthusiasm. They turn away from each other to savor the first food in many hours. Abby motions me away from the others.

"You were right about John and Robert, they already look suspicious," she says. "This won't be easy."

"If they interfere or make you hesitate, Josef will run. You have to do this without them."

"Don't you dare toy with me."

"I'll be in the background if you need me. I give you my word."

"Engage Josef. I've got too many men protecting me right now and they're all wound a little too tight."

Soldiers crowd the Antwerp docks. Buildings show the destructive force of Hitler's V-bombs, a nightmare delivered right into March. Several volunteers relay the sad news that a V-bomb hit the Rex Theater on December 16th. After all the wartime horrors, in a place soldiers could finally relax: a Gary Cooper movie packed the house with soldiers and civilians. Hitler's V-bomb leveled everything. It killed 570 people and announced the start of an offensive meant to capture the city and its valuable seaport. The ensuing Battle of the Bulge further devastated Belgium and hospital necessities still remained in short supply.

Even the smallest donation could help.

I watch Abby's temper rise and fall during the emotional plea. Abby gives what she has, a watch she wore when we first met. Others empty their pockets. This final sin, the destruction of Belgium, seems worse than the other sins, worse than retaliation, a devil's task.

Signs direct us to staging areas for returning servicemen.

The crowd jostles in little knots: the Jarheads and the Seabees, the Squids and Ground Pounders. I know their slang. Each service unit finds their respective comfort. Three men approach, men I know, but I wave them off.

"More friends of yours?" Abby asks.

Despite Hitler's effort, Belgium is not Germany and my control disappeared several hours ago.

"Alder?"

Too many lies cross eventually. The truth is much easier to remember so I search for the right explanation.

"Friends?" she asks again.

A young sergeant interrupts her.

"Sir, ma'am," he says, "are you headed home? Soldiers departing Europe will ship out from France. Daily transports stop in Antwerp mid-morning and the next transport leaves in five minutes. Five minutes. You must hurry if you want to catch that boat."

"Is there another boat later?" Abby asks.

"Not for several hours ma'am. Quickly then, let me walk you there."

He delights in helping a pretty nurse. He assures her that France assembled an organized military installation to process military personnel. Former POWs need their prison ID card, which includes their service ID, rank, nationality and photograph.

Our cards, forged and otherwise, pass inspection.

Abby goes first, watching the two extra men in our company. The others that approached me raised a red flag. She studies these two, learning what she can. I know Abby's look. Robert and John move ahead of us on the gang-plank as Abby falls behind to intercept me.

Sometimes even the best laid plans pick up unexpected wrinkles.

I need her focus.

"Abby," I say, "let's all head up on deck."

"I'll walk with you. And you tell me about the men that approached you on the docks."

"C'mon people. We have a boat to catch," John says.

"Alder?" she asks.

A tall woman grabs my shoulder.

"Over there, sir." She points downship. The woman refuses any further hesitation on my part and I'm happy for her rescue.

On the top deck, a small WAC contingent leads all former prisoners to a delousing area. Inside, we toss our POW rags into trash cans. Two GIs spray our naked bodies outside a long row of hot showers and afterwards, a supply officer issues military uniforms based on each prisoner's dog tags.

Thirty minutes later, Abby finds us eating roast beef and mashed potatoes in the mess hall. She squeezes in beside Josef. Each man eats enough for an entire family. Abby eyes me but I keep my distance.

CHAPTER 15

JOHN

I don't remember the sniper's bullet. I don't remember the battlefield hospital or the doctors in between or the trip to Browning. I don't remember the feeding tubes or the time they say I walked to the window.

My first memory is a memory of light, and in that light, a girl with brilliant red hair.

Robert and I grew up together. We spent every hour near the Rocky Mountains. Nobody told us about the troubles overseas. We lived a rural life, learned ranching skills from our uncle, and found little need for town. Everyone in town referred to Robert as the smart one, and me as the tall one, yet actually, I learned faster than he did, and he stood a hair taller. We didn't talk much, and most people couldn't tell us apart.

Two brothers couldn't grow closer than twins living in Montana. Robert feels like a part of my own arm, my own thoughts, but Abby, the person behind the smile, the light catching her eyes. . .

Abby.

One day after waking up in Browning, I spent eight hours with a girl already so excited about my recovery that she made the impossible tasks seem possible out of my own desire to satisfy her. I never imagined such a girl existed.

Just being with her made me feel cleaner, somehow rid of the dirty killings an ocean away.

That's how it started.

I didn't have room for anyone in my world. Still, Abby slipped in anyway, without even knowing, she stepped right around my defenses. It happened slowly. My brother said this kind of thing is common with a nurse, although, there was nothing common about Abby.

I fought to push her out of my mind and did that the best I could. We traveled to Germany, and as much as I wanted to control every facet of the rescue, I couldn't connect the dots. I couldn't see five moves ahead anymore. I wasn't the man they had sent to coordinate this mission, but Abby immediately filled that void.

In Moosburg, my brother, Robert, played his part: an autonomous part because our roles could not overlap. Robert didn't know how jumbled my brain truly was. Abby did. She orchestrated everything from the Stalag VII-A infirmary, and with little choice, I followed her lead.

She made the impossible possible so efficiently that I just stood there at the end—watching General Rose walk away to freedom.

We had completed our mission, and normally I would remember every tiny detail. More importantly, I would already have a full extraction plan for Abby, Robert, and me.

Instead, I stood there on the Belgium border with little more than whispers moving away in the dark, General Maurice Rose and his Belgian escorts. My memory didn't register an orchestrated mission, more of a confusing sequence that somehow came together. I knew there was much more to it.

I knew Abby took tremendous risks.

The Milky Way sparkled that night, yet its stars didn't seem all that bright compared to Abby.

I felt humbled. I felt scared.

When General Rose reached the Belgium border, I vowed to get Abby out next. I would return to camp like normal after leave. Robert had entertained various ideas for our next move, and I trusted his judgment. Unfortunately, when the danger seemed over, it had really just begun.

We hadn't agreed upon the next step, yet Abby planned it perfectly. She stashed a Russian body so Robert could give up his infirmary role as General Rose. Robert's version of Rose stepped back into guard duty, and we buried the Russian with Rose's camp identity. The countdown began. The danger seemed behind us. We planned a celebratory meal in London with fourteen days until our next leave and our final freedom.

Abby saved Robert. Abby saved us all.

Fourteen days seemed like fourteen years with my life at stake. Fourteen days seemed like an eternity with *Abby's* life at stake. She came into this rescue untrained, just a ranch girl from Browning, Montana. Somehow she played a more significant role than the OSS men sent to rescue General Rose. Abby outshined Robert and me.

I felt guilty about exposing her to this danger and desperate to get her out of Germany. All of these emotions only complicated my hopeless attraction to Abby.

Then a hastily written note appeared in our emergency dropbox.

The countdown stopped when Alder took Abby away.

Abby's note delivered my own personal hell.

When we first arrived in Moosburg, we cut all ties. We trusted Abby to prepare her part of Rose's escape, yet we knew nothing about her work. We performed the rescue like distant spies, working independently, and playing our cards in order, not seeing each other's cards. When the game ended, Alder played a trump card.

He transferred Abby away from Stalag VII-A.

We didn't know what Alder's card meant.

Did Alder suspect our part in Rose's rescue? Did he just move Abby where she could better serve Germany? Did Abby write the letter under duress, or was she still safely in character? If we escaped now, would it put her in danger? How could we escape either way without knowing where Alder took her? Did she make some deal with him?

She left behind a hundred possibilities, and her words did little to eliminate any of them. The note simply said:

John and Robert,

Alder moved me today, no time for discussion, no idea where. Please stay here and wait for me. I'll return as soon as possible.

Abby

We couldn't leave her, and we couldn't ask questions because this letter might be a trap. So we waited. An entire year passed in black and white, no real color in a filthy camp, no joy or hope. I shared a prisoner's unknown future—death could take any of us tomorrow. Robert shared his rations with the prisoners, too, the men suffering the most because they were all our fellow soldiers. He insisted I eat and watched me all this time, to make sure I didn't falter. My misery multiplied tenfold each time I thought of Abby.

Misery steals color because a mind cannot grasp both.

Shades of gray tainted my world now. A passing bird reminds starving men of food, not the colorful creature, not the bird's beautiful song, not the freedom they crave. Misery is all-encompassing. We shared our misery with an increasingly overpopulated prison. The Germans pushed 80,000 men into a ninety-acre compound—too little space for 20,000—with too little food for 10,000.

We took the brunt of their misery. We heard their anguished pleas, watched their endless suffering, and carried their spent bodies out.

I focused away from the misery as best I could. I focused many tedious days on two things: Abby and the dream that led me out of my coma. I sensed something useful waiting just out of reach.

The dream haunts me in disconnected flashbacks, but I know the flashbacks somehow connect. I move about with pad and pencil, because these brief snapshots return without a pattern.

Flashbacks usually occur in a shadowed place that's not quite sleep.

I reassemble the pieces every day.

The mental exercise helps heal my brain. Like a year-long puzzle, I concentrate every waking hour on this mysterious dream. That focus somehow helps realign the future and past within my head. Short-term memory now fills in the gaps. Hunger returns with a vengeance.

And after an entire year of recording and rearranging this sputtering memory, I convince myself that this dream is specific to Abby's final days. So detailed, the only logical explanation involves a Blackfeet vision.

My indoctrination to Blackfeet culture was as passionate as it was fleeting. Our dying Grandfather spent his last healthy summer teaching Robert and me about the ways of our people.

His own vision guided our teachings.

As a young man, he fasted and prayed in the mountains like most young Blackfeet warriors. He sought guidance for his future and found it after four days. The year was 1883, and the previous year's successful bison hunt suggested that the Blackfeet could continue their traditional lifestyles.

Grandfather's vision told him the opposite. The bison would soon disappear, and many would starve.

Grandfather's vision made him prepare for a world without bison. The vision helped his family through hard times and ignited a passion within him to prepare us for our own visions. Life seldom lasts as long as we hope.

Our summer passed quickly near Little Plume Peak.

We learned native plants, shared family stories, hiked, and fished far into the mountains. Each activity somehow tied into finding oneself. Many Blackfeet still sought out visions. He wanted us to understand through his own vision, the sacred bridge we might someday cross.

A dream is not a vision. A vision may feel like a dream.

If my dream truly crossed over to a vision, I knew Abby would return to us alive, and I knew a few things about Abby's final days. I knew danger awaited, and I knew with even more certainty I could not stop her because she would accept the danger as part of something much larger. My dream, my vision, focused on Abby and her eventual death. Still the overwhelming evil that accompanied her made her very determined. Her anger overwhelmed her. Abby would not accept help or tolerate interference and within these constraints I came to realize I could not stop her.

Somehow, I need to save her without stopping her, but, I don't catch Abby in my vision.

So it must be a dream.

I stubbornly try to reason it away.

If Abby returns undamaged, the dream ends.

Visions cannot be shared.

Visions offer insight.

My vision offers me a chance to help Abby. A Blackfeet vision whispers from a world of ancestors and earth; a fleeting opportunity easily lost, a distant truth offered to a single man who must carefully weigh opportunity and risk and timing and choice.

I know I must proceed cautiously.

It might be a vision. My actions could decide Abby's fate if an opportunity arises.

All of these thoughts compete for my sanity, and the more I worry, the more I dread her return.

As much as I try to deny this vision—because hope is human frailty—I know the truth when Abby steps back into our lives.

It happens at shift change.

We always walk by her infirmary, and one day, she's standing there watching the men pass. She looks tired. After our morning rounds, we deliver an unconscious soldier with hours to live. She opens the door for us. I look into her eyes, and I know that evil has touched her, and within that touch, she simmers inside. She makes the dying man comfortable.

We soon cling together in a tight triangle. My heart is about to explode.

"I'm alright," she breathes.

"I'm far from alright," Robert says.

"Maybe alive is a better term," she says.

"Are you in danger?" I ask.

"No. We're in less danger than before."

"For God's sake, what happened to you?" Robert says.

"I spent the year serving at a camp called Auschwitz."

"And it had to be kept from us all this time."

"I don't know you. There's no way to tell you I'm safe. I haven't slept for a year."

"Nor have I," Robert says. "I'm sorry for acting like this. You scared the hell out of us."

"Nothing to be sorry about. We're back where we were with one important change. We're going home. I made a deal."

She turns away from us.

"What kind of deal," I ask.

"I spent the year working for an exceptional doctor named Josef Mengele. I've agreed to escort him out of Germany along with Alder and two associates."

"Why would you agree to help these men?"

"A brilliant scientist wants to defect. How could I refuse?"

"And the others?" I ask.

"Even trade. The three of us will leave, too. I value our lives more than the chance these Germans will someday stand trial."

"You trust Alder?"

"In this case, yes. We talked of Josef's defection at length."

She finally turns back. She turned around for a reason at the beginning, so I couldn't read her emotions, but I see them now before she tucks them away. She's good at that.

She's also not telling us everything.

"So, Alder delivers us to the border, and we deliver him to freedom," I say.

"He could kill us now if that was his desire," Abby says.

"True," Robert says. "And we have the same option across the border, technically speaking. So it's a gentlemen's agreement."

"Yes," Abby says. "A gentlemen's agreement."

"There's so much we don't know."

"And little time to explain," she says. "It's already in motion."

Abby takes charge. She asks about my health, and I assure her that my mind healed in her absence. We ask about her health, and she immediately changes the subject. We will smuggle Alder and two others out of Germany with his help, including a prominent scientist named Josef who wants to defect. She tells us this nervous scientist is a great discovery, and he will need everyone's support, including much of her own time on the voyage. She asks us to maintain Josef's comfort zone by using the German language in private conversations.

She seems relieved. She seems distracted. She seems restless as she secures our allegiance and sends us on our way.

Her poignant dismissal makes it clear. She will tolerate no more discussion.

Abby returned from Auschwitz, and we won't see her again until the final escape. She's bitter and determined, I can tell that much from one brief look.

I have no idea what to do without making it worse.

We sail from Le Havre on April 22, 1945, aboard the *Argentina*, scheduled for a May 5th, New York City arrival. Alder and three other Germans escape Germany too, men still in our company on the ship. Robert and I question her again in private, but she shuts us down. With the war ending, four escaped Germans are a small price to pay for safety. She says the words with certainty, with conviction, her eyes far out on a stormy sea.

We relent.

I have no sense of her danger, of who is dangerous, of who can be trusted. All I can do is stay close every moment of every day.

Onboard, Abby divides her time between Robert and me, Alder, and this scientist named Josef. She stands close to me on launch. I try to pull her closer as the ship accelerates, yet she shakes her head no. She smells of soap and lavender and starched khakis—a wonderful change from the horrid smells back at Stalag VII-A.

I wander the decks alone most of that first day.

The *Argentina's* oil furnaces push gray smoke out her massive funnel. Since the War Administration converted the *Argentina* for soldier transport, few rooms remain off-limits. I explore below deck, near the boilers that power two General Electric steam turbines. I find a room filled with shirtless GIs, treating themselves to a heat-induced sauna, complements of the excess boiler heat.

"Come in," a bald man says. "Nobody here's been warm for years so we're catching up."

I join them for a while. They're a silent group, savoring the quiet hum of the turbines nearby. Krueger's beer covers a shelf to one side, and they pass me a warm can even before I sit down.

"Where you from?" the bald man asks.

"Montana."

"Pittsburgh," he says, "Jersey, Dallas, Kansas, Jersey again, Tennessee," he points at each man in turn.

"Joisey," the first man says.

"Yeah, sorry, Mike, Joisey."

"You came on board with a dame," the Joisey guy says.

"Yes, she's from Montana, too. A nurse."

"Not many dames on board," he says.

"One or two," I say.

"What? There were three of you with her? Seemed like she fancied that dark-haired guy."

"She worked with him over there."

"A doctor or something, huh?"

"Something like that." I take a long pull on my beer.

"He didn't seem like one of us. Seemed kinda wide-eyed, like his first ocean voyage."

"I dunno," I say. "They coulda flew him over to start. Medical people were scarce to start."

"Alright, so you know him. Just makin sure we don't have no spies aboard. Damn Germans always knew everything we were doin' before we did it."

"Yeah, I know him. And you're right about those Germans."

I finish my beer, and wish the men well. Back above deck, Abby finds me leaning along the rail.

"Looks like you found your spot again, just like on our trip over," she says.

"And you, too. What's up?"

"We ate. Josef's asleep, and he'll be out until morning."

"A soldier asked me about him. He saw us all board together, thought Josef looked a little out of place."

"He did. I coached him at supper. He'll blend in better."

"I'm still not sure why you're going so far out of your way for him."

"Revenge. Stealing one of Germany's finest scientists."

I shake my head. "Alright."

"You find anyplace quiet?" she asks. "There's so many men, and they all like to stare at me."

"C'mon."

I grab two cots from a pallet. I lead Abby below deck, clear down to the turbines where the door to a control room full of gauges stands propped open. A man checks some steam valves at the opposite end of the room every hour but never ventures much further. There's enough space in the little control room for two cots.

"With the door closed, you should be able to sleep."

Exhausted, we set up the cots side by side and fall asleep together. Hours later, when I wake, she's watching me.

"I've never watched you sleep, really sleep, John."

"I haven't really slept in years."

"You can catch up now."

"So what happens in New York, Abby?"

"The Germans go their own way, we catch a train west. Simple as that," she says.

"Just realize that I can't let anything happen to you, after all you've done. I'm forever in your debt and quite glad to be there."

"You owe me nothing, John."

"I owe you my life, Abby. I love you."

She stiffens at my words, yet I see the truth in her eyes, in that youthful innocence that slips past her defenses for a moment, her bottom lip quivers. She scoots over and runs her hands through my hair. She tucks her face into my chest. Her breath warms my shirt.

"I mean it, you know. I love you."

She's shaking in my arms, but she doesn't respond.

"So, who are these men with us, Abby–the Germans?"

"You've asked a hundred times. I worked with one of them, and the others are strangers, friends of Alder."

"No regrets helping them? No reservations?"

"None whatsoever."

"Look at me and say that."

"None whatsoever."

"I believe that you believe what you say, although there's more in your eyes."

"Just a long year, John, a long two years."

"Tired?"

"All the time. Let it rest. Hold me a little longer."

"Alright. I promise."

"For now, you have to trust me. I have to stay in character with Josef. I'll tell you when it's over."

"I trust your judgment, but still worry about you."

"As I do about you." She grips me for several minutes. "You're pretty much healed, John. I didn't know if that would happen."

"My memory returned. When we first arrived, things still wouldn't stick day to day."

"Thank God." I think she's crying. "I need to stay with Josef most of the voyage. I should be near him now."

"Brilliant scientist."

"Conspicuous German, too. You said it yourself."

"You sound mysterious again."

"Stop it. You promised."

"Yes."

"We'll have plenty of time to catch up later." She snuggles her head under my chin. "And I can't wait. Please believe me."

"Promise?" I ask.

"Yes. I better get to it then."

She rolls off her cot. She sits facing away from me, still shaking for a moment, rocking, regathering herself, deep breaths, finally standing up.

"We'll see you around on the deck." She won't meet my eyes.

"Please be careful, Abby."

"I'm fine." She kisses my cheek. "Don't worry."

And she's gone. I'm devastated.

When I told her that I love her for the very first time, it caught her unprepared and betrayed her for an instant. I know without a shadow of doubt that she feels the same, but something still exists between us like it did in Germany. She's still not free.

For some reason, the war isn't over for Abby.

Try as I might, I cannot get her alone again.

Abby remains detached after that, strangely disconnected the entire voyage. I watch the Germans, watch Abby, and struggle with my own demons, my own secrets, my absolute adoration, and my desperate concern.

She moves about with Josef.

They know each other very well. He's smitten with her, that's clear in the way he follows her movements, yet she doesn't watch him when he's not looking. With Abby, it seems more of a show. She's always smiling, complimenting, even taking his arm, but something changes when he turns away; a cloud drifts in. Her brow drops then rises again with his next interaction.

I discretely find ways to rest where they walk and observe their interaction from a distance. With so many men on the ship, it's not hard to blend in.

A few days of concern push us across the Atlantic even as I juggle an ocean of concerns. After ten days, an OSS employee escorts us from a busy terminal to a large black car.

Alder and two other Germans depart with a simple wave. I struggle with this agreement, but Alder delivered us from evil, to quote the Bible, and saved Abby, and that's enough for now. I suspect we might see Alder again, yet I can't interfere. Abby said she would tell me when the coast clears, and I promised not to interfere.

Not yet.

The trip through New York refreshes my senses. Europe lies in ruins, but New York City's glitz churns all around us. Well-dressed people move purposefully between cable cars shadowed by skyscrapers all covered with glass and neon and art deco flair. The science defector, Josef, travels with us for safekeeping, according to Abby. He looks about like a child seeing heaven for the first time. The scientist rushes to open doors for all of us at Gimbels. I like Abby's defector more and more, his easy laugh, his refined ways.

At Gimbels, Abby chooses a red dress, sweater, scarf, and a new watch. She wears them right to the cash register. Many other women join her at Gimbels, most of them eager to dress up and meet their returning soldiers. The counter attendant gives her matching red lipstick for free. Abby looks innocent, wistful like she finally found her way home.

Times Square stops us all in a cluster, turning around and around to take it all in. Neon signs advertise a dizzying array of products: Canadian Club whiskey, Planter's peanuts, Admiral Televisions, and Pepsi Cola. A smiling man smokes Camel cigarettes and blows puffs of smoke larger than a locomotive exhaust.

At the Stagedoor Canteen, the Andrews' Sisters' beautiful melodies flow onto the street. One shoulder-worn door away, raucous sailors sing those endearing songs. They crowd their own bar because there's no room left in the Stagedoor. They flow in and out with bottled beer and shoulder slaps. They sing off-key harmony to the perfect harmony next door, and they cry real tears of joy. People pack the adjacent blocks too, an area jammed with bars and hotels and entertainment. Servicemen and the New Yorkers that supported them all celebrate their European victory.

A sign on the Hotel Bristol offers one night free for returning soldiers. Josef insists we accept their offer.

"This is the New York I have always dreamed about, Abby," he says. "The bright lights make it seem that anything is still possible. The world is a wonderful, amazing place."

"He's right, Abby," I say. "What a great way to welcome this man who risked his life to bring his medical research to America. I will buy us all supper in his honor and let me tell you, Josef, I do appreciate your sacrifice."

"Thank you, John, the honor is mine, defecting to this amazing country. It reminds me so much of Germany already. The Caucasian population truly loves New York City. Yes, people of European ancestry thrive here, and it will be my honor to help brighten their future."

Abby's steely gaze softens when I turn to her.

"What's wrong, Abby?"

"Nothing at all, John, a little headache. So, one night at the Hotel Bristol then? One night to celebrate the research Josef brings with him, the work on soldiers exposed to the horrors of war? Yes, those brave soldiers that suffered in battle should not be forgotten. We should celebrate their lives."

"Yes, yes, Abby," Josef said. "The soldiers brought to our ward with such grievous injuries cannot be with us tonight, yet their suffering will make the world a better place. The things we learned studying them will enhance the lives of everyone. I celebrate tonight in their honor. A real celebration, just you wait."

We check into the Bristol. At 7:00 p.m., we stroll into the Pink Elephant Restaurant. Our lavish table includes fresh flowers that match the red floor and Abby's rich red lipstick. Dark wood cloaks the walls extending well above my reach. I spend a wonderful evening staring at Abby: the dress, her beautiful smile, a sprinkling of freckles across high cheekbones, her lips joking and laughing. There is an essence about her like the room itself, both timeless and seductive. She dances with Josef, Robert, and me, like the carefree girl I traveled with eighteen months ago.

At 1:00 in the morning, Josef surprises us with a tray of Cointreau celebrating our liberation of France and the entire European continent. He holds the tray. She hands out the glasses very formally, each including a hug. We stand for the toast, cheering the men who will not return. Another hug from Abby sends us each off to bed in this wonderful hotel, all on the house for the military tonight. We've scheduled a noon lunch and an early afternoon train. I fall asleep with Abby right next door. I fall asleep assured of her safety and the thought that I might never let her out of sight again. I dare to hope that the danger really has passed.

It's light when my eyes flutter open.

I roll into wetness. I pissed the bed. A beautiful bed with soft silky sheets, a feather tic, my head feels groggy, dizzy.

Did we drink that much? I look outside and find the sun partially up, mid-morning. Satisfied, I draw a bath and call room service for coffee. The coffee takes forever, so I leave the bathroom door open. When the knock finally comes, I shout out, "Come on in."

A smartly dressed Asian waiter pushes through the door.

"Leave it on the wardrobe there," I say.

"Sorry, sir, you must sign for it."

"Alright, bring it in here for me. Good, you aren't a young woman, with me here in the tub."

"That's fine sir, we run into room situations much more interesting than a man bathing." He holds a clipboard and a pen for my inspection.

"May 7th, it looks like your kitchen got the day wrong."

"No, sir, today is definitely the 7th."

"Impossible."

"May 7th. Today is my mother's birthday," he says.

The bill finally registers, 10:30, May 7, 1945, a full day and a half since I entered this room. It's 10:30 in the morning.

The Cointreau.

Josef's smile. Abby's careful distribution. The way Josef turned the tray for her. The way his eyes moved about during the toast. Her insistence we all turn-in thereafter.

It all looks different now.

I wake Robert from a similar hangover. We check her empty room and the entire hotel. A busy breakfast room frustrates our efforts, but several frantic loops leave us empty-handed. A tall desk clerk thinks he watched her leave yesterday morning, alone—a stunning redhead walking into the darkness.

MAY 1945

BRIAN STRIEFEL

CHAPTER 16

JOHN

S o, after all the incredible danger in Germany, Robert and I lose Abby in New York City. We search the streets, talk to cab drivers, and hustle into the train station at noon. We find her trail immediately.

At New York Central, the USO escorts veterans to a special window where soldiers receive discounted travel. Inside that travel log, a terrifying puzzle unfolds. Fourteen consecutive names share the destination Browning, Montana, all purchased May 6th.

Yesterday.

Abby's name appears first, written in her own handwriting.

"What on Earth, hey," Robert says.

"She tucked us in our hotel rooms for a reason," I say.

"The next train loads in a few minutes, John. We need to figure this out."

I talk to a clerk at the military ticket booth. Abby's name and description bring instant recognition: a young nurse accompanied by a middle-aged man with dark hair and a gray fedora.

"The early train always has plenty of room, even though it's sometimes booked. Soldiers celebrate too much the night before," the clerk says.

"Eleven military men left for Browning yesterday morning," I say, "and two more travel to Cutbank. There's not a single native name in this group traveling to the Blackfeet reservation, does that make sense?"

The clerk shrugs her shoulders. "I opened the booth yesterday, and these two people bought tickets together," she points to Abby and the name below hers. "They boarded the train before all these others who arrived together." She runs her fingers down the rest of the list. "The second group seemed to know each other."

Abby Erickson   Red Cross Nurse   Browning, Montana

"She left with the scientist," Robert says.

"What would a research doctor want in rural Montana?" I ask.

"We need a fast car," Robert says, "a real fast car, to catch that train."

"Where's the nearest dealership, ma'am?" I ask.

"Go out that door, walk left to the first corner, then straight ahead four blocks. You can't miss it. Gentlemen, you'll never catch the train with a car. From Chicago, the Montana passengers change trains, and the Empire Builder is almost across Minnesota."

We study the train schedule.

"Huh, you're in luck," she says. "There's flooding outside Minot, and they'll be held there overnight."

"What are you saying?" Robert asks.

"Look, it's 900 miles from Chicago to Minot, call it eighteen hours," she says. "Your train will arrive in a few hours, but they will remain in Minot overnight. That's the last place with a decent airport. You might catch them in an airplane."

CHAPTER 17

ABBY

"Here, by the window."

"Thank you, Josef."

"These seats look very comfortable, Abby."

Josef guides me into a train seat with his right hand. I remember that hand guiding a little brother and sister. When the medicine knocked them out, I remember that hand cutting off their toes, and swapping them from one child to another. It didn't work, like the previous time. We seldom saved the foot after the infection set in. Yet, he took failure as a momentary setback, just an alignment error or a patient defect. I worked so hard to save them. I talked Josef out of a few surgeries, but he maintained a full staff, some as dedicated as Josef himself, and I knew I couldn't stop them all. When Josef offers a friendly hand, it could guide you to your deathbed. I plan to arrange the deathbed this time, yet Josef could be plotting something entirely different because he cannot be trusted. Today, his vest pockets bulge with gold rings and fillings, several hundred lives reduced to escape money. I get a glimpse inside one pocket when he sits down.

Bastard.

I smile and pat his hand.

Josef's black hair curls perfectly across his forehead. His fresh shave includes a trim of sideburns and eyebrows.

I know because I study his face all the time, seemingly in admiration, but actually in anticipation. I want to remember everything about him. I want that for all the people he killed, the collective satisfaction they would take in his death.

Old Spice aftershave largely masks the Brylcreem, but not quite. He adopted these two products a few weeks before Auschwitz closed—Josef himself searching through the confiscated possessions of prisoners to find the right products for his own transformation. American aftershave and British hair tonic are two of several changes. He drinks to get a buzz now, and sometimes drinks cheap wine. His clumsy use of American slang might give him away in the right circumstances, although his life expectancy probably won't accommodate such problems.

He revels in his new persona.

Josef polished himself up for this next exciting chapter in his life. I'm memorizing every detail because I remember John's words very clearly.

"Over there, we fight and die and sleep, with no time for anything else," John said. "Back here at home, the voices find you, the dead and dying. You remember last wishes mumbled in words you couldn't understand, but you nodded anyway. Your brain can't process it then, so your mind saves it for later."

I understand John's words far too clearly now.

I know the dead and dying will find me. I'll pull out memories of Josef Mengele and tell the victims everything I couldn't tell them then. I'll relive Josef's last days so his victims can share in his death, and maybe reliving it will help ease my pain. Maybe I had no choice. Maybe the end justifies the means. Maybe his death will be all I have.

What about Alder?

This morning I snuck out of a New York City hotel and purchased a ticket with Josef Mengele. Alder insisted I leave without John and Robert, and his reasoning made sense, yet nothing about Alder comforts me. He's on this train somewhere.

Bastard.

If I can kill them both, and die in the process, I will die happy.

I'll keep Mengele close, so he doesn't get nervous, but I wonder what Alder will do when we arrive in Browning. Is it Alder and me? Is it Alder and Mengele? Will they kill me and wait for John and Robert? Is this all a twisted plot to exact revenge?

We sit among other soldiers. In the next day and a half, the train rolls through trees and meadows and little towns in an endless parade of the eastern United States. I would thoroughly enjoy the ride under other circumstances, but I loathe my companion. The train's dining car is abhorrent to me too, because Josef connects with families at breakfast and grandmothers at lunch.

He's warm, friendly, helpful, disarming. Every kind gesture reminds me of past atrocities that started the very same way—him gaining someone's trust. They let their guard down. He proceeded with his patients, "unencumbered by the stress of knowing" in his words. The procedures were violent. The victims still trusted his judgment afterward because he assured them everything would be alright. It never was.

I proceed with their suffering in mind. I am encumbered by the stress of knowing.

He takes me outside for sherry. We watch the sunset from a tiny platform between cars. It's too loud to talk, so

I drink instead, relieved that I can't converse with Josef. I
watch him admire the land, and I swallow my feelings along
with the sherry. I need to maintain his confidence. There
will be time for bitter memories later.

Sherry finally displaces my hunger enough to sleep before another morning and reality. I feign motion sickness,
so Josef rolls me a cigarette and insists I try it. The smoke
makes me cough, but it calms my hunger and anxiety, my
motion sickness to him. I thank him graciously. By the time
we reach Chicago, I'm ravenous.

One hour between trains allows me time to either purchase food or run for my life, but I can't run because I
escorted Josef Mengele into the United States.

*Second thoughts only work when the first thoughts leave you
a way out.*

I slip my hand under Josef's arm. He smiles that warm,
disarming smile that looks as comforting as it is dangerous.
We walk past a young family gathering their children's belongings: a pillow, a blanket, and a teddy bear. Josef runs
his free hand through the little boy's crewcut, and the child
looks up at him with a surprised smile. They connect like
that—a gentle touch, exchanged smiles—Josef always so
very beguiling.

Several GIs depart with us. They walk from a sandwich
stand without talking for a messy lunch standing under a
long "Empire Builder" sign. Josef grabs three sandwiches
and four Cokes while I watch those other GIs from a distance. They watch me, too. They watch everyone actually,
these older soldiers, polite when approached by well-wish-
ers, quiet otherwise.

I finally realize what bothers me about them. Their
shoulders sag. The youngest soldier can't be less than thirty.

Some men look forty or better—not just war-years and not a single bar among them. All these men survived the war without a bullet or promotion. One soldier may have approached Alder in Belgium although, I can't be sure from this distance. At the time, I asked Alder if they were friends. He never answered.

Alder.

I'm so tired, I can't think. My mind churns in a foggy blur, completely wrung out like the hours after an all-night cram session and a difficult physiology test. I don't have the capacity to add more worries to an already dangerously overloaded basket, so I push the other men out of my mind.

I can't concentrate enough to assemble any further distress.

We board the Empire Builder in the late afternoon, and Josef seats us several rows behind those GIs once again. He quietly babbles about places we might restart his medical testing. He talks about mistakes made when warming patients immersed in ice water. He's proud of the altitude tests that killed a hundred before Josef finally located a bad vacuum gauge and started the testing again. My exhausted head bobs, too nervous to sleep.

At dusk, we step out for sherry at Josef's insistence. The second glass delivers a soothing buzz that calms my nerves. Back inside, he's worried about finding good nurses.

"You always kept me focused, Abby. Your organization skills are next to none. We didn't always agree, but your meticulous records stepped me through my research at a sprinter's pace. How do we find more women like you?"

"It wasn't me, Josef. I just witnessed your miracles."

"Miracles, yes, all those moments you made possible. You pointed out many things I missed. I want you to train the entire staff when we start again. Maybe in Argentina, somewhere we can organize an orphanage in a remote area."

"Argentina?"

"The government is far removed from world politics, so they don't know much about our war. The undereducated population and vast empty spaces fit perfectly into our vision, yet just as important, the landscape matches Germany. Argentina will feel like home."

"I understand."

"So, first, we gather currency. We sell the spoils of war, the gold, where people are wealthy enough to purchase our gold. Then we take hard currency to a poor country. They will welcome us like rich cousins. Our work begins anew."

"I'd be glad to further support your work," I say, though I'd rather pull a grenade pin right now.

"You look tired."

"Yes, the excitement for our future sometimes drains my energy."

"Sleep then, my dear, and we'll plan another day."

Despite the added revulsion, my brain shuts down so completely that I sleep all the way across Minnesota. When I wake up at Grand Forks, I barely make it to the bathroom.

I wash up. I walk to the dining car alone for a cinnamon roll and a pot of coffee. Four old soldiers smoke at a nearby table, their silhouettes back-dropped by stubble fields outside. The caffeine pulls my senses back in line.

I think the man with protruding ears approached Alder in Belgium. I wait an hour until they finally stand up and walk past me. It's definitely him.

That afternoon, the railcar keeps everyone awake except a few GIs accustomed to sleeping through anything. My butt aches, the worn seat bounces, and rail noise all make conversation impossible, and somehow, they sleep. Josef sleeps, and I stare out the window as North Dakota slips by in a mix of tired farmhouses that didn't escape the depression or recover from it since.

I sip a warm Coke.

How many men did Alder sneak out of Germany? More importantly, why is everyone headed west on the train? My eyes wander through the railcar, stopping here and there on little groups of soldiers, finally coming to rest on Josef sleeping at my side.

We boarded the train together, just two travel companions headed west, Abby and Josef, but I can't do it anymore. I should wait, I'm supposed to wait. *I won't.*

Each night we stood outside and sipped sherry, his choice. We stand on the platform, between railcars barreling across Illinois, Minnesota, noise be damned, and we sip sherry and smoke hand-rolled cigarettes. We smoke outside even though everyone else smokes inside.

He *is* rather handsome. He trusts me with every detail, every accomplishment that makes him proud. He keeps sharing details like the death progression inside his gas chambers. Everything he tells me makes my final decision easier.

That night I burn something very important to Josef Mengele. I burn his most precious possession. I burn the notebooks he painstakingly wrote near the conclusion of the war—a file cabinet full of medical research condensed to a single satchel.

I throw Josef's satchel in the engine's boiler. I tell the train worker that my lover left me, and I'm burning all his memories. The flames consume so much more than memories.

I passed this way eighteen months earlier, traveling east through an early blizzard that stranded us in Minot. Today, spring flooding will stop the train in Minot again. We coast into town alongside the Souris River, and many perfect little houses surrounded by their spring finery.

A black porter announces our Minot delay, hopefully just a single day to inspect the tracks west of town. He answers questions about hotels, restaurants, and local landmarks. He laughs easily at any opportunity, and his gentle disposition puts passengers at ease.

None of the soldiers ask him anything.

I take a final inventory of the other men around me, GIs returning from war. I expect men in their early twenties and find men in their forties. I expect jubilation, restless tension, excited chatter, yet quiet glances prevail, and a strange silence somehow amplifies the slowing rail clatter. I've had enough lies.

"Josef, we're in Minot. Are you up for supper? I know an interesting place on High Third."

He adjusts his jacket.

"Let me clean up, Abby. This place on High Third serves good food, then? How long it's been since I sat down in a real restaurant."

"You'll love this place. I ate here before the war when I traveled to see my aunt."

"This sounds like a celebration!" Josef claps his hands together.

"A real celebration, yes. Just you wait."

He walks away opposite the other soldiers, who now mill around for their own belongings. I consider my options here, first Josef, then Alder, maybe his cronies? Minot already entertains its own share of questionable characters, so these odd soldiers will fit in fine until I get to them.

My confidence swells.

I follow Josef outside for a cigarette, a quiet moment shared beyond the crowded platform. I stand in Josef's shadow and watch him smoke while a band plays "God Bless America" near the train. The homecoming celebration includes a half-dozen teary-eyed men holding their families, but none of them are my railcar companions.

A seventh soldier limps toward the waiting throng—everyone parts for a mother and daughter and a brown dog with an American flag in its collar. The dog's tail stops wagging first. The wife hugs him. The daughter and the dog stare up at him expectantly, and another man slaps him on the shoulder, the shoulder he still has, but the seventh man just stares blankly at the sky. The wife gives him a sad smile before taking his hand and leading him away.

With the band now blaring an off-key jazz song, I take Josef's arm and steer him south down Main Street.

"Do you like barbeque, Josef? Maybe a glass of sherry or something stronger? I know just the place."

We walk past Alder. He looks wary, disconcerted. He sent me to Auschwitz for an entire year of hell, and now he's nervous. In my world, there's a lot of reasons to get nervous. In my world, people pay for the wrongs they committed because we're a nation with rules, most of which I will soon break. I imagine his emotion, and it drives me on.

A familiar smell permeates the damp downtown area. Minot burns coal nine months out of the year, a town like Browning—both towns too far north. Snow lasts seven months, then rain and mosquitoes for a month, two months of blazing heat, September, and snow again. Add gusty winds to most days here, something not so prevalent in Browning.

"So, you've eaten here before, Abby?" Josef asks.

"Yes, a place called Saul's Barbeque, wonderful pork, and they have a private little club downstairs that serves anything you'd like to drink."

"I miss my scotch, Abby, miss it something terrible."

"Well scotch, it is then, Josef, and my treat. It's a bit of a hike, but well worth it, and we have some time on our hands."

"The train depot reminds me of Germany, with the cross-gabled roof and the red brick, really a magnificent structure. Did you find the German countryside charming, Abby?"

"The trees and hills reminded me of the foothills near my own home Josef, walk with me now."

A thin drizzle develops, and we stop under the Orpheum Theatre's protective overhang. The drizzle turns everything dark, the cars and street, the brick buildings themselves. Cars pack every parking spot to our right, block after block, finally reaching a gentle rise out of the river bottom. Sears Roebuck does a brisk business. A tall woman in an evening dress carries a lamp from the Goldberg Furniture Store next door. Goldberg's sign proclaims, "Your Credit is Good!" Somehow, I don't think her credit is needed, although you never know. The bank clock next to Goldberg's says 4:00, and further south near the Leland Hotel, a man works on a globe streetlight.

"Ah, this drizzle feels like home. You remembered a hat, Abby, what was I thinking?" Josef shakes his head.

In planning Josef's death, for one second, I feel like a mother about to punish her child, a situation usually equal in resolve and regret. He's just like that excited boy right now, jubilant at my company and the evening ahead. He snaps his fingers.

"I always have my hat; then I walk out in the rain without it."

"Look at all the stores, Josef. Buy yourself a new hat. How about right here?" I turn under the Orpheum canopy to face another bright sign, *Goldberg Clothing Store*.

"Goldberg is a German name, and it means Gold Mountain," Josef says. "These German people did very well in Minot, and I would very much like to visit their store."

We stroll in together and find a half-dozen shoppers browsing trendy clothing. A balding man approaches Josef. His eastern accent befits an outsider here, flawlessly groomed right down to his manicured fingernails. Josef's nails, also, end clean and undamaged, not the hands of local farmers and miners but the hands of the upper class. A couple beside me appreciates fine clothing, yet his hands tell me he works hard for his money. I watch them interact, and I wish for her quiet life. There are pitfalls out there, men with perfect hands, men without a conscience. It is difficult to tell who is whom.

"Yes, a black fedora it is unless we happen to have gray, sir. What was your name then?" The salesman plies his trade well.

"Josef. Call me Josef, and this beautiful young lady accompanying me is Abby."

"I'm pleased to meet you both. Welcome to my store. We received a large shipment this very morning; I haven't even unboxed anything yet. With all the servicemen like yourself back, I can hardly keep hats on the shelf, so if you would accompany me across the street, we have warehouse space, and you can take your pick."

"By all means, Josef, let's join him," I say. Together the three of us turn toward the door.

"Elaine, keep an eye on things while I run across the street with these fine people. Josef, what did you do in the war if I may ask, sir?"

Josef offers me his arm. We cross toward the First National Bank and again over past the Leland Hotel. The variable street noise finally allows Josef's response.

"I was a medic in the Army. I worked to help our boys heal—heartbreaking at times, truly heartbreaking," Josef says. "Our troops fought the good fight, and now with the war behind us, our lives will get back to normal."

"I sure appreciate your sacrifice, sir, and will deduct twenty-five percent off your bill today." He turns left at First Avenue and continues east. A bearded man sits on a wooden crate near the corner. His left leg ends in a wrapped stump that supports a Maxwell House Coffee can. I drop some change inside. My companions act like they don't see him at all.

"Some guys come back like that almost every week," the salesman says. He opens a nondescript door. "What can a man do without a leg? Maybe a desk job, yes, but blue-collar men learned a trade, not an accounting book. There's no desk job for him. Down the stairs here, sir."

"Well, thank you," Josef says. He follows the salesman down a wooden staircase. "I wasn't expecting the damp weather today, and my favorite hat is packed away on the train."

"So, Josef," the bald man says, "Here's the stack I mentioned, all by size. Allow me to look at your head, a fine head of hair indeed. Let's try a seven. Ah, yes, perfect."

The salesman tips his offering at a jaunty angle like Josef placed it himself. A mirror appears from one hip pocket.

"So, tell me how you like it?"

"I like it fine, that light gray one catches my eye; make it gray, and how much do I owe you?"

"Call it two dollars, Josef."

"The rock walls are beautiful," Josef says. "Such massive field stones in all the colors of the world, and such a perfect fit. These beautiful walls seem wasted down here."

I run my hand over the south wall.

"A sturdy foundation and very beautiful, too," the bald man says.

"Abby and I spoke of scotch earlier, and I picture a tavern here someday," Josef says, "with beer taps along that north wall where people come down the stairs."

Josef pays the man two dollars from a roll in his pocket.

"That's a great idea, sir, and something the owners haven't even considered." We scale the stairs and exit together, the salesman balancing a dozen fedoras.

"Thanks so much for your business and have a wonderful night in Minot, Josef and Abby."

"I don't think anything can possibly go wrong," Josef says. He tips his new fedora.

"Except this constant drizzle," I say.

"Your summer days are actually longer than the days in California, Abby. Same thing in Germany, the sun moves so far north in summer that we get more daylight than Italy. This far north, the sun barely gets above the southern hills in winter, but days stretch out eighteen hours in mid-summer. When the Earth spins. . ."

Blah, blah, blah

I let him talk all the way up First Avenue to where it joins the south end of Third Street, "High Third." A 1936 Chevrolet pickup pulls in ahead of us along the curb. We meander around the open door while the passenger, a young woman in black cowboy boots, applies fresh lipstick.

"This is cattle country, Abby. Some breeds came right from Germany."

High Third bustles and Saul's place overflows. I light a cigarette for Josef on the sidewalk and ask him to wait outside. Inside, I seek out our waitress Luella and we meet near the counter.

"Come in, come in, Saul mentioned you this spring, the girl with the long red hair."

"Thank you for remembering me, Luella. I'm with a new man, someone who hasn't been here before. So you remember me from before the war, alright?"

"Oh," she winks, "and who is your date tonight?"

"His name is Josef and we want the very same food and entertainment that makes Saul's so famous."

Saul approaches almost immediately.

"Abby with the red hair, you grace my establishment once again. I understand you have a new companion and that your last visit was actually several years back."

"Yes, yes, and I was hoping we could partake in your hospitality once again, sir."

Josef walks through the door.

"Anything for you Abby, you let Luella know your needs and we will do our best," Saul winks.

"Scotch for Josef's coffee?" I whisper.

"Done."

"He's a black man," Josef says on Saul's departure. "In these United States, men of color can own a business, even run for public office." He looks about the room.

"What do you think of that, Josef?" My question and his answer disappear in the room's chatter.

"That man at the counter, the one in the worn coveralls, he's more deserving of a successful business. He's of good European stock. His ancestors fought the British and the French, and now he's a working man with dirt beneath his fingernails. The negro should do that kind of work."

I remain quiet in my thoughts.

Suits and coveralls and work uniforms crowd the counter. "These customers could own or sweep or steal from any given business, and here they share raucous laughter just the same," he says.

Beside us, a well-dressed older couple orders steak. Her lace hat and matching gloves suggest happiness and comfort, but tonight her reality contradicts the lace. She questions him and he scoffs. She chides him and he's condescending. She growls out a litany about nights down here, weekends somewhere else—temper and women and verbal abuse. He tells her she's nothing without his money. Before the steaks arrive, she throws her handkerchief at his face. She demands a divorce and storms out the door. He glances about, suddenly aware of his audience.

"That was uncomfortable," Josef says. "I suspect a place like this might offer too many options for a married man with a wandering eye."

"I suspect you are right."

"We tested syphilis cures for almost two years, yet nothing worked very well, even on young girls exposed to the disease. Peroxide helped slow the early sores, but not enough to arrest the later stages."

"Order the pork. Here this one," I point. "It's some southern thing. People don't know how it's prepared, only that it's really good." I don't want to hear more about the teenagers Josef killed.

"The things we like, food and work, those things make our lives joyous," Josef says.

As if on cue, two young women walk by, obviously twins, absolutely beautiful. Saul comes around from behind the counter.

"Donna, Delores, welcome ladies," Saul says. "Please sit, come with me."

Josef's eyes follow them, and I don't know if their beauty catches his eye or some potential Frankenstein experiment. It all comes back to me in a wave of nausea, the people, and the reason I'm here with Josef. The food arrives, and my stomach refuses to take it.

"You look peaked, dear," Josef says.

"I'm sorry, just a long day, I guess. You go ahead and eat. Maybe a glass of sherry will bring me around."

"You know it will."

I watch him eat, and try not to remember specifics, but I can't get past the faces. Josef sneaks glances at the twins, Donna and Delores, while he eats pork at Saul's Barbeque in Minot, North Dakota. I smile at Josef while pork juice slowly congeals on my white porcelain plate. Two dozen patrons dine around us, as unaware of my performance as Josef himself.

"Are you sure you feel alright, Abby. This food tastes wonderful."

"Here, eat some of mine. I'm having one of those days, Josef. You eat, don't let it go to waste."

"I'm fascinated by the negro girls and their quick wit. We seldom got any Africans to experiment on, occasionally a drafted soldier, but never more than a half dozen."

"The owner, too, seems quite capable," I say.

"They learn by imitation. The negro race is incapable of original thought."

His blanket judgments reflect the entire Nazi view, and I hate him for it.

"Just like the Jews," he smiles a conspiratorial smile. "They lie and cheat, it's in their blood, and soon they own half the town, and good people wonder why. I can tell you why."

He finishes his drink with a confident flourish.

"The Jewish people, like the Negroes and Russians, they're not exactly human. They see this world through human eyes, but behind those eyes, we find limited capacity. They don't contribute to society, they feed off it, they take from the people who persevere to further civilization."

I nod, fighting back the digust I feel toward his words.

"They're not intelligent enough to hide it," Josef whispers. "And not intelligent enough to see when others come for them. Germany killed many thousands of Jews like sheep to the slaughter. When the world gets overrun with undesirables, a superior race will always repair the damage. It's happened throughout history."

A moment later, and just before I stab Josef with my fork, Luella makes arrangements and Saul leads us downstairs for two glasses of sherry, and maybe a little card game for Josef.

"Ah, the real attraction," Josef says. "Another glass of scotch first."

Soon the twins arrive in their high heels, and the game tables roar. I avoid Josef's eyes. I fixate on the bartender's white shirt. It passed through the wash fifty times, at least, not always successfully, but the black silk tie redeems his look.

A simple tie, a clandestine room, the people around me, the things that happen here out of sight. . .

The bartender's biceps visibly strain against retracted sleeves. He's a giant, a very powerful man hired to make a statement to keep the patrons in check. I think he could just snap the sherry bottle open. With surprising dexterity, he flips a corkscrew from one hand to the next, pulls the cork, and hands it to Josef. Having received a knowing nod, he pours a generous portion. Josef slides it to me. The bartender leans a meaty forearm on the bar, and together they watch me drink.

"Delightful. It's sweeter than the sherry on the train," I say.

"Not a lot of call for sherry, ma'am," the bartender says. "I keeps an Oloroso with jus' enough Muscatel mixed in to please the ladies." He pours for Josef.

"Beautiful color," Josef says. "The Spanish know their grapes."

"Most dessert sherry is composed around an Oloroso, so this mix stops short of a Pedro Ximenez but still delivers a hint o' raisin. I's converted a few wine drinkers at Saul's."

"How did you become well-versed on sherry, living so far from a place one might associate with a cultured palate?" Josef asks. "A bartender in Minot with a nose for sherry, goodness!"

"I bartended at the Green Mill in Chicago," the man says. "Al Capone hung out there all da time an' I treated him real good. Ran into a little money troubles myself an' Mr. Capone put me on da train, right here to Saul's."

Both barmaids converge on their respective stations, and the bartender departs. Josef downs his sherry and pours another.

"This Al Capone even made the news in Europe," he says. "The American gangster that ruled Chicago."

"A lotta his liquor came through Minot here," a waitress says in passing. "Capone kinda ran this town during the dry years."

"America fascinates me," Josef says. "It's still the wild west in many ways, still young and restless. The little man can still make a name for himself. Europe is old and crowded and so very established in comparison."

Someone wins big at poker, eliciting a roar from the players. We're alone at the far end of the bar.

"Steeped in tradition," I say. "War is a tradition, too."

"Yes, a storied history of fighting over a relatively small landmass. Here you ride the train for miles and never see a sign of civilization. I can't wait for Montana. I can't wait to repair my finances and disappear from this great country."

"Montana surely offers plenty of space."

"I think I should like to return eventually. Return the victor."

"Return the victor?"

"We could have taken the United States," he says. "Hitler planned that right after Russia. With Russia's oil and fighting men, we would have crossed the northern Pacific, and crushed Canada. Then, well, with Canada's oil and steel there's little standing in our way."

"Don't underestimate the U.S. people, Josef."

"With Canada in hand, most major U.S. cities are in easy missile range. V-1 and V-2 cruise missiles don't care about a determined people."

"You've thought about this," I say.

"Yes, I have. South America is another young continent ripe for the taking. Without Hitler, and with the right men in charge, the Nazi ideal can still succeed." He winks.

I nod. I hope he can't see my thoughts.

"Bathrooms?" Josef asks.

I finish my sherry with a gulp.

"I'll have to show you, please get my coat," I say.

Josef dutifully stands and walks toward the entrance, I pour a small vial in his sherry and swirl. He returns with all of our over-garments, including that fedora, appropriately placed.

"Don't want anyone grabbing the wrong jacket," he says.

"Drink up Josef, or someone will drink it for you."

"Ah," he turns and downs it in one gulp, "this is truly the best sherry made, a hint of apricot I would say, delicious."

"You noticed that flavor," I say. "Come now."

A familiar blonde hairdo bobs between several taller men across the bar. I escort Josef toward the tunnel, and somehow the blonde picks me out through the crowd. Bernice follows my progress with her eyes, but I shake my head almost imperceptibly. She grips the forearm of a large man and turns away.

I lead Josef down the tunnel, and he's already short of breath.

"Whoa, that sherry packs a punch," he says. Josef sways along beside me, veering wide around a misplaced dishrag, "Yes, yes, I feel a little drunk."

"Right this way, Josef." We walk past the bathroom, and I palm the flashlight where the tunnel forks.

"I think I'm going to be sick," he says.

"Might be the pork, Josef, might be the pork."

Around the corner and further back, the stench of rotting garbage assails my nostrils.

"Oooh," he doubles over.

"Just a little further to the bathroom."

I pull him along to where the wooden walkway ends. He's unable to stand alone now.

A rusty chain separates us from the sinkhole, and a quick flash of my light shows trash floating on black water some twenty feet below.

"Oh, my God, it hurts," he groans.

"That apricot taste and the symptoms of your pain, do they ring any bells, Josef?"

His wide eyes look up in the flashlight's glow.

"Cyanide, yes, your choice for hundreds. . .thousands. Zyklon travels poorly, so it's potassium cyanide today. I saved some from Auschwitz, just for you."

"Why, Abby?" He twists away, clutching at his coat, his muscles writhing in agony.

"Why did you kill all those others, Josef. What gave you the right to play God?"

"The opportunity to engineer a superior race, a better future for the world."

He curls into a ball now.

"One generation later, two generations, everyone benefits, nothing progresses without sacrifice," he moans.

"I don't think the world needed you to perfect our gene pool by torturing children."

"I did it for everyone, for you too, Abby. The patients died for a noble cause, a stronger race."

He convulses.

"What about the people you killed?"

His hand reaches out to grasp my ankle. I jump, surprised at his quickness, jerking as hard as I can, but his grip is too firm. An empty syringe spins away from his opposite hand.

"Sodium thiosulfate and sodium nitrate," he groans. "When cyanide became the poison of choice, I carried the antidote of choice because not all the Nazi family liked each other."

"Abby?"

I turn my head.

"Abby, what are you doing?"

Josef yanks me, tumbling to the ground. My purse spins away.

"Bernice, stay back, this is something you could never understand."

I'm sure I can wrestle free but each time I kick with the opposite leg, he pulls me a little closer. My hands scramble for something to hold onto, a rock or stick or anything at all. I feel a tremendous pain when my right forearm slides across some twisted metal.

The shadows flow, and she's standing over us. Bernice arrives with a large brick.

"Tell me this is what you want," she hisses.

He's got me with both hands now—the hem of my dress tears away. He's moaning something indiscernible, yet his strength returns by the second. I look up into her eyes, and I know there's no choice.

"I've got a little girl," Bernice says.

His hand reaches my throat before I can answer. My breathing stops. I twist within his grip. My eyes bulge, and stars spin all around the dark walls. A shadow expands upon that nearest wall, taller for just a second, then gone.

WHAAACK!

Blood spurts across my face and arms, her legs, and shoes. Josef's hands spasm several seconds then slowly release. My first breath tastes like blood and rot and Josef's cologne, and I vomit sherry on his arm.

"Damn it, Abby," Bernice says.

I can't stop coughing.

"I spotted you in the bar and followed to say, hello. I heard everything you said down here." Her voice is steady.

"He's a Nazi. He ran an experimental clinic."

"Yes, I heard the conversation, Abby, but I find it hard to imagine, especially in Minot."

"If you needed to kill someone, Bernice, where would you go?"

"This is real, what you said and what he said?"

"Yes."

"And you brought him to Minot. You brought him to my town."

"He's untouchable there and unknown over here. It's so complicated. You'll understand when they liberate the concentration camps, Bernice. Someday I'll tell you everything, but right now, please believe in me."

"You forced me to kill a man. Abby, we got a real mess here."

"I know. I'm so, so sorry."

She takes a deep breath. "Alright, wait a second, there's a bigger cinderblock and some wire out there."

My hand slides right and somehow I push myself into a crouch. Blood wells up between my fingers, blood and dirt and my own vomit. I wipe my hand on Josef's trousers, yet the wool does little to absorb anything. I'm on my feet then, moving away from him, fighting the urge to vomit once again.

"C'mon."

She leads me back to the entrance where cinderblocks support several wall timbers. More cinderblocks lay askew along the path. An alcove holds wood and wire and other materials of construction.

"Grab one."

We each pull a block into the tunnel. Bernice returns for rusty project wire, her high heels deftly avoiding cracks between wood floor planks.

"Use both blocks and the wire, and make sure that body sinks, you understand? I'll wait outside and watch." She shakes her head.

I wrap wire around a wrist and ankle; attach a block to each, more wire for good measure. I find a place where the blood hasn't reached and sit down: I push with my legs, sliding the man closer, then a brick, then the other brick, until it all slips over the edge with one loud splash. Several bottles clink off one another in the water. I look down, and my flashlight confirms his fate, just a gray fedora spinning slowly down into filthy water. The man named Josef Mengele disappears forever. I shuffle back on one heel, the other lost with Josef's last push. I toss the second heel in behind it. His body scraped away most blood in passing, but I finish the job with dirt and sand.

"Oh, Abby, you look like you just killed someone and dumped the body," Bernice says. "We're both half-covered in blood, and your arm needs attention. We better sneak out another way. This won't be easy. I'm sure glad we both got our purses out of Saul's."

Bernice leads me down a familiar tunnel.

"Stand right here." She disappears through a narrow door. Five minutes later she returns with a young black woman, the waitress from the Avalon.

"I need to get us cleaned up, Grace."

"Oh my God, Bernice, what you got yourself into?"

"Nothing you want to know about, Grace. Remember the man that beat you up last year, the alderman from town here? That sort of thing, alright? Man got too rough with Abby here."

"Been some new folks comin around. Most 'em are nice, some bad uns. I can't go crossin no law types."

"It wasn't anyone from around here, Grace, and there's no evidence of wrong-doing. Can you help us?"

Grace looks frightened. "Don't tell me no more. I can help ya Bernice 'cept the cops is raidin everything tonight. Sherriff's department too, we's all shut down upstairs. I can run up an' get some clothes, bucket o' water. How's about that?"

"That would suit us fine."

"Wait right here, then!"

I'm shivering so hard my teeth chatter. Bernice's white wool hat still hugs her blonde hair, but dark smudges cover both sides. The blood splatters on her legs look like bullet holes. My own arm alternates from dark red blotches to fresh blood still seeping from an open wound, and my throat burns from strangulation.

Grace returns out of breath. She plops a bucket of soapy water at our feet and lays clothing across an overturned trash can.

"I gotta get back inside and make the business look respectable, Bernice. Sure wish I could help ya more."

"You've done more than enough, Grace, and I thank you."

Grace scurries away.

"I'll wash you up."

Bernice strips my dress off, wipes my exposed skin, and tends my wound. The hot water briefly stops my shivering. She pulls a rusty sliver from my wounded arm and combs my hair.

"There, get into this sweater. She brought a red one to cover your bleeding."

I wash Bernice's legs. We dress in Grace's clean dresses and help each other with buttons and zippers.

"I hate to say it, but we're dressed like prostitutes, and there's a police raid coming. Oh, and you have no shoes."

"Gosh, Bernice, I'm so sorry."

"Gotta hurry, c'mon."

We rush down more tunnels, the walls moldy in some places, oily in others, all reeking in various states of dampness and disrepair. Eventually, Bernice spins into another alcove. She puts her index finger across her lips and slips inside one of two doors. My feet ache from running across broken rock. Minutes later, Bernice slips back into the tunnel.

"Borrowed some shoes I can bring back tomorrow." She takes my hand and pulls me through the opposite door, into a men's restroom with one occupant quietly peeing in a homemade urinal.

"I seen you come in," Bernice says to the man.

"Evening Bernice. How's Alfred?"

"Just about as loud as ever, Leo. How's your daughter?"

"Doctor said she'll be fine. Says the little ones beat pneumonia even faster than a four-year-old."

"You say hi to Helen for me then."

"I'll tell her I ran into you at the grocery."

"Fair enough. I'm going to take my friend through the bar and sneak out the back door."

"Well, don't bother going in 'cause the Mayor called, and we've got a raid comin any minute. They're already in the alley waiting for all the black girls to run."

"Already, Leo?"

"Yes, Bernice. Maybe I can take you out the front myself, but I bet we all get arrested for prostitution. You girls got some pretty provocative dresses there. Even for the Vendome."

"You don't need this trouble, Leo. We'll go back to the tunnel where we came, maybe head toward the river."

"They usually put a couple officers down there, too. You two can't hang out in the tunnel, or you'll freeze to death." My teeth are already chattering, and he looks sympathetic. More than just cold, I'm terrified that this police raid will somehow discover my murder.

"We're in quite a pickle, Leo." Bernice checks her hair in the mirror. Leo finishes his business. My heart races, even as my legs feel rubbery.

"Tell you what. . ." but I don't hear the rest of his words because a million black spots overtake my vision at once.

I wake up in unfamiliar darkness that smells like baby powder. My hand feels a feather pillow and a heavy depression-blanket and eventually, an arm.

"You're safe up here. Just stay quiet." The whisper sounds familiar.

"Where am I?" My whisper sounds scared.

"Erma's house. Upstairs." The whisper is definitely Bernice. "There's four of us hiding here in the baby's room."

"And we don't want to wake the baby," another whispers.

"What did. . ."

"Leo carried you over here before the raid started. The girls insisted."

"There's cops all over Third, even Fourth." That voice comes from another direction. "Sheriff's department on Broadway and down by the river."

"We'll get the all-clear after a bit. After the sheriff's men leave."

"Don't get no white girls up here very often."

All these voices bounce around like so many moths and between them, the shallow breathing of Erma's baby.

"Keep whispering until Erma comes up for us," Bernice says.

"So, everyone got out of the Avalon?" I ask.

"I hope so," Bernice says.

"Yeah. The police station's normally quiet in the evenin' so when there's a bunch o' activity, one of the firemen calls. We always gets us an hour warning."

"Why don't the police come in like a client and then arrest you?" I ask.

"We knows the police. They's only so many, you know, sheriff's deputies, too. We don't do tricks with younger men 'less we know who's they are, lest they be trying to get on at the police station."

I hear voices outside, sirens in the distance. There are footsteps on the back porch and the faint smell of cigarette smoke. I almost doze off before the bedroom door swings open.

"C'mon then," a woman's voice says. Everyone moves through the dim doorway and down some wooden stairs to a kitchen table. Small bread loaves cool on a wire rack.

"Most of you know each other," Erma says, but she doesn't make any further introductions. "I know you probably didn't get supper, so I made my favorite raisin bread." Erma is young, mid-twenties, fair-skinned, and quite attractive. The black girls thank her in turn, their eyes darting about as they sneak out the back door.

That leaves Erma, Bernice, and me standing in the kitchen. Two framed pictures show handsome young men in crisp military dress. I can't help but stare at their confident smiles.

"We lost my brothers last November a few days apart. James and Dalton. Dalton and his wife Irene were the witnesses in my wedding."

"I'm still so very sorry, Erma." Bernice grips her shoulder.

"Sit down, you two, and tell me how you landed up with the whores tonight," Erma says. "I shouldn't use that word, but they use it themselves, and it kinda grows on you."

"We were using the tunnels," Bernice says, "and when we entered the Avalon, Leo said a raid was coming. Dressed like this, he thought we might get busted."

"You've got blood behind your ear, Bernice. Abby's got blood on her ankle. So why were you using the tunnels anyway?"

Bernice takes a long breath. "You don't want to ask questions right now."

In the silence that follows, Erma looks unsurprised.

"Because we couldn't tell you the truth anyway," I say.

She nods. "You didn't bring any danger into my home, did you?"

"No. Everything's over and done with. You would approve if I could explain, but with the police all around, you're better off not knowing." Bernice nods at my appraisal.

"They bring sheriff's deputies sometimes," Erma says. "Otherwise nobody gets arrested. Minot doesn't want to shut Third down, they just need to make it look like they're keeping things clean."

"Third Street's good for business," Bernice says.

"It brings a lot of people to town, and they spend their money," Erma says. "Those rich locals don't mind a little adventure, either. Half the downtown businessmen gamble upstairs at the Coffee Bar every Sunday afternoon."

"Lotsa cops sniffing around all the time."

All this talk after I murdered a man and Erma noticed blood. My heart starts racing again.

"I don't think they found much," Erma says. "Hardly any cars here on Fourth Street. Here's a dishrag, let me get that blood cleaned off the both of you."

"How's your baby?" I ask, trying to calm my nerves.

"He's better every day," Erma says, "with your swaddling and Etta's gripe water and a new hot water bottle he sleeps with."

As if on command, a little voice babbles upstairs.

"It's time to feed him," she tosses the rag toward the sink. "I wish my husband was here to take you home, but he's working nights."

"We'll go back down the tunnels," Bernice says.

"Go out through Stearns' Motors," Erma says, "Here, take this flashlight. Take some bread too, just a little shopping trip in case you meet the cops. Whores aren't out buying bread at this hour."

"I'll tell you my story, Erma. Another night."

"Safe travels then, Abby." She hugs me. "You tell me about it when the time is right."

We thank her for her hospitality and the raisin bread. We scurry across her shadowy yard into the hotel and push back inside the damp tunnel. A rat watches us pass, and I wonder how Bernice hardly notices. Our route soon carries us north beyond proper lighting.

"I've never been down this far, but there must be a door somewhere," Bernice says. "There's a car dealer that runs booze down from Canada. I know Saul brings his whiskey right out of the tunnel. The pimps store their cars here too, all part of the hush-hush business."

"I hope there are no more rats."

"There's always rats, but rats don't bother you. They're part of High Third, part of the underground Minot that people don't see."

I keep glancing over my shoulder.

"Keep your eyes in front of you, Abby. Stay on the cart trails, see? All those handcarts make the trail hard."

She's right. Even in the low muddy areas, a thousand cart tracks form a solid trail. Five minutes later, she surveys two doors and chooses a black door that opens left.

"Careful, if it's the car dealer, there's a big dog in here," she whispers. My flashlight illuminates a cavernous room. Bernice pulls me up a stairway and I hear the rustle of something below, something alive, the sound of claws on concrete.

"Out this door, hurry."

She slips a wooden block up, unbarring a metal door. We creep outside. Moonlight reflects off the river below us, and streetlights follow the main road running north from our perspective.

"We're off High Third by a block. That's Broadway. Where are you staying, Abby?"

"We just pulled in on the train and went out to eat."

"And he won't be missed, this companion of yours?"

"Nobody knows him here. Nobody would ever look for him in Minot."

"Come with me then quickly."

We walk downhill away from the lights. The Souris River runs heavy with spring snowmelt, slipping over its banks, swirling right onto the gravel road.

"We shouldn't see anyone down here this time of night, but you clam up if a cop comes. Pretend you're drunk and let me do all the talking."

"I owe you, Bernice."

"That guy we killed, he's really a Nazi?"

"Yes. I spent the war as a nurse in Europe. It's a long story of how he snuck out of Germany before the war ended. He ran medical experiments in a concentration camp, really sad things with kids and everything. He thought I was German, too, so he told me everything."

"Bad, huh?"

"Intentionally giving kids malaria, spraying them with white phosphorus, swapping fingers child to child; tell me when to stop."

"Stop now. He told you all this?"

"I was taken prisoner and forced to care for his patients."

"Oh, my God."

"Bernice, I poisoned a man with cyanide. It had to be bad."

"I finished him off, you know. I heard his accent so I knew he was a German."

"Doesn't everyone around here have an accent?"

"North Dakota German isn't the same as German German. Half my friends talk North Dakota German."

Three raccoons rush away from the river's edge into nearby foliage. We hardly break stride.

"I give you my word, Bernice. You would definitely want him dead if you knew."

"You owe me the whole story someday."

"We'll spend time together later this year. I promise."

"Erma, too. After she lost both her brothers, she'll want to know."

An open space spreads before us as we emerge beyond the Broadway Bridge.

"How much do the black girls make, Bernice?"

"Oh, they make a lotta money. The pretty ones make $500 week or more. I know one girl that says she makes almost a grand. Of course, that's after the house cut, usually forty percent."

"So this girl makes $1000 a week. That's what a man makes working a whole year."

"So, she makes fifty times what a man makes, and the madam makes even more with two or three girls. Ma Butler has five or six, a pretty lucrative business."

"Before, all I saw were these unfortunate black girls."

"They got more money than anyone," Bernice says. "People say Ma Butler makes more profit selling girls than Westlie Motors makes selling Fords."

"I guess it's worth dancing around the cops."

"Well, all the cops should be headed home right now, so look normal," Bernice says. "We're just friends returning from supper."

She leads on in silence then, back up Main Street and into a small apartment over one of the many businesses.

"My daughter is twelve, and she should be asleep. Our neighbor watches her when I go out, so keep quiet."

Bernice unlocks the door.

"Mom?"

"It's alright, Dorothy, just getting ready for bed."

Bernice approaches a small bed in the same room, a bed surrounded by a draw-curtain. "You got room for me in there tonight?"

"Sure, mom, we can snuggle like when I was little out in Wolfpoint."

"Alright honey."

Bernice brings me a change of clothes. Her trundle bed folds halfway out into the room.

"That one's yours for the night, and if you slip out before we wake up, that would be best. Don't forget your purse."

"I'll tell you everything someday, Bernice, I promise. It's still a really bad situation."

"You better, Abby, and I will trust you. Can you control this situation?"

"Nothing will tie what's left to what's done, so don't worry. I'm gonna try. I dunno if I can control what's left."

"Oh, yes, you can. I have faith in you."

I hug her long and hard.

"Now, get some sleep," she says.

"Mom is that Aunt Bette, it sounds like Aunt Bette."

"No honey, just a friend from another town."

"Alright, but you promised we'd visit Aunt Bette, remember?"

"We visited three days ago Dorothy, remember playing with Lila?"

"You said we would go back soon."

I slip out after several hours of actual sleep. Coal smoke fills my lungs, the aroma now somewhat familiar and somehow comforting. I walk into the U.S. Café, wash my face in the bathroom, and settle in a corner booth. A middle-aged waitress delivers exceptional coffee in an oversized porcelain cup. I plot my next move while sipping coffee and smiling, the first genuine smile in two years.

I don't know how others would describe this smile. Call it devious hatred.

Five young GI's enter the restaurant. They look like some downtown tavern did a brisk business right up until the wee morning hours. My smile grows even wider.

"Are you guys riding the train?" I ask.

"Today's train arrived right after midnight," one man says. "They told us we can get on either one, so we decided to wait. The trains will only be a half-hour apart, traveling west."

"That sounds like a good plan, waiting on the second train. Thank you."

They nod in sequence. They bump into the large corner booth, and I can smell the sweet alcohol still lingering on their breath. An overhead clock ticks—5:15.

Alder finds me there a half-hour later. My hands still grip the same coffee cup and around me: a few pancake crumbs, an empty juice glass, a yolk-smeared plate with dots of bacon grease.

"Good morning, Abby."

"Good morning, Alder."

"You ready to go?"

"Our train is about to leave, but there's another train waiting behind it. We will board that train."

"How about your luggage?"

"Should be there when we arrive."

He nods. "Fair enough, then, did you have a restful evening?"

"Like most nights, not much rest."

He sits down across from me. "Josef is nearby, I assume?"

"Yes."

We stare across the table one minute, two minutes. The first train engine woofs louder.

"He won't be joining us for breakfast?" Alder looks away when he talks.

"Not unless they wake him up. We switched trains, and I left him snoring in his sleeper a few hours ago. I told him that I will bring him a caramel roll."

"And nobody will bother him until you return?"

"No, they will not. He's my problem, and I hate you for putting us together so leave me alone. And go to hell."

Alder takes the news with a small nod, a wistful look out the window. "The river there, I drank ale with a French-Canadian last night who still traps along the river. Surrie he called it, that's mouse in French."

"The sign along the tracks said Souris," I say. "My point is, sometimes words have two meanings. If you need clarification, think hell in the literal sense, not the figurative sense."

The front door of the U.S. Café opens and closes.

"Good morning Abby, who is your handsome companion this morning?"

"Bernice, so nice to see you again. This is my friend, Alder."

"This is my daughter, Dorothy. Nice meeting you, Alder."

He tips his hat; Dorothy murmurs a quiet hello, the waitress rushes by with a tray of dirty dishes.

"Everything alright, Abby?" Bernice asks.

"Everything is good, Bernice, thanks. Say, you run into Al Emil lately?"

"Just this week at Aunt Bette's," Dorothy says. "Al helped work on the barn. He's so nice, and he said to come visit his farm, said I could ride his favorite horse. Can we, Mom, please?"

"Dorothy, we will have this discussion later, right now it's time for breakfast." Her voice is stern, although her controlled smile suggests Al might have a chance.

Alder walks to the bathroom.

"I don't know what's going on this morning, Abby, yet I know you're up to your neck in it. If you're really gonna try, like you said—go all the way, otherwise get out now. I can help you now."

"Thanks for all your advice, Bernice. It pulled me through until today, and I think the worst is behind me." We visit briefly, long enough to put Bernice at ease that I do not need saving once again. Alder could use saving, but Bernice will never know. He returns from the restroom.

"Well, you two have a fine day," Bernice says. "Dorothy and I always eat at the counter so we can look at the pies. Nice seeing you again, Abby, and stay in touch."

They walk to a nearby breakfast counter, and Dorothy spins on the round stool, once, twice.

"I used to do that in my father's ice cream store, Dorothy. You know Grandpa Bill. He had stools like these."

"You've told me that a hundred times, mom."

A shrill train whistle sounds outside.

I pay my check, along with ten extra dollars for Bernice's tab. I add a caramel roll to the bill, too.

"Today's train departs soon, a half-hour behind yesterday's?" he asks.

"You heard the first whistle."

"Ready to leave?" Alder asks.

I laugh. I walk out the door with Alder on my heels. I have no idea what to do next.

Great Northern's first train chugs away from the depot. Morning light touches early risers moving down Main Street. Pigeons, gray and white, *whoosh* across brick buildings where upstairs windows alternate in dark and light.

The hungover servicemen watch our departure. Their muscular arms droop over the corner booth like so many hams displayed in a meat shop. I could bang on the glass and motion them outside. Then I could tell them who Alder is rather than continue this charade, but my instincts say, no. Something still stinks. My gut tells me Alder plans something beyond the plot we shared. He knows others on the train.

I look back toward the window. If I give up Alder now, the other train passengers scatter. If I keep him close, maybe I can take them down too, somehow, one at a time. From inside the diner, a soldier meets my eyes through the glass, he observes my indecision, my discomfort with this older man.

I step forward, and Alder steps in front of me. Behind him, that observant soldier adjusts his sleeves. Separated by thin glass, he watches my face. He pushes up to his feet, his eyes following mine, sensing my conflict.

"Alright, Abby, there are many things you don't know about me," Alder says.

The man inside squeezes past his companion's chair.

"The world is so complex," I say.

The soldier crosses his arms against the glass door. I make eye contact enough to keep him in place for the moment.

"I helped you with Josef. You want him dead, don't you?" Alder's eyes blink.

"Yes, I do. I still don't trust you for a minute."

"What can I do to gain your trust?"

"Give me back the year at Auschwitz."

"Anything else?"

"Why did you do it?"

"The answer will take longer than the time we have. If you insist, I will tell you everything on the train." He drops his head. His right hand shakes as he pulls his collar together against the cold.

"I'm in no danger boarding the train? And if I knew everything, I would still board this train."

"Danger is relative. Some people wouldn't board the train under these circumstances, but you would. John and Robert, too."

This game of cat and mouse keeps our real agendas cleverly hidden. With Josef dead, I can't think of any scenario leaving Alder alive. He's a Nazi officer with far-reaching military ties in Hitler's war machine. He interrogated Allied prisoners before slinking out of his losing war. He snuck out other men too, something I allowed in order to save John and Robert, an act of treason. I can't piece together a single direction where a living Alder might benefit anyone.

I can imagine some very bad scenarios. He can't possibly live.

I nod a thank you to the soldier inside.

The train engines rev. I take Alder's elbow, and together, we walk north with no idea who's fooling whom. Minot's streets grow busier with the morning rush.

Two black girls stand near a department store window. I recognize them from High Third, a waitress from Saul's and the girl that saved me last night, Grace. They stare at a dress display, and despite the early hour, each girl looks dressed for a dinner date. This is their daily time off. They eye a beautiful dress, not with bitterness but in awe with the cut and color, each remarking on a detail in turn. I wish them good morning, and Grace returns my greeting. They don't acknowledge any familiarity as their world dictates.

At sunrise, I lead Alder aboard the second train. Alder carries a duffle bag on board. I left mine on the first train. My entire future fits into this day, everything I can comprehend, everything I can foresee.

He follows me, quietly motioning off three men. I catch the exchange in my peripheral vision. They disappear back into the steam.

We find a seat together near the sleeper cars. He smiles a fake smile.

"Josef's in the next car," I say. "We boarded the first car in early morning, after the taverns closed. He couldn't get comfortable, and all the sleepers were taken there so we checked this train."

"Lucky break," Alder says. "What about you sleeping?"

"I slept fine from 1:00 until 5:00. After Europe, I can sleep anywhere."

"So, you tucked him in at 1:00."

"He never sleeps right away. He brought some scotch along, and I know how much he loves it. We won't see Josef until noon, at least. Get some sleep yourself, Alder."

To my surprise, before the train pulls out, Alder closes his eyes and falls asleep.

I stare out the window at passing strangers. I wonder how mundane their lives seem right now, just living another day like the last one. I still don't trust Alder, not a bit, yet I'm worried about John and Robert. He mentioned their names. My routine back in Browning sounds like Heaven on Earth, but right now, I need to plan another murder.

CHAPTER 18

JOHN

The train clerk estimates fifteen hours before Abby leaves Minot—our last airport option before Browning. A cab ride chews up the first half-hour.

New York Municipal Airport offers a single flight to Minot with a connection in Minneapolis, together, an all-day affair not much faster than driving.

Robert finds a charter plane instead.

The aging pilot moves slowly through fueling and checkout, yet we leave the runway in just over an hour. His bright red Cessna Airmaster feels more airworthy than some of the military transports flying the skies.

"So, what's the rush to get to Minot?" the old man asks. "I took a man named Clarence Parker home from a conference one time. We hit it off so well that I stayed a few days, right at his hotel actually, although I wouldn't hurry back to Minot."

"We're trying to catch up with a friend that took the train out of New York," I say.

"Well, it's good you said so. Full throttle's one hundred forty miles an hour. From Chicago, we follow the tracks all the way to Minot, so you know exactly where we're going. Sound like a good plan?"

"That would be great. It seems like you've been flying a long time."

"I flew with Eddie Rickenbacker in World War I. My guns shot down eleven German planes, but I couldn't keep up with Rickenbacker. He shot down twenty-six, so if you see any German Fokkers today, let me know because I'm still fifteen behind."

"We'll definitely keep our eyes open," I say.

He pats me on the shoulder. "You did some battlewatch over there, I can tell. Where at?"

"Italy, Germany, Belgium, and home. One big loop."

"Sounds like a nasty tour. You boys brothers or something?"

"Yes, sir, we are."

"You're chasing after a dame, aren't you?"

"Yes, sir, we are."

"You met her over there. A nurse or something, right?"

"Pretty close."

"Well, let me tell you, I did the same thing. I married a nurse from London after my war. Best decision of my life. Nothing rattles her because she got rattled a lot over there."

"This girl got rattled a lot over there, too," I say.

"Women are tougher than men. There, I said it. What makes them tougher is that they're not in control of their lives, most of 'em, not to start with. They hafta deal with whatever they marry, whatever they can grab onto because men run the businesses and the homes."

"I never thought of it that way."

"Might be different someday, but not in 1945. Women develop their instincts, and those instincts keep the world going."

"Sounds like you speak from experience."

"I sure do. When our oldest daughter died, I picked up a bottle. My wife dealt with everything, including me. You boys don't want to go it alone. You go about your job and whatever you think is important. Leave the real decisions up to a good woman."

"This girl we're chasing, we did a mission together in Europe," I say. "We left the real decisions up to her, even though we didn't know it."

"You're good men, I can tell. Don't let her go."

The flight takes all night, but we're too anxious to sleep, or so I think. Sleep comes all the same, and in the middle of it, some unexpected turbulence.

Abby's near the church. She's crying. Alder's apologizing, "So, so sorry."

I awake to that memory: the dream vision of Abby. No wonder it stays fresh. It finds me at night, those precious moments I never remember in the morning.

Alder. He's been in the dream all along; I just didn't recognize his voice. *Why is he apologizing?*

"You alright?" the pilot asks. "Looks like you spotted a ghost."

"Maybe I did."

"We've reached Chicago if you wanna look down. She's beautiful at night."

Our pilot follows the railroad tracks out of Chicago. A full moon lights our way—the same moon that comforted me in Stalag VII-A when I needed a friend. Forested farmsteads crowd Minnesota, right up to the Red River Valley where trees almost disappear completely. North Dakota runoff pours across gravel roads, visible even in the moonlight. More farms dot the land between occasional towns of a hundred houses or less.

"Quite a country," the pilot says, "that you boys fought to protect."

"You fought the same war, just twenty-five years earlier," Robert says.

"It seems even longer. To think I was once your age seems impossible now. War does that to a man; it accelerates your life because you want to forget."

"The war memories erase what came before?"

"It all goes away together. You don't want to risk stumbling into the war years, so your memories start over afterward."

"I can see that," Robert says. "All that suffering took a toll. If I start reliving my wartime, eventually it'll kill me."

"I can let my memories out here, with you boys. It's good for us to talk, but they go right back in a box when I leave Minot. War memories *will* kill you if you let 'em."

"This country of ours feels more precious now." Robert stares outside. "We heard stories over there. Like if Germany would take Russia, the oil and steel and eastern seaports would deliver them right here."

"There's no doubt in my mind. Take Russia, take China, then all those men fight for Germany."

His comment hits home. Nobody talks that last hour, our minds each entertaining demons and tucking them away. We spot Minot's glow fifty miles out.

"There she is, boys," the pilot says, "I'll have you on the ground in plenty of time to catch her." Morning light touches the eastern sky behind us.

Our flight lands with time to spare, but no cab service serves the airport. I beg a ride from a wealthy couple waiting on an early flight from Florida. Their daughter won't arrive for an hour. We share their back seat with a county atlas and an International Harvester oil filter. They farm near Towner, the lady says, right along the river. All trade for a hundred miles passes through Minot, according to her husband.

We arrive at the Minot train station already bustling with activity. In the predawn light, Minot feels like a much larger city. Warehouses stretch east along the railroad tracks, and businesses vie for space south and west. Trucks and pedestrians fill the streets in all directions, a throng doing the business of 10,000 farms and coal mines and wholesalers and retailers.

We scan the railway crowd, an overwhelming task. Two familiar men approach the train, men Alder included in our Germany escape. They still wear their military uniforms. Their downcast stares serve them poorly in a crowd. A man flinches as one of Alder's men bumps into him.

"There, those two. What are Alder's men doing halfway across the country, John?"

"No coincidence, Abby's tied in somehow. These two must be part of the New York Central list."

We watch the soldiers step onboard.

"Their bags are already inside."

"Well, this is the train she boarded. So Abby came with these men, at least some of these men, or she followed them," I say.

"Probably. The train's leaving now so decide."

"Too many people to find her."

Dawn silhouettes two low warehouses behind us, and in the glare and steam and smoke, we make our decision. The porter waves us on with our military IDs, and we seat ourselves a few rows behind those familiar men. Empire Builder seats, however crowded, feel luxurious after twelve hours in a Cessna Airmaster.

One hour later, I search every passenger seat front to back, then every private berth back to front. I describe Abby to each porter. One porter remembers her before Minot but hasn't seen her since.

Robert searches the train twice more. He returns to our seats with a frustrated huff.

"Abby's not on this train," he agrees. "They could have stopped someplace between here and New York, but the porter thinks she made it to Minot. Abby could be anywhere in the country by now, or dead in a shallow grave."

"She's still alive," I say. "The porter described her companion, and it sounded like Josef."

"Abby's very capable," Robert says. "Why would she miss the train? Why would Josef travel west, when all the major medical centers are out east?"

"This scientist, this Josef, maybe he's not who we think he is. The soldiers in front of us might know more."

"I don't like those two, either," Robert says. "I know an imposter by looking in my mirror. Those men wear Army fatigues the way I wear a tuxedo."

"So, what do we do with these imposters?" I ask.

"What choice do we have? They're our only possible connection to her now, and if we confront them, their plans might change. We have to follow along and hope they lead us to Abby, or that Abby comes to them."

My brother looks ten years older than his age. The lines around his eyes frame the same shared worry. We face each other from the train's double seats, an arrangement meant to encourage travel interaction, yet I feel alone. Without Abby, all seems lost.

"We're not the same without Abby," Robert says.

"I was thinking the same."

"This war never ends," he says. "I should be glad that we both survived, but I don't care. This thing with Abby scares me more than anything in Germany."

"It's worse than before. At least when Alder moved her, we had some warning."

"Seems like she has a stake in this one," Robert says.

"The players are no less dangerous."

"Why didn't she talk to us?"

"We're overprotective. She's up to something, and we would get in the way."

"I think you're right."

"Her war isn't over," I say. "There's something about that man Josef, something she didn't want to share. You know she is hiding things from us."

"I didn't want to believe it."

"Me neither. When we danced in New York, I wanted to think it was over."

"Yes. Yes." Robert nods his head.

"She let us think that. Then she slipped away."

Robert eyes the mysterious soldiers.

"I sure hope they know what happened to her."

"They know something," he says.

We watch the other men for a clue or contact all across Montana. They're young, these Germans, although in uniform it's hard to tell exactly how young.

When the train reaches Cutbank, they rise to leave. Nobody else on the entire train departs in Cutbank.

Without other options, we slip out behind them.

Both men carry small duffle bags. They walk with downcast faces rather than take in the curiosities of this interesting little village—a child with a rambunctious dog, flowery bouquets around an American flag, three teenage girls riding horses.

A farmer shouts, "Welcome back, soldiers!" Yet even his enthusiastic wave draws no response.

And nobody recognizes them. Some middle-aged women part for their passage. The women turn as one and quiz each other. "Josh Anderson? No, he died on Normandy." We approach the women, too, but our passage elicits hugs and tears and a straightened collar for me.

"Welcome home, boys," they all coo. One knows our names. Another knows our aunt.

Those Germans march through an unfamiliar town, into a small diner. The women around us resume another round of name-that-soldier because everyone knows everyone around here. Nobody ever gets off in Cutbank without some local tie. We shrug our shoulders, so the conversation turns back to Robert and me, twenty minutes more, family connections, all the memories these women share. No reason to hurry in Cutbank. This unexpected visit will entertain them for days.

A train whistle sounds from the east, then an expected roar, a second passenger train approaching Cutbank with no customer stops.

"Another train already?" Robert mumbles.

The train's metallic din takes center stage. Citizens stop what they're doing to watch it pass. Pigeons fly a broad circle around Cutbank's only elevator, a towering brown rectangle that hugs the railroad track. When the train passes, the pigeons return to their roost, and Cutbank's people return to their everyday activities.

Our welcoming committee looks ready to move on, so we wish them well. The last of them, a teary-eyed grandmother with thick glasses, hugs us both upon departure.

The Germans haven't stirred.

Cutbank's diner occupies three or four lots. Behind it lays the town's namesake, a precipitous riverbank that guarantees the Germans will revisit Main Street. We watch from the shade of a nearby building. Sometime later, both men hurry back across the street to a cheap-looking hotel. They visit the office, emerge without talking, slide a key into one of six visible rooms, and slam the door.

"They're nervous," I say.

"They seem driven to me. Like they're on a mission."

"In Cutbank."

"I can't imagine two men leaving Germany and traveling to Cutbank under any circumstance," Robert says. "There's nothing here except cattle."

"They know what happened to Abby."

"They have to, John. You got most of the cash. Go find a gun, and I'll watch their room."

Cutbank's hardware store flows right out onto the sidewalk. Bicycles, mowers, and wheelbarrows line the street, leaving space for the rural explosion inside. A man in bib overalls inspects an auction notice fastened to the door. He taps ashes off his cigarette when I pass by.

"Welcome home, soldier."

"Thank you, sir."

Seed racks surround a tub of baby chicks. Their peeping blends with the *whir* of a key grinder—cutting and polishing—the worker soon finished. I gather a bath towel, and a box of .22 shells. The crowded gun case features Colt revolvers alongside several more cost-conscious choices. I pick out a little Sedgley.

"Gonna shoot some rabbits?" The man in bib overalls strolls past. "Ain't got no Nazis to shoot at anymore, thank God."

"Amen to that," I say.

He squeezes around an older man loading a chest style soda machine. "Can I buy you a Coke, soldier?" the worker asks.

"I'll buy it," the overall guy says. "Gotta pay for this key anyway."

"Thank you, gentlemen," I say.

"No, thank YOU," the worker says.

"We're mighty thankful for your service."

Money changes hands with a female cashier. She opens the Coke and hands it to me.

"Anything else, sir?" She tallies my purchases. She wears a tiny American flag and a silver locket showing two little boys.

"Ring me up another Coke for my brother."

"He's a serviceman, too?"

"Yes, ma'am."

"On the house then. Thanks for your business and have a great day." She grips my hand for a moment. She's teary-eyed, this young mother, and I wonder if she, too, has somebody at war, or just lives the war like everyone, from the newspaper. These gripping headlines that haunt our entire country.

A Red Wing crock sweats beside the counter, offering cold water for free—a metal sleeve holds pointy paper cups. I push the little spout, splashing several drops on the adjacent block wall. Downing the water, I gather my items and step outside.

Hopefully, the Germans don't own a bigger gun.

Walking toward my brother, I notice similarities between the hotel and hardware store. Small towns often lost entire business districts to fire, when men built wooden structures side by side. Masons often rebuilt those buildings with sturdy blocks, creating utilitarian structures like the hardware store.

The same concrete block, probably laid by the same mason, built Cutbank's rectangular hotel. Owners painted it turquoise once, then white, then tan, as new hotel owners refreshed it in turn. Unfortunately, the paint didn't stick. Each block peels differently to expose a crazy camouflage pattern that hides nothing. The hotel will change hands again soon. Tourists only stop in Cutbank by accident, and locals won't spend money on hotel rooms because every dollar represents more potential livestock. A six-hour drive back to the ranch is fine, even on dark rutted roads.

Robert stands waiting.

We walk through thin dust raised by a passing truck. The hotel room has no windows to the front. A knock at the door, a few mumbled words from within, I hear the latch *click*.

One man cracks the door. Afternoon sun casts his profile across the tile floor behind him. He shields his eyes. All he sees is a towel and a hand.

"The manager sent me down with extra towels, sir, and another welcome back from that terrible war. I sure hope you both had a nice trip here."

Now he opens the door further, and I ram it with my elbow. The door swings left. My towel drops away to reveal a gun leveled at his chest. He stumbles backward over some shoes and onto the bed. Beyond the bed, another man stares wide-eyed.

Robert slips into the room.

And my jaw drops at the sight before us.

"*Herr bitte helfen Sie mir*," Robert repeats the words I uttered almost two years ago, the week I first met Abby.

Lord, help us.

CHAPTER 19

ABBY

With Josef rotting in a watery grave, I followed Alder onto the train.

Josef's murder brings profound relief. The thought alone bothers me, but the killing does not. A thousand worries followed Josef into that water, and with those worries, my humanity. I'll never see the world in quite the same way.

How can anyone feel elated killing another person?

Empathy will find me again. Right now, it's a distant notion, smothered in resolve. I feel satisfied knowing Josef will never torture anyone again, and that satisfaction enticed me to join Alder. Something tells me the killing isn't over.

Alder probably spent the entire night looking for Josef and me. Today, he smiled before he sat down, yet his eyes darted about. His rapid breathing suggested both relief and apprehension—relief in finally locating me, but apprehension, too. His tentative questions changed our relationship. Alder can't control this speeding train he's boarded.

Such a handy metaphor for this dangerous journey.

When the train rolled out of Minot, his forced cheer told me the worst is yet to come, a possibility I can't imagine. Now he sleeps with his hand on my forearm, a reassurance that I won't leave, yet where would I go?

I recheck the facts but left alone with my imagination, too many memories crash together.

The train moves through a flooded valley. The tracks stand three feet higher, a serpentine trail cutting through submerged trees and occasional farmsteads—some perched above the waterline and others not. The only other notable presence outside are thousands and thousands of ducks enjoying their temporary refuge.

Before Minot, Josef occupied my thoughts. Other soldiers moved about, but I pushed them out of my mind so I could focus. I believe those men are connected to Alder.

Today, Alder chose the third passenger car.

I rode the third car into Minot, only a different train and a different companion. Josef didn't survive to reboard either train.

Funny, I never spotted Alder on the other train.

Josef's imminent death blocked out everything.

Today, several familiar men populate the third passenger car, the same men that accompanied Josef and me on the other train, all sitting as before, like church people populating the same pew. They seem to know each other except nobody talks. They stare out the window, stare about the train, and exchange little nods each time another passes. I would expect returning soldiers to greet each other. Still their subtle acknowledgment looks more like an inward smile—a secret among friends.

I don't know them, yet their presence stirs my anger. Why did they switch trains? I feel the same dysfunction as before. Military men, eight or ten, none of them young, none of them speaking, comparing stories, writing letters, gazing at photographs—nothing. We should all rejoice at the end of the war.

I want to rejoice at the end of the war.

A tiny spider tends her web between the window and seatback in front of us. She can't be larger than a pencil eraser. She hopes this space will entice a passing fly into her web, so she can eat and grow and spin a larger web to capture even more flies. Her world exists in a realm of possibilities.

Alder enticed me with the possibility of killing Josef.

In turn, Alder's possible murder enticed me onto this train, but I can't kill him here. My web can't unfold in the open like the one woven by this spider.

Alder turns his head my way.

I get up and walk east.

Alder finds me in the observation car five minutes later. Stubble fields and pastures flash by. I jerk my arm away when he touches it. An old woman looks uncomfortable with our tension and she shuffles away, her departure providing distance between the nearest passenger and us. Alder slides down next to me.

"Coffee?" I ask. Two steaming mugs and an insulated pot wait on an adjacent seat.

"Yeah, sure." He looks exhausted, and I know I look the same.

"It's still too hot, give it a minute."

"Fair enough."

Can he read me already? Deceit takes on a whole new dimension when it seems your plan might be discovered. Changes in dialog, things you probably observed a thousand times now feel out of character. Offhand remarks sound like hidden accusations. A simple phrase like, "fair enough," feels blasé from a man that never relaxes, and you wonder if his cool remark is really meant to taunt.

"The soldiers in that car don't talk, don't laugh. It all seems strange, doesn't it? They should rejoice at the war's end."

"I didn't notice." He gazes at a passing farm.

"One looked familiar. I thought maybe you knew him."

"Just another tired soldier. They're all tired."

"You're right, Alder. They all look the same after a winter in Europe." The rings around Alder's eyes look even darker against his white skin.

"Awful winter." He shakes his head.

"This coffee is almost cool enough now."

Our game of cat and mouse drifts along, the innuendo rising. I offer a mug.

"Thank you, Abby. I can sure use some coffee."

"My pleasure. Look, here comes a river stretch. It looks like the train follows it several miles through the trees. It's quite beautiful."

The car holds a half dozen people, all well ahead of our seat.

He accepts the mug.

"A toast to our sleeping companion Josef and his impending demise," Alder says. He doesn't make eye contact like he's playing along.

"Here, here, and thank God there are no more like him on this train," I say.

Outside, two whitetail deer watch the train from a hidden meadow. Scruffy winter coats hang in clumps from their gaunt ribs, a reflection of their own difficult winter.

Alder lifts his mug for my toast.

"There aren't," I ask, "more men like Josef on the train?"

The train rocks. Mugs clink. We both spill some coffee.

Alder's eyes meet mine. We stare like that long enough to know that we're both hiding something. I reach for the insulated pot.

"Do you trust me?" He holds his porcelain mug between us. His eyes hold my gaze.

"I don't know." I swing the coffee pot over and tilt it to refill his cup. We watch the steamy brown liquid flow.

"You said I was a man of my word back in Germany. Do you still trust me?"

I'm sure the cyanide will kill him, even with only one sip.

I'm sure that sip will end our conversation forever, too, and now I'm not sure. Outside, the river dances in white cloud-reflections. Behind it, a layered hillside rises abruptly to several cattle, indifferent to our passing.

"Those men that never talk; they aren't soldiers returning home," I say with an air of utmost confidence.

"Sometimes it's best if you don't grasp everything, Abby. After Auschwitz, you know this is true."

"Don't patronize me."

"I didn't mean it that way." He lifts his cup again. "What I mean is that you're right. There's more to this."

I reach over and hook my finger on the rim of Alder's cup. His mouth hangs open for the first sip. Our eyes lock again.

"There's always more to it," I say.

"He's already dead, isn't he?" Alder's face stays expressionless.

"I thought you knew."

"I didn't even suspect it until now."

"Those other men on the train, the ones that don't talk, they're not servicemen going home to their families are they?"

"Abby, if I tell you anything, I have to tell you everything, and I don't want you in that far. If I tell you everything, you will have much more to worry about."

"You already got me in this far. Think about it, Alder, how much worse can it get?"

"One hell of a lot worse, I'm afraid."

"I can take it."

"You killed Josef."

"Good guess." I release the finger on his cup. He drops the cup a little below his chin and closes his eyes.

"Oh, no."

"So that ends this thing between you and me, Alder."

"Abby, please understand I need you on the train all the way to Browning. Sit with me, that's all I ask, and all you need to know." His eyes plead in a way I never expected. That look makes me all the more suspicious.

"You're helping those men escape, and I want no part of that."

"It isn't what you think. I swear to God."

I take his cup away and hand him my own.

"Do you want to know what happens when I get off this train? I can tell you how this is going to work, Abby, but telling you will make you part of it. Do you really want that?"

He lifts my coffee for a drink. I pick up sincerity in that brief exchange, something I can't quite grasp that leads to a split-second decision I might regret.

"Yes, I do."

He savors the coffee. He sets it aside. I spill the other cup onto the floor.

"Alright, I can't say I didn't deserve that." He stares at the puddle on the floor. He runs his hands through his hair, closes his eyes.

"I planned this the day I discovered Rose missing," Alder says.

"Revenge."

"Call it what you want, Abby. You are a woman of incredible character."

CHAPTER 20

JOHN

The Sedgley revolver feels comfortable in my hand. Guns of this caliber don't pack too much punch, but at this range any gun will do. I lower my arm. Both men we followed to the hotel sit motionless. A leaky faucet drips somewhere to my left.

"Take a quick look around, Robert."

He circles through the small hotel room and glances in the bathroom.

"All clear."

"Where are your weapons?" I ask.

"We do not have any," the taller one says.

Both men stare up at me, the closer one is only five feet away. He's crying. I point my pistol at his chest, and he breaks down; this man, this Nazi I followed halfway across the country.

Only this is not a man.

This is a boy.

They look young, fourteen, maybe fifteen years old, tall for their age, able to pass for men in military uniforms, yet, very young.

"When I call the local sheriffs' department, the *Polizei*, how will you explain your visit? You arrived in the uniform of an American soldier."

The farther one raises his hands, almost like an afterthought. A wet circle spreads down the closer boy's trousers.

I point the gun at the floor.

"Who are you, and what are you doing in Cutbank, Montana?" Robert asks.

The closer and younger boy stutters and sniffles, "We, we, we, we. . ."

"Why did you have to point a gun at him?" the other asks.

"Because you escaped Germany with Colonel Alder, and I know damn well you're not American soldiers," Robert says.

"We've never done anything to you," the boy says. "You don't know anything about us." He's scared, not accusatory. His voice wavers in that place between puberty and adulthood.

"I'm more worried about your plans here."

"We aren't planning to do anything except wait for our father."

"Who's your father?"

"Colonel Alder, s-s-sir," the younger boy stutters.

"Colonel Alder is your father," I say.

"He told us to stay in Cutbank until he came to get us," the other boy says. "We aren't doing anything else, I promise."

Alder's eyes and nose, his dimpled chin, yes, they could be his sons.

"How old are you?" I ask the younger boy.

"I'm fifteen, and my brother is fourteen," the other says. "We're supposed to prepare for Hitler's army this month, but our father snuck us away."

"That's all Hitler has left," the younger boy says. "K-kids and grandpas."

"What's your father doing right now?"

"He wouldn't tell us."

"And you have no guesses."

"No, sir."

"Where is he?"

"In a place called Dupuyer, sir. He talked about some unfinished business in Browning and Dupuyer. He told us to stay here a few days. He said that if he didn't return, well, I can't tell you that part."

"Tell me, anyway."

"No, sir."

"He has unfinished business from the war. How do I know that you aren't backing him up, somehow part of this unfinished business?"

"That is not it, sir, I promise you. Alright, I'll tell you. He told us what to do if he doesn't make it back, you know, how to survive, that's all, how to live in Montana by ourselves."

"Does he have Abby?"

"Yes, sir, he does. They boarded the train behind us, the one that just passed through."

"And they will get off in Browning."

"Yes." The boy's shoulders slump. "Browning and on to Dupuyer."

Everyone leaves their keys in the car here. We steal a dirty coupe from the rail station, a car with several dirt lines on the windshield. Since the owners left, at least three storms delivered snow. Sunshine removed the snow each time, yet the dirt left behind shows me nobody needs this car today. We speed west on Highway 2. Robert drives, and I allow myself a chance to believe we can overtake them. After all, a car will outrun a train.

This bastard Alder tricked us, but we can catch them, and save Abby despite my dreams, nothing more than dreams. A

Blackfeet vision takes weeks of preparation, time to purify one's thoughts, fasting and focus, certainly a coma wouldn't put my mind in order.

Or would it?

If it's important to my future and I don't have the proper time or take the proper time, would my vision find the proper moment?

Abby's life hangs in the balance.

All this time, Alder waited to even the score, and he plotted the ultimate revenge because we helped Rose escape. We helped Alder escape to exact his revenge on us.

Lord, help us all. God only knows what he tells Abby, what lies he uses.

"I knew Alder had Abby," Robert says.

"Abby said Alder was furious about Rose," I say. "He made her describe our ranch; now he'll kill her and leave her for us. I don't know how we missed all of this."

"How did he get her out of New York?"

"She felt distant on the ship, who knows what deal she made. Maybe in her mind, she's still paying him back. Remember, they had her a whole year. After all she's been through, he found a weak spot, something she wants to believe."

"She left the hotel alone," Robert says, "so, he convinced her of something. I can't imagine holding her captive all the way west. She's way too crafty for that."

"And Alder told the boys how to survive here if he doesn't return. He assumes the worst."

"He's afraid of her."

"I can't blame him."

"Maybe she set him up."

"I can't rule that out either," I say, "but everyone runs out of luck eventually."

The gravel road south offers a shorter drive to Dupuyer, half the distance even, rutted, and dangerous in spring. Robert speeds down Highway 2. Browning grows in our field of view until we can distinguish individual buildings. Somewhere ahead, Abby and Alder play a deadly game of wits.

An explosion sounds one mile from town. The car lurches hard right, down into the ditch with Robert fighting the steering wheel and narrowly avoiding a rollover.

"What was that?" he yells, wrestling our car to a halt.

I leap out and find a baseball-sized hole in the front passenger tire.

"Sidewall's blown," I say. "Did someone shoot it out?"

"Oh, damn it, no." Robert points up on the roadbed. A twisted muffler clamp lays a few feet behind us.

"I spotted it a second before we hit it. Our momentum bounced it clear up here."

"Seems a cruel coincidence, Robert."

He opens the trunk.

"The spare looks about ninety-eight percent shot, too."

"Pull the jack, and let's do it quickly."

"He'll tell her anything to get what he wants," Robert says. "Alder's a master at his trade."

The jack, the tire, the lugnuts, all speed through their respective tasks. Spring winds dimple the water below us, a temporary pool for two greenwing teal watching us work. Blackbirds chatter in the nearby cattails. Puffy clouds pass west to east, and it's their movement that captures my overstressed mind. *If the world spins toward the morning sun, shouldn't the clouds go east to west like the sun? Why do they move against the flow? Why does everything move opposite the way you plan when you're in a panic? Why are so many unusual obstacles blocking our chase to catch Abby?*

Robert slings the flat tire into the trunk.

"You drive, John."

I slam the driver's door, and the door bounces right back open. In my hurry, I didn't let my coattail clear the latch.

The train is long gone, and the station is abandoned when we reach Browning. A spin around the parking lot guides us right back onto the road.

Nobody in their right mind could drive from Cutbank to Dupuyer in an hour, including a flat tire, but I pin the gas pedal to the floor. Highway 89 flashes past in a blurry series of pastures and cattle. Whitecalf Coulee overflows its banks into the road ditch. Soon we fly through Dupuyer, racing west on the final stretch, a ten-mile road leading to our ranch and not much else. Prairie roads sneak off at regular intervals. Ranchers and hunters access these remote canyons seasonally, although, by Thanksgiving, snow fills most trails.

Halfway up our road, we spot dust in the distance.

"There," Robert says, "can't be anyone else."

The front-end wobbles, and the car sweeps right.

"Slow down, John. What happens if you roll this thing?"

"I didn't do that," I say—the front end sweeps hard left. "That other tire gave out." I coast to the shoulder.

"Are you sure?" He jumps out and finds the same tire down. "Damn it. Anyway, I didn't actually think it would get us this far. Why does it seem we're not meant to catch her?"

"We have to," I say—the hot engine ticks in the cool air.

"That's a long run."

"We did it as kids, and we'll do it again. Get the pistol. We got four or five miles unless someone comes along."

"Nobody ever comes along."

My memory starts here.

Nineteen months ago, I awoke from a dream-filled sleep, a coma in medical terms. I woke up on this road. A scene played out in my head, like a dream that wakes you and quickly fades, but this one didn't fade. It returned every night.

At Stalag VII-A, I spent an entire year organizing these moments that followed me out—running down this road, spotting the church, hearing Abby's voice. Within those dreams, Alder appears too, by the door. I'm hidden from view on the west trail, yet I hear him apologizing. *Why is he apologizing?* Maybe I'll know when the time comes.

For now, I run.

The presence of green in a usually brown world tells me winter dumped plenty of snow here. Our ranch produces according to the snow. Wet years start out good and typically feed the cattle well into the fall. Dry years just get dryer.

Running this road always cleared my mind. Thirty minutes out, I try to capture that reset, to clear my mind of Abby's dire circumstance, and arrive without crippling worry. We always ran it together, Robert and I, before we could drive. We lived a few miles south and often escaped to the ranch. We could always hitch a ride to Dupuyer.

Our uncle ran cattle up here in the summer, and we kept track of them, but in early spring and after roundup, we had the place to ourselves. We stocked the cabin with cooking staples, guns, and fishing rods. As often as not, our uncle wasn't around because a rancher and his wife always have too much to do, and too little time to do it. Left to our own means, on Friday nights after school, we caught a ride to Dupuyer.

And we ran.

Ten miles took two and a half hours.

We ran together, always a little competitive right down to the number of mule deer spotted and toward dark, nighthawks and falling stars. The ranch belonged to us, according to our aunt. It held magical secrets. We knew about our parents, about the wonderful life they envisioned, and we felt their presence around us. The cabin, the church, the high pines and low meadows, the crystal-clear streams, and the wildlife all captured our imagination. Sometimes we thought we spotted our mother walking along the treeline. Sometimes the howling wolves and bugling elk moved right down into our meadows, and sometimes we hiked up in the dead of winter just to be there.

The run conditioned us, all part of a sheltered world, our idyllic teenage years.

World War II erupted after we turned nineteen, and our father's legend ensured our sense of duty. Off we went. At nineteen, the Army trains you for war, but maturity still waits around the next bend. War changes that. War throws innocence aside, and offers terror, focus, survival, in that order—if you reach survival.

Somehow we reached survival.

Abby's survival swims back into focus along with overwhelming regret. I should have never taken her from Montana. I should have never allowed her across the German border. I had so many chances to keep her from danger. Yet, I missed every opportunity in my desperation to rescue Rose. Once she stepped into the Nazi war machine, she came out a different person, and even then, I failed to protect her. In New York City, I slept while she crept away. She doesn't belong in any of this, but here I am again, knowing this would happen, failing to act. My vision foretold this exact ending, and somehow the end is here. I couldn't stop her once the world swallowed her up. Abby moved beyond my grasp. I failed her.

"Slow down a little, hey," Robert says. "If you die on the road, nobody gains anything."

I let him catch up a bit right toward the end. Our run leaves us breathless. A small ridge hides our ranch from the road until a quarter mile out, and when we clear the ridge, I spot someone walking uphill.

Toward the church.

A blue 1940 Panel Van sits below the tiny makeshift church. Nothing brings vehicles to this church except for a wedding or a funeral. Nobody married here since 1918, and only five people attended the bride's funeral. Two were her babies, now World War II veterans returning to a place our father left long, long ago.

From the parking area below, a steep grade hides most of the church from view.

We huff up alongside the van. Above us, only the roof rises over the rocky trail. Beyond the church, clear skies spread out in every direction except for one lone cloud high on the mountain.

"You take the pistol," I say, "and come in over there. I'll circle around and come in from the west, and Robert, she's here but don't rush. We're coming into something complicated."

"You know something?"

"All I know is that Abby's in danger, but if we rush in. . ."

"We'll make it worse." He slips around the hospital's panel van.

Our church lies fifty yards up two rugged trails. Germany lies 5,000 miles east. If only we could have finished the war there.

I start my ascent. The element of surprise allows no mistakes, no clattering rocks.

The last time I visited, Abby cried in the church. My mother's grave made her sad too, and with my twin brother missing in Europe. Our visit only lasted an hour. More than once this last winter, I assumed we would join my mother beyond this world.

If I lose Abby now, nothing will stop me from joining her. I could never live with myself, knowing that I caused her death.

Runoff rearranged portions of the west trail. My heart pounds as the little church bounces in my vision, only another thirty yards.

Ed anchored pulleys inside to wrestle rock from a hole below, a mine shaft carved of muscle and sweat. Without a church for miles, Ed painted the building white and put up a cross for his wedding. Several years later he shipped out, and never returned.

Lord, help me today.

CHAPTER 21

ALDER

*E*verything's in place.

Abby and the men, this remote ranch, all in place as planned.

It's time to make things right.

They started up here several minutes ago, and Abby is here. She made my scheme possible: Abby with the long red hair, the impossibly green eyes, and the disarming smile. I planned very carefully around Abby, this ranch, their overconfidence.

They had no idea what they were getting into.

She fooled me in Moosburg, and the thought gives me a chuckle, how people are fooled, and how those same people always obsess with their mistake.

I can't say killing gives me pleasure, yet in this case, I will make an exception.

I stand around the corner of the church. It's a symbol of God, but the church won't save anyone today. I can hear footsteps now. Some see church as their salvation.

Several crows fly west to east. I like the silence in this place, these trees, and rocks, a lack of human influence. After serving Adolf Hitler, the quiet sounds of a world moving through the ages remind me not everyone is at war.

Now, I slip around the side, quietly press the door shut and slip a padlock into the hasp.

Abby made it all possible. Abby sealed everyone's fate.

CHAPTER 22

JOHN

When I near the crest, I hear murmuring. Gravel crunches underfoot there too, slow and deliberate. Tiny green lichen covers most permanent rock, so I use lichen to muffle my own footfalls. It's so quiet that I'm afraid someone will hear me breathing.

Solvent odors float down the trail: kerosene, lots, and lots of kerosene.

My toe catches some protruding shale. The trip almost sends me down on all fours. I drop down anyway and creep ahead through the kerosene fumes. My hand pushes into sand. Everything started as a mountain here, from fine-grained sand to the bedrock itself and every rock in between the freeze and thaw cycles slowly destroying our mountain.

I push up, staring around the little church.

Alder stands near the door. His military uniform looks tired like Alder himself. His haggard cheeks droop under gray stubble. Shiny streaks reflect sunshine off the church behind him, the kerosene I smell splashed all over the wood. A white matchbook appears in one hand.

"I'm sorry about this, Abby," he says. "I wish there was some other way."

He's too close for me to reach him in time. A quick slip of the match will ignite the church before I reach him. He

beat us, Alder beat us, and there is no way I can save Abby.
I crouch anyway to spring ahead, slam him into the burning church, and send him directly to hell. We'll all die
together.

In that instant, Abby walks out from behind the church,
a few feet south of Alder.

What? What on Earth?

Her hair droops over one shoulder, and a military fuel
can dangles from two fingers. She bounces it up and down
near her hip. She watches Alder as he stares at the church
door.

She snuck out when he wasn't looking?

Abby freezes. She looks over her shoulder toward the
mountain, away from me, listening, turning her head by de-
gree. Behind her, a light breeze rustles tiny aspen leaves.

I slip up against the church, Alder opposite me and Abby
slightly right, within my field of view. She cranes her head
toward the washout.

Yelling erupts inside the church.

With a fluid motion, Abby tosses the can straight ahead
onto a small ledge overlooking the ravine. The can bounces with a distinct metallic *clank*, once, twice, then spins in
a circle and comes to rest. Beyond the can, another man
stands up, his white hair askew, his pants still hanging
around his knees. He lifts them slowly under a coat of U.S.
Army issue. His face looks puzzled. Everything falls within
this new man's line of sight. He takes it in with one swoop-
ing glance.

The yelling stops. The aspen whisper. It all happens in
seconds.

He fumbles for a handgun. Abby hesitates, frozen in the
middle.

I see the gun rise. With Abby directly between them, I spring forward. The uneven ground throws me left, but I recover direction across the rocky flat that separates us. I know I can't reach her in time, and I know exactly what will happen if I don't.

Robert crests the opposite bank, revolver in hand, firing wildly in the air. Alder glances aside. His focus briefly interrupted, the white-haired man snaps off a quick shot. Robert tumbles back over the edge.

In that instant, Alder slams into Abby.

Boom, boom-boom, boom. My dive catches her mid-air, behind Alder, his own gun now roaring. I feel burning pain across one shoulder. My fingers pull Abby tightly against my chest, torso twisting, absorbing the ground impact with my opposite shoulder.

Military men know their pistols and several bullets race home. Both gunmen spin to the ground. Stars flood my vision, and at that moment, I lose consciousness.

CHAPTER 23

ABBY

He's slinking away!

Everyone else is down, maybe dead, and he's slinking away.

The very thought ignites me. Nothing can contain my rage.

I grab the gun where Robert lost it. Robert claws at the gravel thirty feet below me, but he can't stand up. John hasn't moved. One man did this to all of us, and now he thinks I won't follow. The gun gives me little comfort because I'm a lousy shot. My father owns a crazy-loud handgun. Most bullets never land anywhere on the target.

If this bastard reaches the trees, we'll never find him. I can't stand the thought of him loose out there, no matter how gravely injured. Irrational thought drives me up the mountain, toward a dangerous man with advantages in both marksmanship and patience. He's a highly trained officer. I'm just mad.

There's little I can do for Robert or John, right now.

I should give up. Not much blood. Not much time. *Damn it.*

He took a wound high on his leg, and the limp worsens as he gains altitude. He glances across his shoulder. His progress urges me into a run because wolves or no wolves I refuse to let him go. I'll get ahead of him somewhere in the trees. He's not moving that fast anymore.

A small dark cloud tumbles down the face of the mountain. The Rockies scratch their own weather out of the heavens sometimes. They reach up, where the air is thin and twist it in passing.

He picks his footfalls carefully. Terrain grows ever steeper near a treeline edged in gnarled roots. Erosion carved the landscape here, leaving roots exposed and vulnerable. He quarters left around a small washout.

How did I let this happen? My anger urges me on.

He looks around again. I'm closer now, running uphill, assuming I can beat him to the trees and wait in ambush, but suddenly that looks impossible. He stops a hundred feet from the trees. He could just slip inside and disappear because the pines form a dense wall, yet he stops and turns his gun instead. I stop too, aware of my exposure. He's forty yards out with his Luger and years of practice.

I look left and right for a boulder, yet nothing larger than a softball holds this steep slope. He changes positions, a crouch now, and the gun comes to rest across one forearm. I scramble toward the trees. Loose rocks scatter behind my feet, and I tumble in a heap. He's ready with that gun now. I claw forward, hand over hand. His surroundings go from light to dark, the cloud shading him even as I fall flat once again.

I am so dead.

BOOOooM!

I wait for the bullet, yet instead, the sound registers a thousand times louder than any gun. Blinding light accompanies a monotone scream within my head.

A spectacular lightning bolt strikes the forest's edge.

The largest pine tree, a hundred-foot giant, disintegrates before my eyes—its trunk exploding into twisted slabs tumbling and cascading down the mountain. Within that chaos, the gunman's head turns skyward, and I see my chance. His hunched figure provides a reasonable target, rendered much less reasonable with a gun barrel five inches long. I pull Robert's gun into position. My father taught me how to shoot, a long exhale, if only a bullet remains in the gun, slow trigger squeeze, my target rising to leap away from some flying debris. . .

BAM. BAM. Click.

The impact sends him sprawling, and in that instant, a wooden slab smashes into his upper chest with such force, he cartwheels a complete circle. A separated arm bounces down the slope once, twice, and disappears in the ravine. Above me, the tree roars, and nothing else escapes the devastation. I watch it burn in a glowing yellow firestorm. Flames reach up twenty feet, and I wonder how or why a tree would burn so ferociously after a lightning strike, but I already know.

Welcome to Hell.

I watch spellbound this amazing sight. The cloud pushes south with this black smoke now arcing up to meet it. I'm emotional then, appreciating my life, overwhelmed by John and Robert's arrival. I brush sand from bloody elbows and balance on both knees. Turning to slide downhill, the loose gravel parts around my legs until one foot catches solid ground, a chunk of the mountain, layered and beautiful.

One knee scarcely supports my weight.

My walk back takes a little longer than the uphill run. I can see someone standing below, the ranch spread all around and endless Montana prairie beyond. My eyes keep checking upslope too, where smoke still drifts among granite rocks.

More movement below. They're both alive.

John meets me near the washout. He offers an arm. We navigate the trail together, several hundred feet, back to Robert, resting on one knee, kerosene still tainting the air, pounding now weaker inside.

My boot sends one last rock tumbling downhill—*click, click, click, click*. Behind me, the world waits in hopeful witness to whatever comes next.

"Are you hurt, Abby?" Robert stands. He balances his weight on one leg.

"No, not really hurt."

"What happened up there? We heard thunder."

"I killed him."

More pounding erupts inside the church.

"Your knees are bloody."

"A tumble in the rocks," I say. "My Lord, John, Robert, are you alright?"

"They nicked my shoulder," John says. "We landed hard and I blacked out."

"John, you're bleeding." Indifferent to the world around us, I spin him around. "And what about your head?"

"Just grazed me, Abby." I pull at his shirt and inspect his wounds. "Robert sprained his ankle pretty bad, too."

"Abby, what on Earth happened?" Robert asks.

Pounding continues from within the church, and another sound in between—*shuffle, drag, shuffle, drag*. All three of us turn to look.

Alder stares across the stench of kerosene and blood. He stares without movement, without emotion. He holds a matchbook in one hand, partially stained in his own blood, and resting unceremoniously on his chest.

A bright red bubble drips from one nostril.

"I thought he was dead," Robert says.

I hear myself scream.

"Ed, oh my God, Ed!" I rush to wrap my arms around him.

BRIAN STRIEFEL

CHAPTER 24

JOHN

White flower petals litter the ground below Alder's arms and across the bloody trail that marks his progress. His ribcage rises and falls, but the blood trickling from his nose tells me his breathing won't last. Inside the church, a steady hammering echoes—*wham, wham, wham*—muffled and almost indiscernible through the heavy timbers.

We walk to Alder. Blood covers his chest, and Abby talks into his ear, her fingers picking dry flower petals off his shirt.

"Abby," he says, "oh Abby, thank you, my dear, thank you." He struggles to inhale. "I watched you go running up the mountain."

"He's dead, Alder. God helped me." Abby grips his hand.

"What are you doing here, Alder?" I ask.

"Not right now," Abby cries. "Oh, Alder, what can I do?" She stares at his bloody chest.

"Right now, you need to light a match," he says. "There's nothing to do for me, Abby, except finish this, once and for all."

Alder glances back at the church door, and the padlock holding it in place.

"None of you should have come up here," he says.

The pounding inside intensifies.

"What am I going to do with you?" he whispers. "Is anyone else coming John, anybody else on the way?"

"I don't think so. What in God's name?"

"When you learn the truth: that will be the end of it." Alder coughs up blood. "It all ends right here."

BOOM, BOOM, BOOM, from inside the church.

I step over to the door.

"Stop, John," Abby says.

"You're gonna burn this church with people inside? Have you lost your mind?"

"Trust me," she says.

She kisses Alder on the cheek. She wraps her arms around him again and holds him through a teary embrace. I'm suddenly aware of the true depth of Abby's sorrow.

Alder turns his head to her and smiles.

"You are very special, Abby. I wish I could stick around, but I know you will take care of everything like you always have. I am so thankful that John saved your life. I will die a very happy man today."

She struggles to shift his hips. Robert braces his good leg, and together, we lift enough to place Alder into a better sitting position. Abby grabs our hands, holding us in place, crouched in front of him. She gives Alder a look I can only describe as pity.

He coughs up blood. She wipes his lips with her sleeve. He nods a thank you, his face now gray-blue.

"It seems we were on the same side all along," Abby says.

"I knew you were capable of saving a man, but I didn't know if you were capable of killing a man," Alder says. "I'm so very sorry about what I put you through."

"Auschwitz gave me the hate I needed—the focus. Without it, Josef may have sensed my deceit." She says the words and squeezes Alder's shoulder.

"What are you talking about?" Robert asks.

"I'd explain it all, but there's no time," Alder says. "Please stay with me, John, Robert."

We both look over at Abby.

She nods.

Two flower petals cling to the blood on his neck.

"They threw the flowers and the picture outside before you arrived," Abby says. "I'm sorry."

"It won't matter in a few minutes," Alder says. "Thank you for explaining the flowers to me all the same."

Lightning flashes in the mountains.

"They threw the flowers out? They, meaning who, the men in the church?" I ask.

Alder looks us over, and Abby sobs. He strokes her hair.

"You can tell them everything. Please be kind," he whispers.

"I can't do it alone."

"Yes, you can. And you must." Alder lifts his head for one more look, not a look of defiance, but a look of wonder at the three of us.

Beside him, my parent's wedding picture lays askew.

"Who's in the church?" I ask.

"Enough evil to start it all again."

Robert lifts the wedding picture.

"She was beautiful, your mother," Alder whispers.

Robert nods.

"She'd be furious that they buried her in the tomato patch."

Robert looks at Alder inquisitively.

Lightning slices the distant sky.

He looks us over one last time, his eyes wide for a moment, another word on his lips, then a bittersweet sigh. Nothing more.

Abby outlines the sign of a crucifix on his chest. She closes his eyes.

"He's dead," she whispers. Her hands flutter, trying to straighten his mussed hair. "I almost killed him on the train."

The thunder finally arrives in several successive echoes.

"You can tell us everything like he asked?" Robert's low voice breaks the moment.

"First, I need to light a fire. Can you please move Alder's body away from the building?" She squeezes his hand one more time.

Abby grabs the matches and the picture next to him. She steps over to the rocky dropoff, where kerosene still shines on the rocks. We follow her down the slope several yards with Alder's body in tow. Robert's limp seems less noticeable, but he might just be soldiering on.

"Abby, you can't undo what you're about to do," I say.

She nods her head. "Alder was supposed to light this match. He planned to do everything by himself in case something went wrong."

Abby touches a match and tosses it ahead.

"Trust me," she repeats.

Kerosene takes time, never hurried like gasoline. The match lies there a few seconds until a small flame pops up beside it. That flame expands. Heat increases the pace, accelerating up the shining trail and over the ledge where the fumes hang thick around the little white church.

The resulting concussion detonates, and within the concussion, a roar as all that kerosene-soaked wood ignites at once, and flames move a quarter-mile into the sky. Smoke rushes over our heads, then disappears with a *whoosh*, a massive updraft grabbing all the air around us to fuel this spectacular inferno.

Cold air rushing in from below gives Abby a shiver. I wrap my arms around her shoulders. Shattered from the heat above, rock shards arc over our heads.

"I don't know what comes next," she whispers.

Robert crouches opposite her.

"We'll take care of whatever comes next," he says. "You lead the way."

Black smoke soon turns gray, billowing east. Footsteps crunch, and together, we help each other up. We navigate the slope, back onto the flat, where a few orange flames consume what little remains. I spot the wooden cross several yards east, and I step over to hold it above my head.

Somehow the cross survived and little else.

A light breeze flaps my shirt collar. Nothing seems out of order at our ranch below. Though the skeletons in front of me suggest otherwise.

"They all liked Josef. They rallied around him," Abby says. "He actually had more personality than the rest."

"So, what happened to Josef?" Robert asks.

"He died unexpectedly in Minot."

"Natural causes?"

"Cyanide."

"In Minot?"

"Alder wanted to do this alone, using Josef to reassure the others, but I killed Josef."

"You killed Josef," Robert repeats.

"I didn't know what Alder was up to. He played me from the start, sending me to Auschwitz. Josef worked with all these men. He coordinated their escape, planned their great resurgence in some backward country."

"Abby. . ." I stare at her, lost for words.

"These monsters represented the remaining Nazi party," Abby says. "At least the important ones."

"I'll get a lantern." Robert limps toward the cabin, and I take Abby's hand.

"Alder discussed each man on the train," Abby says. "I met them all when we arrived. They were proud of Josef's work. Our ward was a source of inspiration for the self-proclaimed superior race."

We stand quietly until Robert returns.

"I can't believe the destruction inside here," he says.

The church burned completely. Only a fine powder remains scattered near the outer walls. The Nazis' bodies burned, too, leaving behind skeletons roasted a luminous white like the original church itself. Eight skeletons sprawl around a steel table that survived the blaze. The table bows in the middle, and stretching almost side to side, a brilliant yellow reflection holds the last colors of dusk.

"They all came up a few minutes ahead of me, every one of them so anxious to get started," Abby says. "They moved this metal assay table to the middle of the room, it swayed in the middle from the breaking of so many rocks. They moved it and threw the flowers outside."

I run my finger over the brilliant surface.

"This tabletop cradles all their stolen gold."

My reflection looks strained and tired.

"Gold melts at a lower temperature than steel," Abby says.

"I've heard that." Robert sets down his lantern.

"Gold. Pure gold," she points, "melts at 1,945°F. I remember that from Chemistry class."

"Nineteen forty-five."

"Nazis looted most of Europe. The most valuable property they took was gold, something they could melt to a form indistinguishable from the original jewelry and fillings and artwork. Gold could become their most valuable currency because the world could never track their gold, but this stolen gold didn't reach its melting point in Germany. . ."

"Because the world reached its own melting point in nineteen forty-five," Robert finishes her thought. "Irony or divine providence?"

"Some of both," she says. "I believe God was angry today."

"I believe you are right."

"Either way," Abby says, "Hitler's top men died here, and the only thing left is their gold reformed within a hallowed church. Alder set them up."

"So, if Alder could get Josef to Montana, the others would follow?" I ask.

"That's what Alder told me on the train. He recruited me to deliver Josef to Montana."

"And you killed Josef en route."

"I would have waited if I knew the whole thing, but I would have killed him just the same."

"Killing Josef early caused a problem?"

"Alder explained everything the next day, and none too soon. The other Germans were following Josef so I had to set aside my hatred for Alder and assume a new role. I assured the others that Josef missed the train and would join us soon. I said I could take them to the ranch."

One corner still smolders. Timbers a foot thick burn like prairie grass.

"I told them I was grateful to see the Nazi dream back on track."

"They believed you," Robert says.

"I sold it. Right now, I need to see what's left of them."

"You must have poured kerosene down in the cave, too, I've never witnessed anything like it," I say.

"No, we didn't pour anything inside. We just locked the men inside. They died an easier death than the thousands they killed."

Robert lifts the lantern, further illuminating the snow-white skeletons alongside a spectacular gold tabletop. "If the fire lasted a few more minutes, the skeletons would have disintegrated, too." Robert staggers on his bad leg, and I hurry to support him.

"Alder finished the Nazi party in Dupuyer, Montana. One man and the world will never know," I say.

"Only his sons," Abby speaks to no one in particular.

"We met his sons in Cutbank," I say. "They're teenage boys, tall and handsome."

"John, he told me about the boys in Cutbank," Abby says. "That was after I told him all about you. Ed actually had four boys."

That flickering lantern will stay with me forever. After all this time, Robert and I still didn't know.

I stare back across our father's mining table. A few more puzzle pieces shuffle about, some of those pieces now snapping into place. Robert's eyes betray a similar cognitive journey. Abby's too emotional for words, so she steps away and retrieves the framed portrait. She places it on the table and points to the woman in the picture.

"I sure wish she were here," she whispers.

The man in the picture smiles back at us from happier times, long ago. The decades changed many things about Ed Alder but not the unmistakable eyes and cheekbones. Suddenly I realize that my vision wasn't meant to save Abby because Alder saved Abby. My vision prepared me to cherish and mourn my father.

"I had an eerie feeling that he had more to say. He just ran out of time," Robert says. "The way he looked at us, the regret—his mouth tried another sentence, yet his eyes said what he wanted to say. His eyes said he would miss getting to know us. That's what it was."

"Ed Meyer, your father, was best man in his cousin's wedding before his first voyage to America," Abby says. "Ed learned about that cousin's death before he returned to Germany as a U.S. soldier."

A late-season avalanche rumbles somewhere south.

"After World War I, Ed Meyer reconnected with Johanna Adler, his cousin's widow. Fighting largely destroyed Germany, and when the snow melted in 1919, Ed stayed to help Johanna keep the family farm. They fell in love."

"So why did he change his name?" Robert asks.

"Ed Meyer took his cousin's name, Alder, so his cousin's widow could stay on the farm. The government took farms away from widows and sent families to Berlin for subsistence jobs. Ed Meyer knew about his dead wife back in Montana, but Ed Meyer did not know about his children."

"He saved Johanna's farm?" I ask.

"They struggled like every German between wars. Johanna brought two sons into a loving household wrapped in a difficult world. Joe and Wendelin grew up too quickly to escape Hilter's disastrous war, and when Hitler's war imploded, Ed made plans for their sons and for the Nazi war criminals he hated."

"It's hard to wrap my mind around all this," Robert says. "It's hard to imagine him in Germany raising a family."

"Ed Meyer became Ed Alder after World War I, and he never knew about you two."

"So, when did he learn about us?" Robert asks.

"Let's finish here then walk to the house. I'm freezing."

Together we toss every skeleton down the mineshaft. The bones clatter into their final resting place, and in that sound, I hear closure.

"Ed's got a beautiful view this evening. Leave his body alone 'til morning," Abby says.

I walk ahead, Robert behind, a solemn procession in the purple twilight.

The fireplace glows thirty minutes later. Ed built it from local quartz: white and gray and pink, his own mountain capturing heat from local pines. Three worn leather chairs and three glasses of brandy surround the fire. Our parent's wedding picture reflects firelight to our left.

"Shall I start from scratch?" Abby asks.

With no response and none expected, she continues.

"Alright, let me start by saying that all ten men planned to escape Germany separately and meet down in Argentina. Your father knew them all, knew about their plans. They blamed Hitler for defeat. They believed in his vision, but not in the man."

"So, they would meet in Argentina and start again," Robert says.

"Properly managed, their goals were still in reach, or so they thought. Ed convinced Josef first, then Josef convinced the rest. South America is poor, so if they could sell their gold in Montana, the cash would finance their efforts anywhere. American currency is more valuable than gold in developing nations."

"Ed knew the men and had to stop them," I say.

"He didn't know about us," Robert says.

"That's the interesting part. When he interrogated me about General Rose, he said we would all die if I lied. I told him everything, yes, yet it all started when he spotted that tack on Burger's map. That tack opened up our first conversation."

"He might have never caught us without the tack."

"Probably not. That tack caught his eye because of what he lost in Browning. The idea Burger had actually found someone from Browning, well, I'm sure it brought back memories."

"So, he asked about you, Abby, visited with you," Robert says.

"And I failed miserably at playing the Italian nurse, but his emotions let me slip. He needed more from me, and by the time his mind cleared, we already took Rose."

"And he still had no idea who we were."

"Until the interrogation. Suddenly, you were two young men from Dupuyer, Montana, whose father disappeared in WWI. I'm sure it seemed too much of a coincidence."

"So, he left us in Stalag VII-A," I say.

"The safest place in the war until he could learn the truth. He didn't learn the truth until after Minot. I don't think he was ready for those emotions. He knew these Nazis as Hitler's real talent, so he focused his energy on stopping them."

Robert nods. "He saved all of us, but he needed to save the world, too."

"He explained many details on the train," Abby says. "He talked for two hours about his clandestine work during the war and about these specific Nazis. I recognized some of the names from Auschwitz, names Mengele held dear."

"And they followed him?"

"It took some convincing. This German bunch spent time together and organized, but they needed up-front money."

"Guys like Mengele had gold," Robert says. "Most of them had gold."

"If gold appears where gold isn't common, it attracts attention. Men finding gold in the Rocky Mountains—that's another story. They brought gold from Germany, and this mine provided an opportunity to sell it," Abby says.

"So, why did Alder target Mengele? Mengele wasn't a military man."

"The men who died here didn't fight, they killed the innocents—the real Nazi mantra—everyone dies except the superior race. They killed the women and children. They organized the medical experiments and gas chambers."

"They weren't military men," I say. "Men drafted into duty fight for family and home against enemy troops. They fight for a noble cause."

"Exactly. And sometimes those men fight unaware of the wickedness behind their conquest. Sometimes evil men operate in the background, driving the real agenda under the cloak of war. Josef and the others here, encompass the Nazi evil that spread behind the war."

"Our father supported them, in a sense," Robert says.

"Germany drafted Ed Meyer. They assigned him as an interrogator because of his perfect English."

"Dad started as a military man."

"Yes, doing his job, interrogating the enemy. His job exposed him to the evil within the Nazi party. He was still very bitter about World War I, bitter about government officials staging a war with only their own financial interests in mind. By the end of World War II, Ed reported disinformation and undermined the Nazi party because he hated what they stood for. Your father helped the Allies win."

"He interrogated and interpreted."

"He figured out the D-day ruse. The Allies made it look like they would attack at Calais so the Nazis would focus there. Ed interrogated so many captured men that he read between the lines and suspected the deception. He support-ed the deception, even fueled it with Hitler. That was one of his proudest moments."

"So in defeat, the Nazi party went underground," Robert says. "How did Alder decide who to take?"

"Heinrich Müller ran the *Gestapo* and really enabled the entire holocaust. He adored Josef. When Müller hired a double and slipped out of Berlin, everyone else did the same."

"So, these people worked for Müller one way or another."

"Yes, Alois Brunner and Rolf Günther deported Jews from half of Europe. Glücks led the concentration camp in-spectors, coordinating human experiments, and perfecting the gas chambers. Josef Mengele and Aribert Heim were medical doctors who carried out the medical experiments."

"Impressive group."

"Yes. Then we have the mass murderers. Gustav Wagner was a brutal extermination camp officer with an unmatched lust to kill. Klaus Barbie was a *Gestapo* head in France, the *Butcher of Lyon*: a man who tortured and killed at least 10,000. Eduard Roschmann managed ghettos in Latvia and organized thousands of deaths. Walter Rauff was respon-sible for mobile gas chambers that killed 100,000 or more."

"They all planned their escape until Ed changed their plan."

"We told Josef that I inherited a Montana ranch with a little gold vein. Together they could break up some rock, dirty up a bunch of holocaust gold, and cash in."

"I'm proud of the man I hated an hour ago," Robert says.

"The Allies plan to hunt down Nazi war criminals and prosecute them. You'll see these names many years from now, men still at large, maybe a sighting now and then, but they all have doubles instructed to act the part until death. That commitment ensures the lifelong safety and security of their family. Ed described each man on the train and their complex identity changes."

"Ed witnessed their crimes first-hand and took the responsibility of prosecution," Robert says.

"He made sure the world wouldn't suffer through this again," Abby says.

The fireplace crackles through several minutes of silent reflection. Abby stares at a mantle clock showing 9:15, the time its internal springs gave up.

"Beautiful, isn't it?" I say. "I like to look at it, too. We never wound it. The last person to wind it was our mother."

"My God, John, that's so sad. We haven't talked about her. She gave up everything, too."

"I never felt that way. Everyone dies eventually."

"You left the clock alone, right where she left it. You walked around that clock for many years."

"Yes. There wasn't much here after our aunt cleaned the house. Lois meant well. She scrubbed the house of clothing, pictures; she wanted to get the sorrow out so we could get on with our lives. The clock stayed along with the dishes."

"It's a real connection to her," Abby says. "And it is time to get on with your lives. You grew up into war. Today there's closure."

"It goes back to our birth," I say. "The world stood still here since our birth."

"We owe them something, both of my parents," Robert says. "I don't feel closure yet. We should bury him now, rather than leave him out there all night."

We both stand and Robert touches her shoulder.

"I knew you were freezing, Abby. The fireplace has never been this hot."

"It's wonderful."

"Keep an eye on it. We'll be back in a while."

BRIAN STRIEFEL

CHAPTER 25

ABBY

They walk up a moonlit trail that I can see from my chair.

Everything in the room glows orange-yellow. Long shadows stretch out behind leather chairs. Radiant heat almost burns my skin, but I remain stubbornly close to the fire, willing away the deep chill in my bones, and thinking about a young mother who once braved a winter here alone.

As if on command, the clock turns my head.

Tick. Tick tick tick tick.

My eyes come up to catch movement. From this angle, only the gold second-hand slips through the dark space above our fire. I look down and find my watch just arrived at the very same time: 9:15.

"The fireplace has never been this hot," I repeat. "The clock spring got warm, Abby."

The second-hand remains still.

"You know it was the fire, Abby." My voice cracks.

I'm much more emotional than that. A few quick steps, and I'm winding the mantle clock spring. Once again, the clock ticks away precious seconds, seconds spent together in this room, seconds Agnes Meyer didn't get to spend with her boys. Time at the ranch just started again.

"Oh, bullshit on the warm fire," I say. "She was so young."

Outside, John and Robert carry their father toward a cross sheathed in delicate white beads.

"She'll always be here," I say, even though the men can't hear me. "They both will."

I scoot the chair back. The warm fire eventually lulls me to sleep in Dupuyer, Montana, on May 12, 1945.

An empty stomach wakes me a half hour before my companions. If hunger had a voice, the words would come out of my lungs, screaming. The Meyer cupboards hold bulging canned food, honey, rice, bouillon, and some petrified jerky. I remember spotting some chives outside. Somehow the Perfection #32 kerosene stove lights, and an hour later, I serve the most amazing hotdish ever.

"This isn't exactly the most amazing hotdish ever," Robert says. "I could eat the bark off a tree right now, so it's still pretty good."

"Sorry, guys. No hollandaise sauce in your pantry. It kinda tastes like sweet dirt, but I'm starving. I hardly ate anything since New York."

"Those cans look like they're about to explode," John says. "Van Camp's bombs."

We eye the open cupboard via kerosene lantern.

"Kind of a bachelor assortment. Beans and corn and Spam."

"Open a beer, and you get four courses," John says. "The last time I drank beer was a warm one on the ship. Some soldiers kinda made a sauna to warm up."

"I didn't think I'd ever warm up after that winter," Robert says. "I will say something, though. Otto Burger saved a lot of men."

"How so?" I ask.

"He'd give us days off to find food. With so many abandoned farms in the area, we found standing crops, feral livestock, enough food to help get the men through. Enough to keep the guards healthy."

"Men got anxious with the war ending, too," John says. "Burger made it clear that escaping posed more danger than waiting. Patriotism ran high around Moosburg, and with all the heartbreak, escaped soldiers would be shot on sight."

"He delivered an allied officer to the border himself. That's what I heard." Robert walks over to the window. "He gave the man a map to share with Allied command—a map so they wouldn't bomb Moosburg. Saved the prison and a lot of civilians, too."

"He always treated me very well," I say.

"So, what are we going to do about that hospital panel?" Robert points out the window.

"I borrowed the hospital panel, well, I stole the hospital panel, so we need to get it back this morning first-thing. It hauled some German men to the morgue yesterday."

"So, how did that go?" he asks.

"Pretty easy. They waited at the train station. I stole the van."

"Not exactly the church-lady crowd either."

"Not exactly. We drove down, unloaded their gear at the house—they all kept their gold hidden. Some boasted how much they carried. Buncha pricks. The good-old-boys club walked around admiring the view and smoking cigarettes."

"So, how would you describe them as a group?"

"Snobby. They talked down to each other by rank. Men accustomed to leadership should appreciate those around them, but arrogance from the top always trickles down."

"Hitler's arrogance led right into Russia," Robert says. "He owned Europe until his ego outgrew his army. Thank God for arrogance at the top."

"I felt that arrogance when the men arrived here," I say. "Then, they gathered to celebrate."

"A successful escape."

"Yes. Alder announced we would meet in the church. At 6:00 p.m., they all hiked up there and proudly dumped their gold on the table."

"I'm trying to picture it," John says.

"Well, your father described it quite well, a table covered with wedding rings and dental fillings, a thousand lives surrounded by the men that took those lives. The smug looks made it all the worse. Your father came around and stood next to me in the doorway a minute, then quietly closed and barred the door."

"With one man still outside," Robert says.

"I escorted those men up to the church, and then I walked back a few yards to look for Alder. One man slipped out of sight."

"We don't blame you, Abby, not for a minute," Robert says.

"I blame me, though. I could have saved Alder if I paid closer attention."

"Ed coulda counted to nine before he locked the door," John says. "We all coulda twisted this thing a hundred different ways at one point or another."

"Sometimes fate doesn't care," Robert says. "Ed locked the door."

"I poured kerosene all over the church, and then I heard something. When I tossed the can, it bounced right up to the ninth man, buttoning up his pants. The man pulled a gun, Alder pulled his own gun, and they destroyed each other."

"And somehow Alder saved you," Robert says.

"You all saved me, and I'm so sorry about your father. If I only knew."

"We lost him the first time because he didn't know he had two sons on his ranch," John says. "We lost him the second time because he didn't know about another man on his ranch. Maybe it was all fate like Robert said. Maybe this is bigger than all of us."

"These men walked right into the church," Robert says.

"Just like the Jews in Europe," I say. "Sometimes, the most human of traits, trust, is our undoing. We used their own weapon against these men. Fate doesn't choose favorites."

"What shall we do over Ed's grave?" Robert asks.

"The mine gets backfilled with tailings, and that closes one story," John says.

Robert nods. "I agree. Then we'll put another cross right next to our mother's. We never knew the man, so he still seems lost, but I'm very proud. I'm sure glad he's home."

"I'll start backfilling the mineshaft right now," Robert says, "I'm not sure about the gold."

"I thought about the gold," John says. "The irony of that gold almost overshadows the irony of our father's death. He worked so hard to fill that table with gold, and he finally succeeded, yet the last thing he would want is Nazi gold buying the land he always wanted."

"May I make a suggestion?" I ask.

"Please do."

"When I left you two in the New York hotel, I had an extra hour, and I stopped in front of a synagogue to pray, the Eldridge Street Synagogue. I don't know anything about that institution, but it gave me strength, and somehow I believe the gold would be properly spent there."

John takes my hand and leads me outside. The eastern sky glows yellow-orange where the sun will soon light another Montana day.

"It's over, John. I said I'd tell you, and I feel terrible for all the deception."

We stand alone beyond the reach of evil. I crumble into his arms.

"Please forgive me, John. I love you, too, and I've always loved you. I couldn't say it because, in love, I couldn't function. I couldn't keep my emotions and our danger separate."

"I know, Abby, and there's nothing to forgive."

"When you told me that you loved me on the ship, I danced inside, really danced."

"I watched you dance. I watched your eyes."

"Then I stopped dancing until we could dance together, John."

The creek nearby rushes, and in the sound, we find a waltz, just a few turns and back into his arms laughing out loud.

"I'm so very, very glad to be here with you, John. You can't imagine."

"Walk with me, Abby." He wraps his arm around my waist.

"Where are we going?"

"There's an overlook nearby, one of my favorite places. I need to ask you a question."

"Does it involve a train ride? I don't want another train ride."

"It doesn't involve a train ride."

"Good. I doubt any of us will ever ride the train again."

"I've never doubted that I loved you, and I waited over a year to ask you this question. It can't wait one more minute."

A covey of ruffed grouse break cover at our feet, startling me into John's arms. He kisses the top of my head.

"Do you know what the answer will be?" I ask.

"The most important things are always the hardest to say. You could never describe the fire we witnessed yesterday. Simple words sometimes make something spectacular sound infinitely smaller."

"Well, I know for sure what the answer will be."

"You do, huh?" He holds me out at arm's length.

I smile up at him, as if it's not already blindingly obvious.

John and I deliver the hospital van back to Browning later that morning, May 13, 1945, one hour before Mother's Day church, so nobody misses it. We stop for breakfast at the Teepee Café.

"I wasn't completely honest with you last time we ate here," I say. "We did the same thing I always do, the same thing my father and I always did. We perused the menu like we planned to try something different, then we ordered burgers and fries. I don't know if anything else is any good because all I've ever eaten is burgers and fries."

"I don't think that's on the menu this early."

"Oh, John, maybe if I asked really nice?"

"Maybe."

The fries take a little extra time because both deep fryers are still cold. We drink coffee like nothing happened, like we never left Montana, like the rural people around us with a routine, with a wonderful day ahead of them. Our corner booth keeps us hidden for a while.

"Robert said you remind him of the little sister we never had. You do the kind of things he would like to think our sister would have done."

"I appreciate Robert's sentiment. I had a little brother, you know."

"You never mentioned that."

"He died when he was four."

"What happened, Abby?"

"He choked to death on a vitamin pill. I was at school."

"Oh, my God."

"Our little family never recovered, that's why I don't talk about it. There wasn't much happiness in the house for many years afterward. A farm needs a boy to carry on, but they got me, kind of their second-place prize. My parents always treated me great, don't get me wrong, even though his death put a big hole in our family that we still walk around."

"I'm sorry."

"I wanted to warn you in case something awkward comes up."

Someone notices us before the food arrives. Everyone stops by our booth then to welcome us home. They're relieved to see John both alive and healthy. They stare wide-eyed through the same questions, always hurried, so as not to disturb us, happy like their own close relatives returned from war. In a way, they did.

"Robert's fine, too, yes."

"The Germans put up a helluva fight."

"Yes, we'd love to stop for supper sometime."

"Together, yes, but my parents don't know, so keep it quiet for today."

I know that last one won't work out, so a call to my parents brings them directly to the Teepee. They had my car at home and our Mother's Day reunion shocks my mother so much that she faints. When she comes to, I introduce John as my fiancé, and she faints again. The drive back to the ranch reminds me how much I had missed Montana. The rural place that I thought I outgrew looks very inviting after New York City. There's a certain glamorous charm in the big world, but way too many people to share it with.

Later that morning, John asks my father about the transmission spread all over the garage. Pretty soon, they roll up their sleeves. Dad can't remember how something fits together, yet John knows, and that fix makes them instant friends. They reassemble an entire John Deere transmission in less than three hours when I announce our late lunch; they stand over it together, sharing a beer.

Dad got his boy at last.

When I left Browning suddenly in 1943, I told my parents about nursing in Europe. I come home with a soldier, a local soldier, and my parent's lives click back into place.

After fried chicken that afternoon, if the day isn't already crazy, we meet Robert on his way back to Cutbank. Robert returns that car to the railway station, and together, we visit Cutbank's only hotel.

I knock on the door alone.

"Yes?" A tentative response comes from inside.

"Joe, Wendelin, I need to speak to you."

The door opens wide, and they stand there together. Worry slumps their shoulders.

"He's dead, isn't he?" the tall boy, Joe, asks.

"Yes, Joe, I'm so sorry."

"We knew that when he didn't come yesterday. You're Abby, right?"

So little emotion left. These boys already lived through a lot in their young lives.

"Yes, I'm Abby, and I have John and Robert with me."

"We know they're our brothers. Dad told us." They stare at the floor like the world might end. In some ways, it already has.

"And we're here to take you back to the ranch."

Joe nods. "We packed this morning and paid the owner here. Dad told us that you might come for us. Otherwise, we were supposed to visit you in Browning, you or our brothers. We probably can make it on our own, though."

His younger brother finally speaks.

"We w'woulda visited you first, Abby," Wendelin says. "The brothers weren't too h'happy the last time they saw us."

"Well, that's all over now. John and Robert are both anxious to get to know you boys. I can grab a bag if you want."

"No, we got it. Dad described that ranch right down to the rocks on the fireplace."

Robert and John stand somewhere behind me.

"Are you guys alright?" I ask.

"Yes, we both cried all morning, sorry to tell you that, not the kind of things a man should do."

"Well, I've seen your big brothers tear up, too, so don't worry about sharing your sorrow. Your father told you about the ranch, huh?"

"He told us a lot more, too," Joe says, "about his first wife Agnes, John and Robert's mother. He told us about places she liked in the forest and the prairies, like a little fishing hole only she could find."

"Well, your brothers will need to catch up," I say.

"Did Ed tell you where Agnes' fishing hole is?" Robert asks.

"Yeah," Wendelin says.

Joe squints one eye. "He said she found the fishing hole the year he went off to war. She'd get out of bed early and sneak down there because it drove him crazy how she always out-fished him. He followed her one day, and he figured it out, but he didn't let on."

"He told her at supper the last night, that he would join her there after the war," Wendelin says.

"It was her special place," Joe says. "and he wanted to look forward to seeing her there, something he could dream about."

"Dad said she wasn't feeling well some mornings, and he thought it was nerves because of his draft notice," Wendelin says.

"This week, he told us it was morning sickness," Joe says. "He figured that out when he learned about you two."

Wendelin nods. "Yes, he was sure you were his s'sons when he rode with us on the ocean liner going to New York. He talked about your ranch all day. He loved the p'place."

"He always thought he'd find enough gold to buy more land. That's what he told us," Joe says.

"I'd like to see it through his eyes," John says. "You boys can show us around from Ed's memory, and we can show you around, too."

He wraps an arm around Wendelin, and I grip Joe's shoulder. We shuffle out to my car together.

"Our aunt told us about this fishing hole when we were kids, too," Robert says. "Lois said she came to stay with our mother before our birth. Our mother told Lois she spent every morning by the fishing hole after Ed left, just her and a horse. Supposedly there's still a chair there, where the trout bit best."

That day, my car transports us back in time to Ed and Agnes' ranch.

In many ways, the ranch renews all five of our lives.

Ed's death blends in with the horrors of war, the physical and psychological scars, yet, our mountains capture new imaginations. Joe and Wendelin's youthful exuberance saves us all. Their energy wrestles away dark thoughts and puts a bright future into perspective.

Each boy remembers a dozen "Ed stories" like building the house, chasing lost cattle, little mountain lakes, and Agnes' favorite foods. The ranch feels fresh and exciting again.

In turn, Robert and John dote on their new brothers. They immediately send for Johanna, Joe and Wendelin's mother, because the boys are worried about her. Johanna Alder sheltered Jews on and off throughout the war. This letter is the first attempt at contact since the armistice.

The most amazing moment is when the boys show John and Robert their mother's fishing hole.

It happens the third day after dawn. The five of us are eating breakfast outside, where sunshine first reaches the log porch. Lilac blossoms flavor the air from a forgotten hedge. Full plates of bacon, eggs, fried potatoes, and toast give way to good cowboy-coffee and a discussion of the day's activities.

"I've got a plan today," Joe announces.

"Alright, you better tell us about it," Robert says.

"The fishing hole."

"Whatever directions you have probably won't help much. We spent many years searching every nook and cranny for miles up there." Robert waves his hand west over the vast mountain range.

"Then you looked in the wrong place," Joe says. "Come here."

Joe and Wendelin walk around the corner together. They move west, beyond the house's shadow.

"Alright, we have to stand right here," Joe says. "On a summer morning, line up the chimney with the chimney's shadow and it points to the fishing hole."

Robert and John look at each other.

"Down there?" John asks.

"Must be," Joe says. "I'm just repeating what he said."

"In the horse thicket?" Robert asks. "John, were you ever inside there?"

"No. I mean, not really inside. I rounded up cattle along the little openings. I tried crawling in there once, and it liked to tear my clothes off."

"I did the same thing, bled for a week," Robert says.

"Jump in the back of the truck, boys, and let's go for a ride," I say.

I sit between John and Robert up front, with Joe and Wendelin in the box of the truck. We bounce across the pasture a quarter-mile to a little creek that flows northwest to southeast. Stunted trees crowd much of the shoreline. John drives to a massive thicket, with undergrowth so dense a rabbit could hardly penetrate.

"We always pictured her up high, not out in the pasture," John says. "That tree is a thorn-apple, those are buffalo berries. Every tree and bush here protects itself with a thousand thorns. Riding past, this is a solid thicket, an impenetrable fortress."

"A creek runs in one side and out the other. Even there you can barely see under the branches," Robert says. "It's whitewater everywhere upstream."

"It sounds like someone found their way in," I say.

"We never paid it any attention with all the beautiful places up high," John says.

"It looks like the water's down this morning until sunlight warms the mountain snow," Robert says.

A meadowlark calls from somewhere behind us, while several sharp-tail grouse sail overhead, alternately pummeling the cool air and then gliding long distances. I envy their birds-eye view.

"I'm going in," Joe says. "Might be easier looking inside out."

"That stream's like ice."

He's already gone, belly-crawling through the dense overgrowth. From our perspective, the thicket stretches 150 yards downstream and almost that distance wide. Heavy underbrush crowds the circumference, giving way to a few large spreading trees in the middle—but gusty winds don't allow these trees much height. Prairie trees grow low and sturdy in Montana.

"It's more open in here, I can stand now," Joe yells. His voice causes a commotion from inside. Two coyotes break cover. A whitetail buck slips across the creek to our left.

"You OK in there?" John shouts.

"I found something. This is quite a place."

"Can you find a way in that doesn't involve ice water?"

"I'll find the easiest way. There's a waterfall and everything."

A few minutes later, Joe approaches us from the opposite side.

"Wow, you won't believe it."

"Wow, as in what?" I say.

"You'll hafta come see."

He flops his wet shirt off. His scratched shoulders look like they slept on an angry cat.

"I've got two shirts. Here." John pulls off a flannel shirt and hands it over.

Joe slips it on. His skinny white arms jockey for the sleeve holes even as he motions us ahead. Fifty yards downstream he stops.

"You can get in here. I broke some branches, follow me."

Together we squeeze between crowded little trees. The thicket absorbs sunshine very efficiently near the outside, where thorns scratch any exposed skin, but foliage soon thins. Our route drops away toward the creek. Ash trees now control the skyline. They get enough water down here to outcompete the stubborn prairie shrubs. They're cautious of late frost too, their branches covered with swollen buds, the leaves of summer-ready to burst forward.

We hear the little waterfall before we reach its pool.

On the upstream side, a rock shelf runs perpendicular to the stream. The shelf dips in the middle where water passes through mountain rock, effectively trapping the stream passage in place. Clear water fades to unknown depths below. Cedar trees dot open spaces around the pond, and cottontail rabbits abound near the fringes.

"This is the first place that water gets to rest. It's all pretty much whitewater from here on up," Robert says.

"Come over this way." Joe motions further down the rock shelf.

We converge on a single chair resting well above the pond. Somehow it survived two decades of heavy winter snow. Wood ducks bank overhead: finding their little paradise in the company of strangers. Wendelin comments on the drake's spectacular colors, but Agnes Meyer's hand-built chair rivals the beautiful drake. Cedar branches curve from backrest to seat. More cedar widens the seat and curves downward into handmade rockers.

"This spot gets direct sun every morning," Robert says, circling the chair. "Crafted of cedar and sinew. Beautiful work."

"There's still a rope where she tied her horse. This rock slab stretches almost completely through the thicket."

"What's on the chair, Abby?" Wendelin asks.

"A gold pan," I say. "I think we're all pretty curious about that."

An upside-down pan covers the chair seat. Long ago, the pan gave up any normal color to seasonal dampness, yet the rusty shell remains solid. John lifts the pan straight up. He uncovers a flute, and two shiny rocks. I lift a small rock and confirm its unusual weight.

"Gold," I say. "Just another woman locating stuff her man couldn't find."

"This little waterfall could run a gold sluice," John says. He stops a few feet short of the waterfall's spray. From my elevated position I notice the natural part in his hair, that bullet scar is almost hidden now. He carries no outward sign of injury, no headaches, or memory lapses. John lifts the flute to his lips for a mournful song.

"Our Aunt taught us to play," Robert says. "That's a very old flute."

John's fingers grasp worn areas where generations of players held this instrument. I imagine its journey through homes and forests and reverent hands. Music accompanies my retreat toward their cabin, and the boys stay close at my side. I can feel their struggle to belong.

"You look like a skinny lumberjack in that buffalo plaid shirt, Joe."

"At least I don't have food on my shirt from breakfast."

"Whoops. Didn't see that." I laugh at myself.

"Maybe you need to use a s'spoon instead of a fork." Wendelin tries his hand at humor, an opportunity largely absent through his adolescent years.

"You too? Who the heck cut your hair?" I ask.

When I ruffle his hair, he leans into the contact.

"Dad cut it with a scissors before we l'left Germany," Wendelin says. "He said it was too long for a military man."

"It's good you wore a hat because it looks like some dogs chewed it off."

"Dad used to trim our dogs in the spring, too," he laughs. "They looked pretty awful."

"I cut my own hair when I was three."

Joe takes my elbow and guides me around a protruding rock.

"Thank you, Joe. I cut my bangs because they were easy to reach. My mother smiled and took pictures."

"You know what?" Joe asks.

"What?" I reply.

"If I were John, I'd definitely marry you, too."

"Why's that, Joe?"

" 'Cause you're pretty. Pretty and a little salty. You're not afraid of anything, are you?"

"I'm afraid of singing at church. I'm terrible."

"I'm terrible, too. Terrible at singing. Terrible at talking to girls."

"You're both very handsome young men. You look a lot like your brothers."

"No way," Joe says.

"I'm serious. Working on the ranch will build your muscles like them, too. You won't even need to open your mouth because the girls will chase you. That is if your hair grows back."

"Yeah, he cut it pretty bad. You think we'll go off to war like John and Robert?"

"The world's done fighting for a while."

"You think we look like them, huh?"

"C'mon Joe, lighter skin and different hair, but it's obvious. Right down to the dimples when you smile."

"My dimples look better than yours, so you'll get the second choice on the girls," Wendelin says. "That is if I ever want a girlfriend, which I certainly don't."

His lopsided smirk makes me laugh.

"What would your mother say about all this girl talk?"

"She's a redhead like you," Joe says. "She'd tell us to stay the heck away from girls until we're at least twenty-five, so we're good and scared like we should be."

"Words of wisdom. A good friend told me that all redheads are salty, so I can't wait to meet your mother."

We place Ed's pewter cross the next evening. After John reads the litany, a crazy lightning storm erupts across Mount Richmond. The peak glows a brief instant, and thunder echoes all around.

We never see a cloud.

The very next day, I witness something so unexpected that I cry like a little girl. Somehow the crying pleases me because I didn't know I still had much emotion left.

It starts out with a dusty horizon at dawn.

"Hey everybody, you better come outside," Joe says. "There's a prairie fire coming."

"Maybe," Robert says. "Could be dust too, a windstorm blowing in."

We join Joe in a tight cluster.

"Kinda strange coming from the east," John says, "yet, it does happen. Let's finish breakfast. We might need to tie things down."

We learn the truth an hour later when 200 head of cattle and a half dozen mounted riders come into view. Robert scans the procession with binoculars and names four neighbors riding with his aunt and uncle. He then names two familiar cows, Lena and Gretchen, leading the herd.

Robert whoops and dances around the kitchen until he runs into John. They hug, and not an awkward hug but a genuine emotional hug that gets the best of me.

"Are those your cattle?" I ask.

"Ours and more," John says. "We told our uncle to sell them when we enlisted. Everything happened so suddenly that we couldn't get them to auction. It looks like everyone took a few and kept 'em for us."

"And it looks like the cows got along with the bulls."

"Can we get a dog?" Wendelin asks.

"Gotta have a dog with cattle," Joe says.

Summer rushes by much too quickly, but the mountains more than compensate for our short season. We spend every daylight hour outside.

John and I marry that September, and honeymoon in Minot, where I reconnect with Bernice. The four of us celebrate together at Saul's Barbeque. Afterward we slip downstairs for some poker, but John loses this time. He explained later that Al's the best poker player he ever met because Al kept everyone laughing and bought several rounds of whiskey, too. With all the distractions, Al rakes in almost $100 and pays for our entire evening. He tells John that Dorothy's getting awfully attached to his farm dog.

I promise Bernice that I will return alone to explain Josef's murder. I tell her the story will take an entire day, and that it didn't end in Minot.

Back in Montana, the boys name our dog, Alice. She's a blue heeler of local breeding, which means she can move an entire heard of cattle through a kitchen without breaking a saucer, according to John. His prognostication proves very accurate. Alice retrains the herd herself. They soon know exactly what she wants as soon as she arrives, often a predictable pasture change accomplished with little more than some gentle steering.

Johanna's boys ranch with their brothers and chase gold upstream, usually in the company of Alice—most days their chase leads them right back to the pond. The boys work into October when the first blizzard finally locks everything down. The pond yields almost $1,000 that year, enough to purchase the pasture Ed always wanted.

Somehow, between all the other activities, John and Robert build another cabin on John's overlook. We like Ed's original cabin so much, that they build an identical replica, right down to the fieldstone fireplace. John moves me in on Thanksgiving weekend, and I cook everyone a wild turkey in the process.

The men spend Thanksgiving contemplating the remaining gravel, deep in Agnes's pool.

"Ten feet deep at least," Joe says. "We got through everything else."

"We got a plan, too," Wendelin says. "I found an irrigation pump at the scrap dealer in town. He said we could have it for five dollars."

"You gonna drain the pond?" John asks.

"Oh, no. I read about how they do this up in Alaska. You make a suction pump by pushing water into one arm of a Y..."

MAY 1946

Twelve months after we bury Ed, his wife Johanna Alder finally arrives.

Johanna waited helplessly in Germany after learning of Ed's death and her son's freedom. Through me, and assuming the worst, Ed had asked that his four sons bring Johanna over, but Johanna postponed the trip several times.

She had a secret of her own.

Joe and Wendelin said the Jewish plight horrified their mother. Before her boys fled Germany, Johanna joined forces with people smuggling Jews to safety. She helped hide several people and became attached to a young Jewish woman. Johanna told the boys she would wait at home until she could take the girl with her to America.

Eventually, Johanna agrees to travel. We know nothing of her efforts in Europe, and the very first night, we all gather for a joyous celebration.

I invite fifty people, and at least 100 attend. Johanna's honored and overwhelmed.

We look a bit alike, Johanna and I, so when I introduce her around, many people ask about the connection. "She's my mother-in-law," I explain. Local people that don't already know the story soon gather it from others. The evening ends with a heartfelt toast, welcoming Johanna to Dupuyer.

The next day, I find her standing at Ed's grave in the morning light.

"Good morning, Abby," she says.

She turns back to his grave several long minutes. It's a cool morning under slate-gray skies that threaten the first spring rain. A single snowdrift still extends several feet from the nearest cabin.

"This place reminds me so much of Germany," she says. "The trees and valleys and the snow itself. I know Ed loved his ranch."

"He made it back here, too," I say.

"Please tell me he killed those bastards."

She whispers the words like they've waited in her heart for an eternity.

I'm caught off-guard. Instinctively, I turn toward the missing church.

"There, huh?"

I nod my head.

"Ed told me about the little church. He had it all planned. He didn't mention you, though."

"Oh?"

"Did you help him?"

I nod my head again. "He made me think it was my idea."

"Everything went somewhat as planned?"

"Somewhat, yes. The church stood right between those trails."

I look back at her face. She waits for me to continue.

"You knew his plans?" I ask.

"Get our sons out, then kill the swine that destroyed our country. Yes, I knew everything."

"He succeeded on both accounts."

"Good. At least his death has meaning."

"Joe worried about you a lot. He said you helped several Jews."

She hangs her head.

"Oh no, I'm so sorry I asked."

"No, it's alright. Funny, I haven't cried about Ed, but Elfriede, she almost made it out. She was a Jew, yes, a wonderful girl who survived the entire war in cellars only to die last month. She'd be with me today because we had her emigration's papers all lined up."

"How old was she?"

"Twenty-three. The Nazis killed her entire family."

"Your family made so many sacrifices, Johanna."

"I'll have none of that. You risked as much as any of us, according to my Joe."

"Ed rescued everyone. You're all wonderful."

"Ed's death is partially my fault because I encouraged him."

"He didn't need encouragement. He needed understanding."

"I understood. I urged him on."

"I'm glad you did. The world is so glad you did."

"I have one single question, Abby."

"Ask me anything."

"What happened to Josef Mengele? We entertained him in our home once, and that visit convinced me. I want to know how that dreadful murderer died."

I stare up into the sky.

"Abby?"

"Josef came to your home?"

"He was in town for meetings, with Ed already working on this elaborate scheme. Ed needed a closer bond with Josef. At supper, he got Josef talking about his work."

"I hope he didn't go into detail."

"He told us all about a young Jewish mother who survived a high-altitude experiment. She wanted to live for her children. She did live longer than any other test subject, almost a week of tremendous pain. Josef proudly determined that as a mother, her will to live for her children gave this woman a hormonal boost previously unknown to science. He vowed to bravely continue such experiments so he could discover, through autopsy, what kind of biochemical agents made this woman so brave."

"It's a true story," I say. "He wanted to give those chemicals to front line soldiers so they could fight through mortal wounds."

"I wanted to kill him with my bare hands," Johanna says. "Every morning, I still wish I had killed him. Every morning I think of that devil loose on our world."

"Josef isn't out there anymore."

"You know this with certainty?"

"I killed him myself."

She smiles a sweet smile. She looks incredulous.

"I'm serious. Dead serious."

Another look overtakes her.

"Dead serious?"

"Uh-huh."

"Impossible."

"You woulda killed him, too. I don't feel bad."

"Tell me how he died. I know it's an awful thing to ask, but you can't possibly imagine how the story will heal me." Her eyes grow expectant.

"If I tell you any of it, I have to tell you all of it. Death is never pleasant."

"I disagree. I will take unbridled delight in the details of Josef's death."

The lines in her face deepen. Her fists slowly clench, and she leans forward slightly.

"He was the devil," she says. "You know it's true."

"Josef worked for other evil men. He worked for Hitler."

"Josef was Hitler's golden boy, his continual inspiration. Josef convinced Hitler that they could perfect the human race by eliminating everything and everyone that did not fit their shared vision."

"I think you're right."

"I know damn well I'm right," Johanna says, "but there's a deep dark hole in my soul where his death belongs. Just knowing he died doesn't fill that hole. I'm sorry for talking like this."

"Don't be sorry. I filled the very same hole one year ago. Our dance took all evening."

"I wish I had been there."

"The details feel good now. I'm glad you asked."

"You must share them."

"The details would fill a well."

"Please tell me, Abby."

"There might be a way."

"Anything."

"Are you up for another train ride?"

"I could ride a train again."

"Can you live outside the law for an evening?"

"Yes, I can."

"Then plan a little trip next week. We'll be gone for four days."

"A hotel stay?"

"I haven't decided between a friend's place or the whore-house behind it."

"I've never stayed in a whorehouse. Shall I pack anything special?"

"A dress and heels. We can buy what you need in town— something dark in case you spill your sherry."

"I owe myself some sherry after the last twenty years," she says.

"And I owe two friends this story. The four of us might drink a lot of sherry."

"This sounds like a celebration," Johanna says.

"A celebration, yes. Just you wait."

1918

A million distant stars crowded the horizon at dusk, shimmering against a cold wind. For a moment, he was back in Montana, admiring the same celestial patterns on a lonely ridge near Dupuyer. The North Star always conjured up thoughts of early winter: of elk gathering in low-lying meadows along icy streams.

Ed's current surroundings looked much the same: rugged foothills of the Ardennes not far from Bitburg, Germany. A square foxhole limited his panorama, just as it protected him from a sniper some 300 yards south. He knew several snipers along the allied front, yet this particular foxhole belonged to the Germans, a perilous situation indeed.

World War I roared well into 1918, but the Germans were losing.

The war took Ed from Montana. His young wife died after he reached Europe. On the German side, Ed's cousin lost her husband before Ed even arrived in Europe. German politicians and their war destroyed both families.

Tonight, Ed wore a wrinkled uniform and carried the identification of a man named Adolf Wenger. The real Wenger died a quiet death in another foxhole several miles north, minutes after Wenger's commanding officer suffered a similar fate.

Despite obvious danger, Ed relaxed completely as lesser men shivered nervously up and down both lines. Not a single soldier on either side had spent more time living outdoors in tough weather. Back home, Ed preferred secluded mountain places that sharpened the senses and cleared the mind.

The U.S. Army had no idea where he was. Although intercepted messages made it clear, his work continued to wreak havoc on the German frontline. Each officer's death put another nail in the collective psyche of tired frontline troops, especially on the young troops Ludendorff now chose to continue this hopeless war. By necessity, frontline officers came from far away, where stories of these bizarre killings didn't haunt each and every foxhole.

Sporadic firing pierced the night air as Ed dozed. It would be noon in Montana. His wife lay under some remote cross there, dead to the beautiful world she cherished so much.

His cousin's widow would need help with her farm south of Dusseldorf. No point in returning to the United States after the war. Ed might as well stay in Germany, providing he didn't get shot while killing every German officer he could find.

His cousin's name was Alder, and he looked a bit like Ed. Ed could assume Alder's identity, probably the only way Alder's widow could hold onto the land. Since they purchased the property before the war, nobody in the area would know any differently.

Ed Meyer thought about his wife and hated the German military every waking hour of every day with rage he would never be able to control.

The Gypsy Family Camp at Auschwitz housed entire families. All arrivals received a tattoo with a Z (*Zigeuner*–Gypsy) followed by a number: babies on their thighs because of fit and on everyone else's forearms. This rare case of family incarceration shows an attempt to convince visiting organizations like the Red Cross that Nazi prisoners were treated fairly, humanely, but family incarceration meant little more than just words. Food supplies were terribly inadequate and living conditions horrible. The camp measured 170x150 yards and buildings designed to hold 300 held over 1,000. In some cases, fifteen people shared a bunk bed.

The real horror lay with the camp's assigned doctor: Josef Mengele. Experiments depicted in this novel accurately describe Mengele's work, his enthusiasm, his callous disregard for human life and suffering. Josef Mengele once had an entire family of eight murdered so he could study their variously colored eyes. He sewed together four-year-old twin children, and connected their veins to see if they could survive. They didn't, but their suffering continued until their mother found some morphine and permanently ended their pain. Near the close of war, Mengele gave his medical research to a trusted nurse for safekeeping. Nothing is known about the nurse or her life after the war. Josef Mengele fled Europe and tentatively drowned in a swimming accident in Brazil, or was it Minot?

Minot's Red-Light District boomed during prohibition, partially because of its proximity to the Canadian border. Capone and other bootleggers took advantage of a very rural border, and Minot served those men very well. Restaurants along "High Third" provided cover for illegal gambling and prostitution, usually downstairs, often connected business to business to private home by secret tunnels.

Al Emil and Bernice are real people, doing what they did in downtown Minot. Emil bootlegged during prohibition, getting his Canadian whiskey at a Minot car dealership. Emil claimed that when he requested the correct "service," his car went upstairs on a lift, and came down with a package in the trunk and a service bill. When Bernice and Dorothy moved from Main Street, Minot, to share Al's farm, they changed his bachelor ways, too, all for the better. Al and Bernice lived happily together into their 80s.

As a single mother, Bernice once worked in the railroad station in Wolf Point, Montana.

The Blackfeet Tribe lived on native lands just to the west, deeded, and then reduced by the U.S. government. Blackfeet soldiers fought tirelessly in World War II. Brave men like Robert Paul, Forrest Gerard, Jesse LaBuff, Floyd Monroe, Warren Adams, and Myron Anderson returned as decorated heroes. Even more Blackfeet men left us as fallen heroes, proud of their heritage, proud to serve.

When World War I started, Native Americans were not considered citizens of the United States, but 12,000 signed up to fight anyway. During World War II, the War Department said that if the general population had enlisted at the same rate as Native Americans, Selective Service would have been unnecessary. By the end of World War II, 44,500

Native Americans had served in the military effort—one-third of all of their able-bodied men, eighteen to fifty years old.

According to military experts, Native American men fought courageously with a sense of honor.

"The real secret which makes the Indian such an outstanding soldier is his enthusiasm for the fight." –U.S. Army Major, 1912

"When I went to Germany, I never thought about war honors, or the four 'coups' which an old-time Crow warrior had to earn in battle. . .But afterward, when I came back and went through this telling of war deeds ceremony. . .lo and behold I [had] completed the four requirements to become a chief." –Crow World War II Veteran

Other nationalities found honor on World War II battlefields, among them, **a Jewish general named Maurice Rose.**

On March 30, 1945, a few miles south of the city of Paderborn, in a rural forested area, General Rose was riding at the front of the Task Force Welborn column. The front of this column consisted of his own jeep, a jeep in front of him, a tank at the head of the column, an armored car behind him, and a motorcycle messenger bringing up the rear. Suddenly they began taking small arms fire as well as tank and anti-tank fire. General Rose, along with the other men, jumped into a nearby ditch with his Thompson sub-machine gun as the lead tank took a direct hit and was destroyed. When they realized that they were being surrounded by German tanks, they re-entered their jeeps and tried to escape. They drove off the road and through a nearby field before heading back towards the road. When arriving back at the road, they realized it was occupied by numerous German Tiger tanks. The lead jeep gunned its engine and narrowly made it past the Tiger tanks and escaped to the other side. The driver of General Rose's jeep attempted to do the same, but one of the German Tigers turned to cut them off, and as Rose's jeep was passing the Tiger tank wedged the jeep against a tree. The top hatch of the Tiger tank flung open and a German soldier appeared pointing a machine pistol at the group in the jeep. General Rose reached towards his pistol holster (either to throw it to the ground or in an attempt to fight back). The German soldier shot him several times with at least one round hitting Rose in the head. It is believed that the German tank crews never had any idea that the man they killed was a general because sensitive documents, as well as General Rose's body, were not removed from his jeep.

(https://en.wikipedia.org/wiki/Maurice_Rose)

From 1942 until the end of the war, the war widow, **Johanna Eck** (b. 1888) sheltered, successively, four Nazi persecution victims. Eck came to be acquainted with Elfriede Guttmann, a Jewish girl hiding in another home. In December 1943, the *Gestapo* raided that house. Elfriede, who had been hiding under one of the beds, barely managed to escape detection. Shattered by this traumatic experience, the Jewish girl visited Eck and told her what had happened. Eck, who had in the meantime been assigned a single-room apartment, immediately agreed to offer her refuge.

Elfriede's end was very tragic. The Jewish girl, who survived the horrors of the war intact, succumbed to a sudden stomach constriction shortly after the liberation. She passed away in June 1946, on the eve of her projected emigration to the United States. Eck, a nurse by training, sat at her bedside at the hospital until she passed away. She later inquired with the Jewish community as to the names of Elfriede's parents and brother. Although they had all perished, she had the names inscribed on the gravestone that she set up at her own expense.

"The motives for my help? Nothing special in a particular case. In principle, what I think is this: If a fellow human being is in distress and I can help him, then it becomes my duty and responsibility. Were I to refrain from doing so, then I would betray the task that life—or perhaps God?—demands from me. Human beings—so it seems to me—make up a big unity; they strike themselves and all in the face when they do injustice to each other. These are my motives." –Johanna Eck

(http://www.yadvashem.org/yv/en/exhibitions/righteous-women/eck.asp)

BRIAN STRIEFEL

BRIAN STRIEFEL

B rian is a demanding reader and author, especially incensed by lousy endings. His character-driven thrill rides hold your attention long after the end. Each story seamlessly blends into real events, sometimes literary in message yet wildly original in direction. Brian once spent time scientificating coal. Along with his wife Anita, he now travels, golfs poorly when the fish aren't biting, and often chases a mule deer named Thelma from an untended garden.

Check out his Facebook page: "Dust Cover Intros."

WHY MARY
FORGOT

When you doubt the thing you want to believe most,
you're usually right. — Hanna Johnson, Bismarck Police

In 1927, Calvin Coolidge located his summer White-house in the Black Hills, where the Sioux made him an honorary chief. Up in North Dakota, the KKK ran Grand Forks, a Catholic Mission served Ft. Yates, a speak-easy thrived in Bismarck's Patterson Hotel, and Miss Delia Gransberg was Miss North Dakota.

Hanna's that young detective that desperately needs a break. In 2005, she records a wild murder confession involving President Calvin Coolidge, Miss North Dakota 1927, some Sioux Indians, and a chef named Pierre. Another crackpot case could doom Hanna's career, so she must quickly prove that Sister Mary Murphy didn't really kill anyone in 1927. Sister Mary's case looks open and shut—unfortunately, the little nun forgot some very important details.

Pope Benedict desperately needs a hero. He discovers that opportunity with Sister Mary Murphy's upcoming 100th birthday celebration involving the church's highest missionary honor: the Lumen Christi. Her audience will include a hundred dignitaries and every resident of Fort Yates, North Dakota, the rural community she served almost eighty years.

If Hanna can't convince Sister Mary Murphy of her innocence, Mary will also admit to murder.

This lighthearted thriller unfolds in two timeframes from the present-day perspective of Hanna Johnson and that of Delia Gransberg, Miss North Dakota 1927. Hanna meets a handsome history professor who helps and distracts her as she rushes through the case–on her week off–without her supervisor's knowledge. The trail may be eighty years old, but what starts out as a dead-end case quickly escalates into the crime of the century—albeit the previous century.

Stir together Janet Evanovich's *One for the Money* and Margaret Atwood's *The Blind Assassin* to find this novel's feel. Though fictional, this novel contains many actual events that happened during Prohibition in North Dakota.